Praise for Gail Gaymer Martin

"This touching finale to the Dreams Come True series proves the power of faith."
—*RT Book Reviews* on *A Dream of His Own*

"Martin's story contains strong characters and touching scenes."
—*RT Book Reviews* on "Small Town Christmas" in *Christmas Gifts*

"Gail Gaymer Martin probes the depths of love and forgiveness. A tender and heartwarming read."
—Lyn Cote on *The Christmas Kite*

"Settle into your favorite chair and enjoy."
—Robin Lee Hatcher on *The Christmas Kite*

Gail Gaymer Martin is a multi-award-winning novelist and writer of contemporary Christian fiction with fifty-five published novels and four million books sold. *CBS News* listed her among the four best writers in the Detroit area. Gail is a cofounder of American Christian Fiction Writers, a keynote speaker at women's events, and she presents workshops at writers' conferences. She lives in Michigan. Visit her at gailgaymermartin.com. Write to her online or at PO Box 760063, Lathrup Village, MI, 48076.

Finding Christmas

Gail Gaymer Martin

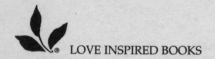

Recycling programs
for this product may
not exist in your area.

LOVE INSPIRED BOOKS

ISBN-13: 978-1-335-04479-2

Finding Christmas

Copyright © 2005 by Gail Gaymer Martin

All rights reserved. Except for use in any review, the reproduction or utilization of this work in whole or in part in any form by any electronic, mechanical or other means, now known or hereafter invented, including xerography, photocopying and recording, or in any information storage or retrieval system, is forbidden without the written permission of the editorial office, Love Inspired Books, 195 Broadway, New York, NY 10007 U.S.A.

This is a work of fiction. Names, characters, places and incidents are either the product of the author's imagination or are used fictitiously, and any resemblance to actual persons, living or dead, business establishments, events or locales is entirely coincidental.

This edition published by arrangement with Love Inspired Books.

® and TM are trademarks of Love Inspired Books, used under license. Trademarks indicated with ® are registered in the United States Patent and Trademark Office, the Canadian Intellectual Property Office and in other countries.

www.Harlequin.com

Printed in U.S.A.

For the Son of Man came to seek
and to save what was lost.
—*Luke* 19:10

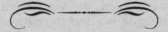

To Bob with much love
for making every Christmas a delight.

Many thanks to Marvel Erdodi for her banking
information and to Detective Ron Wieczorek
of the Grosse Pointe City Department of Public
Safety for helping me find the perfect place for
a murder. Thanks also to Jennifer Wells at The
Parade Company for details on the Michigan
Thanksgiving Parade. Finally, to my Chi Libris
pals: Robert Whitlow, Jim Bell and Tom Morrisey,
who provided helpful law firm info.

Chapter One

"Mommy!"

The plea whispered in her mind. Not a voice exactly, but a feeling.

Joanne Fuller spun around, overwhelmed by the sensation. "Mandy?" A chill rolled down her back.

Her legs gave way and she sank to the floor, covering her face with her hands. Her three-year-old's image hung in her thoughts like a star, once shining but now dimmed.

"Mommy!"

The fear-filled voice resounded in her head again.

Joanne pressed her hand against her heart to steady the beat. Why now, after three years? She knew it couldn't be real. Yet lately, the cry had come to her in the night more than once.

Steadying herself against a chair, Joanne pushed herself up from the floor and waited for the dizziness to pass. Why was this happening? She'd gone through counseling, and the horrifying nightmares had passed. She'd become stronger, but she'd begun to question her sanity since the night her daughter's cry had come to her in a dream.

The telephone's ring pierced the silence and Joanne's heart rose to her throat. She darted across the room and grasped the receiver, and when she said hello her voice came out breathless and strained.

"Joanne?"

She heard her name reverberating through the line across a canyon.

"Benjamin?"

"It's me. What in the world is wrong?"

She crumpled into a chair, clutched her chest to calm the thudding that felt as if it would break her ribs. "It's a long story. I can't talk about it now." Tears filled her eyes— tears of relief and anxiety.

"It's okay," he said, his voice as reassuring as a morning cup of coffee.

"Where are you?" she asked, trying to get her thoughts together.

"Here in Detroit. I'm back."

"Will you be here for the holidays?" *Christmas*. The vision rose in Joanne's mind, and she felt overcome by the feeling of loneliness.

"I sure will. I'm here for good, I hope."

The news settled over her, and she relaxed her shoulders. "That's wonderful news. Will I see you soon?"

His warm chuckle met her ear.

"That's why I'm calling. How about dinner? Tonight."

Her stomach churned at the thought of food. Stress always affected her that way, but to see her old friend, she would force herself to eat. "Tonight's good. I need company."

"It sounds like it," he said. His voice radiated tenderness. "I'll pick you up in an hour."

After she hung up, Joanne sat without moving, amazed at the emotion that filled her. Benjamin Drake. She hadn't seen him since the funeral. Gooseflesh rolled down her arms at the memory. She, Greg and Mandy. Such joy. She'd expected it to last a lifetime. A perfect husband, a perfect child—both taken one cold November night. She'd begged God to tell her why, but she'd never heard His answer.

Joanne's gaze shifted to the calendar stuck to the side of the refrigerator next to the curled, yellowed page of crayon scribbles. Tears pressed against her eyes again, and she tugged her focus from her three-year-old daughter's drawing to the November dates. They'd died nearly three years ago today.

Drawing back her shoulders, Joanne hoisted herself from the chair, suddenly feeling tired, but thoughts of Benjamin returned and so did a smile. She hurried into her bedroom and pulled off her business suit, then rummaged through her closet and slipped on a skirt and sweater. She replaced her pumps with casual slip-ons, and her knotted calves eased as she settled into the soft suede shoes.

Joanne moved to the vanity and eyed her once-neat hair. She pulled out the clasps and brushed the long strands, ready to capture the wispy ends, but taking another look, she let it fall around her shoulders. Thinking of her old friend, she felt younger than she had in years.

As she turned toward the door, Joanne's gaze fell on a small photo on her dresser of Mandy playing in a pile of autumn leaves. She'd taken the picture a month before her daughter's death. Joanne picked up the photo and studied it. She could see Greg's rake at the edge of the picture. Now she wished she'd stepped back to capture them both, but in those days, she and Greg only had eyes for Mandy. Joanne's heart felt heavy again as she set the frame on the dresser top and left the room.

While she searched for her handbag, the doorbell rang. When Joanne opened the door she caught her breath. "Benjamin." A rush of admiration washed over her—his dark wavy hair and chocolate-brown eyes, his familiar easy smile. "You look wonderful."

His gaze drifted over her as he grinned. "You look beautiful as always." He grasped her shoulders and pressed his wind-cooled lips against her cheek. "Ready?"

"I am," she said, lifting a hand to capture his chin. "It's so good to see you."

She opened the closet and pulled out her jacket. Benjamin held it while she pushed her arms into the sleeves, then shrugged it on. She tossed her purse over her shoulder and checked the door lock before pulling the door closed.

Benjamin clasped her elbow as she moved down the snowy steps to the sidewalk. He opened the passenger door for Joanne, then rounded the car to the driver side. "What are you in the mood for? Italian? Mexican? American?"

"I'm in the mood to visit," she said, patting his arm. "Whatever you'd like is fine."

"Let's try Jimmy's," he said, backing out of the driveway. "They have fish and Black Angus. Even pasta if you prefer it."

As he drove through Grosse Pointe, they caught up on the past couple of years.

"Are you still at Solutions, Incorporated?"

"What else?" She smiled, realizing her job had become her life. "I just got a promotion. I'm heading the think tank. It's exciting, and I have my own office with a window."

"Good for you. And a window—now that's really something." He paused for a moment and his smile faded. "Are you seeing anyone?"

The question surprised her. "You mean dating?"

He nodded.

"No. I'm not ready for that."

"It's been three years. I thought maybe…"

"No, I—" Dating hadn't entered her mind. Ever.

The conversation lulled. Joanne didn't mention the disturbing sensations she'd been feeling and Benjamin didn't ask why she'd sounded stressed on the phone. She knew he would, sometime before the evening ended, but she was willing to wait.

They'd settled at a table and made their selections from the menu before Benjamin slid his hand over hers and gave it a squeeze. "So what's all this about?"

For a moment she didn't understand his question, but when she studied his face, she knew. "It's difficult to explain."

"Give me a try," he said, releasing her hand to pick up his water glass.

Joanne lowered her head. She formed the words in her mind though they made little sense. "I hear Mandy's voice calling to me."

A frown pulled at his mouth and his eyes darkened. "I'm so sorry, Joanne. I'd hoped—"

"I know," she said. "I have been doing well until the past couple of weeks." Her pulse skipped. "Greg and Mandy have been gone for three years…almost to the day."

He slid his hand over hers again comfortingly. "I know. It's tomorrow. It hit me this morning."

A feeling of desperation hit her. "Sometimes I'm drowned by the loss, Benjamin. I awake disbelieving, praying it was only a bad dream, but the bed is empty beside me, no dent in the pillow. Mandy's room is silent, and

I know it's true." She glanced at the patrons around her, realizing her volume had risen.

She released a sigh. "This isn't the place to talk about that, but I have no one really who'd understand." She looked so deeply into his eyes that she felt lost in them. "Except you. They were part of your life, too."

He wrapped his fingers around her hand and gave it a squeeze. The warmth filled her with memories, and she realized how much she'd missed his friendship. Benjamin had been such a good and faithful friend, always there when she or Greg needed him, and he had doted on Mandy.

"Thanks," she said. "It's wonderful that you're back in Detroit." She tried to smile. "I'm praying the weird feelings go away. I should be over my grief by now."

"Don't expect so much of yourself," Benjamin said, still holding her hand. "You lost a husband and child in the blink of an eye, and you've never had…" He paused as if not knowing what to say.

"Never had closure," she said, knowing that's what he meant. "I buried a husband and a tiny empty casket holding some of Mandy's toys. That was all." She felt tears surfacing on her lashes, and Joanne knew she had to stop.

"If they'd found her body—if only they'd found her, at least I'd believe it happened."

"I know. I wish I could make it better for you."

He looked as desperate as she felt, and Joanne's good sense and social graces returned. This was no time or place to talk about something so heart wrenching. She pulled herself together and drew in a deep breath.

"So how was Seattle?" she asked.

"Wet. Foggy."

She grinned, and the experience felt wonderful—though it faded too quickly. "I didn't realize you would be gone so long." She hesitated and then added, "And with so few visits."

His expression changed, and she sensed he was avoiding something he wanted to say. "You knew the firm opened a branch there. It took time. I had an opportunity to return earlier, but I decided to stick it out and finish the project."

"I see," she said, confused by the look on his face.

After the waiter arrived with their food, Joanne only shifted the pasta around on her plate, curious about Benjamin. He focused on

his steak. She had many things to ask him—
for one, why he'd kept such a low profile after
he moved to Seattle. After attending the funeral, he'd called a couple of times, but as
time passed, she rarely heard from him other
than an occasional brief call or an e-mail at
her office. He'd been Greg's friend, a fellow
attorney, but Joanne had always considered
him her friend, too.

As she pondered, the answer fell into her
mind. She spiraled the pasta around her fork,
wondering if she should say what she was
thinking. "Losing Greg was hard on you, too,
I guess. Avoidance makes it easier."

His head jerked upward as if he was surprised at her comment.

"I hadn't really thought about that before,"
she said.

Benjamin held his fork suspended in the air
and didn't say anything for a moment. "Greg
was closer than a brother. It hurt." He lowered
the fork and set it on his plate. "But nothing
like what you went through, Joanne. I felt lost
on how to respond to you. I'd never known
the kind of emptiness you had to deal with."

"I thought you'd come home for another
visit after the funeral. I was disappointed."
Disappointment had been her mainstay, she

realized. Not only Benjamin, but her whole family had let her down.

He glanced away without speaking, looked back at her, taking a sip of water as he regarded her over the glass. "I wanted to. I wanted to be here more than I can ever explain, but..."

His voice faded, and she tried to read his expression. "But?"

"It didn't seem right. You were a new widow, and I was a—"

"Friend. I considered you my friend, too, not just Greg's."

"You know you are, Joanne. You can't think differently."

"But I thought friends were supposed to be there when you needed them." She heard the bitterness in her words and wished she could take them back, but she'd been hurt by so many people and hadn't expected him to be one of them. "Benjamin, I'm sorry. Forget what I said. I'm having a pity-party here."

"No apology necessary. You're right. I let my own fears stop me."

Fears? She didn't know what to say.

"I was afraid people would talk."

"Talk? I don't understand."

"About you and me. I worried about gossip—that Greg had been gone only a few weeks and his best friend was already hitting on his wife."

She felt a flush crawl up her neckline. *Hitting on his wife?* She would never have thought that, and no one else would have, either. "You were nothing but a wonderful friend, Benjamin. Mandy loved you. Greg loved you and so did I." She caught his look. "So *do* I," she corrected. "I haven't changed. You were always there for us. You even babysat Mandy once. Remember?"

A crooked grin brightened his face. "How could I forget? It was my first experience changing diapers."

Joanne laughed, her body relaxing with the lighthearted feeling. "I didn't know that."

He set the glass back on the table. "I'm sorry about the past, Joanne. I'm here now, and maybe I can make it up to you."

"You don't owe me anything, my dear friend." This time she slid her hand over his. "I was just telling you my feelings. You're here now, and I feel better knowing that. It's been lonely. I miss them both so much."

"I missed all of you."

He turned his attention to his dinner while Joanne clung to his comment. Being missed felt good. Her family lived out of state, and while they'd been attentive for a short while, their lives had gone on, and they had healed, while Joanne still worked at it. She'd struggled with the resentment until she hardened her heart to them, just as her family seemed to have done to her.

She tore off a crusty hunk of bread and nibbled on the corner as she watched Benjamin devour the rare steak. The red juice ran onto his plate, making her think of her own life juices that had drained away for so long until she'd started to heal.

Her work had saved her. At Solutions, she delved into other people's problems. It was easier than dealing with her own issues. She could hand over a well-tuned plan to a customer for developing a new company policy or rejuvenating a sluggish business and feel good about what she'd accomplished. She'd started to feel at least halfway alive again—until she heard Mandy's cry in her head.

After Benjamin finished his dinner and Joanne maneuvered her food to appear as if she'd eaten, he suggested they leave. They spoke little on the ride home, and when they pulled into her driveway, Joanne didn't want to part company.

"This is the best I've felt in a couple of weeks. Come in for coffee?"

He sat without moving, then turned off the ignition. "Sure. Why not?"

Benjamin followed her inside to the kitchen and slipped his jacket over the back of a chair. "So tell me what else is going on in your life. No dating…so what keeps you busy besides work?"

The question surprised her, and she edged around to face him, holding the canister of coffee. "Not much, but I'm doing okay. Really." She returned to her task and spooned grounds into the basket, poured in the water and hit the brewing button. When she turned back, he stood behind her, so close she stopped breathing.

"You can't fool me," he said, resting his hands on her shoulders.

"I—I…" She didn't want to talk about all the old feelings, and she tried to sum it up in a few words. "It's hard being a widow, that's all."

"I'm sure it is. Life changed for you."

His searching gaze made her uncomfortable.

"What about your family?" he asked. "Do you see them?"

Her stomach tightened. "No, not really. I went home for Christmas last year but it wasn't the same. We've drifted. They all have their lives." She stopped herself from saying *self-centered lives.* "I just don't relate to them. They seem to avoid most topics as if they're afraid to remind me I've lost a husband and child."

His hands tightened against her shoulders and his palms warmed her skin through her sweater.

"People can't handle others' pain, Joanne. I guess you just have to forgive them."

She tensed with his comment. Forgiving was something she couldn't bring herself to do, and it wasn't only about her parents. Joanne truly felt alone but she'd finally accepted it. She had her work and, lately, her church. Now Benjamin had come back into her life—a real friend. That was all she needed.

"I'm sure the voice bothers you."

"I'm just jumpy. I'm not sleeping well, afraid I'll hear the crying again. I can't explain it, Benjamin. It's a feeling. It's hushed, but I sense it, and I don't understand it."

"It's the anniversary, I suppose."

He backed away and leaned against the counter.

"I know," she said, watching the coffee drain into the pot. She reached into the cabinet and pulled out two cups, set them on the counter and, when the decaf had brewed, lifted the pot. As she poured, the telephone's peal startled her. Hot coffee splashed onto her hand and over the counter, searing her skin, and she let out a cry.

"Careful," Benjamin said, hurrying to her side.

She scooted past him and turned on the cold water, then shoved her hand beneath the tap while the ringing continued.

"Want me to get it?" Benjamin asked, glancing at the phone but seeming more concerned by her burn.

"Please." She studied her throbbing red skin, as the cool water washed over it, and listened to Benjamin's voice as he answered the telephone.

"It's a woman from your office," he said, holding the receiver out to her. "Do you want to call her back?"

"No. I'll take it." She grasped the phone, already guessing what the caller wanted. She listened, then said, "I'll remember, Nita.

Thanks." Joanne glanced Benjamin's way and felt an embarrassed grin grow on her face. "No, you didn't interrupt anything. An old friend is visiting. I'll see you tomorrow."

She felt uneasy at her friend's teasing as she hung up the phone and gazed at the reddened flesh of her hand. "I'll live."

"This isn't good, Joanne. You need to calm down. Your blood pressure will be sky high if you panic at every little sound."

"I can't help it. The phone rings. Someone knocks on the door. Anything that breaks the silence, I jump. It's awful."

Her gaze shifted from his concerned look to the counter, then to the table. He'd already poured the coffee and wiped up the spill. "Thanks," she said, joining him.

He took her hand in his and eyed the burn. "Should you put something on that?"

"It's fine." She withdrew her hand, then lifted the cup, surprised he'd remembered she liked milk in her coffee. "Cheers."

They clinked cups with a chuckle, then fell silent again. She and Greg had often sat at this table with Benjamin. He'd never married for some reason, and Joanne had often wanted to ask why but had decided it wasn't her business. If he wanted to tell her, he would.

"After I dealt with my grief, do you know what's been the hardest for me?" She surprised herself with the question and immediately wished she could draw it back.

"I could never guess. You've coped with too much."

She bit the edge of her lip. Knowing Benjamin's spiritual strength, she knew she'd brought up a touchy subject. "My faith."

A scowl settled on his face.

"For the first year, I was angry at God. I couldn't understand how a loving God could be so cruel. I wanted Greg alive. I wanted Mandy alive. I wanted to see her play with her little friends. I want to know what she looks like now and hold her against me and smell the shampoo in her hair. I know I shouldn't be angry with God, but it's been difficult."

Tears pooled in her eyes. Benjamin reached over and used a finger to brush them away.

"I won't argue with you, Joanne. You've been through so much, but you can't blame God for all the evil in the world. Sin causes evil, and makes us trip and fall."

"I know, and I feel ashamed that I've had to struggle to face that. Every time I think of my little girl's body lost somewhere in Lake

St. Clair, my heart aches. If only they could have—" She stopped and shook her head.

"Don't chastise yourself. Remember that God doesn't promise us a life without sorrow or pain. He does promise He'll be with us always. We have to have faith."

"Faith. We've gone full circle and we're back to that. I'm hanging on, dear friend, but sometimes my grip weakens. I do a lot of praying."

"You can't go wrong with prayer," he said, digging into his memory for a Scripture that had risen to the fringes of his mind. "I'm thinking of a verse in Isaiah. 'Then you will call, and the Lord will answer; you will cry for help, and He will say: Here am I.' That's what prayer is, Joanne. It's your cry for help, and God hears it. He's with you."

She closed her eyes for a moment. "Thanks for reminding me," she whispered. She raised her coffee cup and took a slow drink, then lowered it. Her expression appeared faraway and thoughtful. "It's lonely going to church without Greg and Mandy. I still haven't gotten used to that. If you ever want to join me, let me know."

"How about this Sunday?"

Her look of gratitude rolled over him and

roused his emotions. He'd tried to prepare himself for seeing Joanne again, but he hadn't succeeded. The feelings he'd bound so tightly had loosened their bonds.

He needed to guard his heart and his good sense. She'd always been Greg's wife, and she still was. He'd cared so deeply for her and Mandy, just as he'd loved his friend, Greg, but Joanne had always held a special place. Tonight his feelings were growing like vines of morning glories entwining through the secret places in his heart.

"I'd better go," he said, pushing his chair back with such speed that he surprised himself.

"Did I say something?" Joanne looked startled by his abruptness.

"No. I have a busy day tomorrow and it's getting late."

He rose, and she stood, too, gathering their cups and placing them in the sink.

Joanne came around to his side of the table and touched his arm. "Thanks for being a good friend, Benjamin. I'm so happy you're home."

"Me, too," he said, giving her a quick embrace. "Now, don't worry about the dreams."

"It's not just dreams. I hear it when I'm awake."

He forced himself to let her go. "After tomorrow, it'll pass. The anniversary will be over, and then you'll move ahead again."

"I hope so," she said, but a look on her face said she didn't believe it.

As he stepped outside, her voice followed him through the doorway.

"It means something, Benjamin. I feel it in my heart."

An uneasy sensation crept over him as he descended the porch steps, but he covered his concern and waved.

Joanne waved back and then closed the door.

Before Benjamin slipped into his car, the wind caught his jacket, and a chill gripped him—the wind, or was it apprehension?

It means something. The words echoed in his mind.

Chapter Two

Headlights glinted off the snow, and Benjamin squinted to shield his eyes from the glare. He had a headache. His feelings had knotted throughout the evening like a noose. Joanne seemed troubled. He recalled she'd seen a therapist after the accident, and maybe it was time for her to have a therapy booster shot.

Yet that wasn't all that concerned him. Joanne had grown even more beautiful since he'd seen her at the funeral. Maturity and grief had added lines to her face, making her more real, more vulnerable, and the look touched him deeply.

As they'd talked this evening, his mind had journeyed back to that horrible night when Joanne called him. He had barely grasped what she'd told him through her sobs. Greg and Mandy drowned. *No,* he'd thought. *The police have to be wrong. They made a mistake,* he'd told himself over and over as he raced to her house through snowfall so similar to tonight's.

But they hadn't been wrong. The next morning Greg's body had been found in icy Lake St. Clair, his still belted into his car. And Mandy…the divers never found her.

Pain knifed Benjamin's heart at the thought. The beautiful child gone, her car seat still attached to the back seat, the belt unbuckled… The police said she must have disappeared through a partially opened window. The horror of it washed over him now, as icy as Lake St. Clair must have been. If he still felt the powerful emotion of Mandy's death, he couldn't imagine what Joanne must feel.

He drew in a ragged breath and tried to push the vision of that night from his mind. His headache thumped in his temples, and he pushed his fingers against one side to ease the ache.

Everything had seemed confused tonight. For years, he'd had strong feelings for Joanne, but he'd controlled them. She was his good friend's wife—charming, amiable and lovely. Her mothering skills had amazed him. When

Mandy was born, it seemed as though God had created Joanne for motherhood.

Though Greg had worked long hours, Joanne had never complained. She had done all she could to support his career and still have interests of her own. She'd been active at church and had participated in community drives and so many activities, Benjamin was amazed. He had always admired her, but then one day, he realized that Joanne also had begun to fill his dreams.

He felt ashamed when he finally admitted to himself that he was attracted to his best friend's wife. The emotions had sneaked up on him. He'd thought his admiration was friendship, but it had become far more than that. He'd prayed, asking God to help him find a solution. Benjamin couldn't stop being Greg's friend without an explanation, and he couldn't avoid Joanne if he was Greg's friend.

The answer came at the law firm with the out-of-state project. He'd jumped at it. After Greg's death, he left his heart in Detroit and moved to Seattle, built a life there. Women came and went, but no one captured his heart. He left the problem in God's hands—he hadn't known what else to do.

Now, project completed, he was back home

where he belonged, and the same problem faced him. How could he be Joanne's friend when he wanted so much more?

Donna Angelo stood inside the bedroom door and looked at her stepdaughter nestled in bed. Connie's deep breathing assured Donna she was asleep. Her heart eased at the sight of the child so warm and cozy. Donna hadn't felt warm and cozy for a long time.

She stepped into the hallway and closed Connie's bedroom door. If her husband came home tonight with too much to drink and more ranting, she hoped Connie wouldn't hear the noise. The child needed to sleep in peace—something rare for their household.

No matter how many times Donna waded through the details, she could never figure out when it had happened. She guessed their problems had begun slowly and built into a frightening undertone in their relationship.

Donna's hands trembled as she headed down the long hallway to the kitchen. She wanted to have Carl's plate ready when he arrived, hoped that the scent of food would make him less irritable. She rubbed her upper arm, feeling the tenderness resulting from last night's fiasco.

Most every evening, Carl arrived home late. Sometimes he smelled of liquor, but she'd learned not to say anything. He always insisted his business had kept him out late. She never understood why the owner of a trucking company didn't have someone who worked the night shift.

Then, when she caught sight of his duffel bag filled with hundred-dollar bills, she'd begun to wonder if the business fronted something illegal—but Donna knew better than to ask questions.

Yet tonight she had questions, not about his business, but about a restraining order she'd found in an old metal box in a basement storage closet. Why had his first wife obtained an order to keep him away? Had he knocked her around, too? Finally she decided the order had to mean Carl and his wife had separated. Yet Donna knew that Carl had been a widower. Nothing made sense. She wasn't sure she could hold back her curiosity—although if she had any brains, she would.

The garage door rumbled open, and Donna hurried to the refrigerator. Before the door had opened, she'd popped Carl's meal into the microwave. She hoped he would be in one of his rare good moods tonight.

When the back door opened, she glanced toward the sound.

Carl lumbered inside and tossed his keys on the counter by the door. "What you gawkin' at?" he asked.

"Nothing." She rubbed the bruise on her arm and studied his expression. Then she turned away to pull his salad from the refrigerator.

What had happened to the man she'd met? Carl—a widower with a small child—had swept her off her feet. Her heart had gone out to the little girl. Connie had seemed so timid, and Donna had realized the loss of a mother must have been devastating for the child.

When they'd met, Carl had shown Donna a good time. Though unpolished in many ways, he knew about fine restaurants and bought her expensive gifts, and before she knew it, he'd asked her to marry him. The courtship had been too short, Donna realized now.

The buzzer sounded on the microwave, and Donna opened the door and carried the plate to the table. Carl didn't look up. He grabbed the fork and speared a hunk of beef.

"Get me a beer," he said between chews.

Donna opened her mouth to tell him he shouldn't drink so much. Then she closed it.

One of her Christian friends had told her how much better her life had become since she and her husband had accepted Jesus, and Donna longed to share that with Carl. If he stopped drinking and developed a personal relationship with the Lord, maybe he'd stop pushing her around.

Knowing today wasn't the day to make the suggestion, Donna retrieved the beer, snapped open the lid and set it beside his plate. She pulled out a chair and joined him, hoping he'd ask about Connie.

For a father, Carl showed little interest in his daughter. And that wasn't all that bothered Donna. She could handle being pushed around, but sometimes he got rough with Connie. Nothing terrible, but just too threatening, and Donna felt fear each time she thought about what he could do to a six-year-old.

Carl finally lifted his head and focused on her. His eyes narrowed. "What's bugging you?"

"Nothing. I just thought we'd talk."

"About what?"

"Anything, Carl. Talk like most husbands and wives do. Tell me about your day."

He snorted and dug into another piece of meat. "You want money, I suppose?"

She did. She wanted lots of money. Then she could take Connie and go far away where no one could find them. "No. That's not what I was thinking, but it would help if I had a little pocket money."

"I earn the money, and I pay the bills," Carl said. "If you need some cash, ask me. Don't I give you enough for groceries."

Donna knew she was on dangerous ground. "Yes, but if I need clothes or—"

"Why do you need clothes? You don't go anywhere."

That wasn't what she wanted. "A credit card would be nice." She held her breath.

Carl's hate-filled eyes sought hers. "You women are all alike—money-grubbing, unappreciative wenches. You and my mother. She drove my father to drink, and then he'd take it out on…"

The determined set of his jaw warned Donna she was in trouble. His hand snapped out, but she ducked back and he missed her.

"I don't need anything, Carl." Her voice pierced the air, and she feared Connie could hear them. "I—I just wish you'd come home earlier so you could spend time with Connie. She hardly knows you anymore."

"That's your job. Why do you think I married you?"

His caustic remark felt like a punch in her belly, and Donna drew back. "I thought you loved me," she said, now realizing her belief was a fairy tale.

"You thought wrong," he spat. "You're the housekeeper and baby-sitter. I don't even want to look at you."

She calculated he wasn't drunk tonight, just spiteful and he hadn't hit her. Now seemed her best chance of having her curiosity answered about what she'd seen in the basement. "I found a paper in the basement today."

His head shot upward. "What kind of paper?"

"A restraining order—a permanent order to keep you from going near Connie and her mother. What was that about? I thought you and—"

His fist smashed down on the table, lifting the plate from the surface and sending his butter knife clattering to the floor. He snatched it up and pointed it at her.

"Carl, I'm just confused. You said you were

a widower, but if you and she weren't together, then why do you have custody now?"

He leaned across the table and poked the knife at her chest. "Are you stupid? Her mother's dead—and that's where you're going to be if you don't quit snooping. Why were you in the basement? Stay out of there."

"I'm sorry. I wasn't snooping. I was looking for my stuff, and I have to go there to do the laundry." The look in his eye frightened her. "I suppose the question was stupid. Where else would Connie go but with her father?"

"Connie can go to her grave with you for all I care. You're both a weight around my neck. Women are worthless."

He eased the knife away from her chest, and Donna caught her breath. Another question about his name nudged her, but she wouldn't ask, not if she wanted to live another day. "I can heat up some more stew."

"It's garbage," he said, giving the plate an angry shove across the table. "Anyway, who can eat with your puss gapin' at me?"

She started to say she was sorry again, but stopped herself. Donna wasn't sorry. She'd put up with too much, and if she didn't love Connie so much, she'd pack her bags and leave. If only Connie were her child, they could make their escape together—but she had no rights.

For the sake of Connie, she was stuck.

"So who was your friend last night?" Nita Wolfe asked.

Joanne swiveled in her desk chair and faced her co-worker, who was standing in her office doorway. Nita was one of those women with a good heart and the spirit of Cupid. If Joanne spent too much time talking with the copy machine repairman, Nita assumed it was a budding romance.

"Actually, an old friend of Greg's," she said.

Nita's conspiratorial expression shriveled to one of disappointment. "That's it?"

"That's it. He's a longtime friend who's been away. Now he's back in town."

Nita perked up as she moved closer. "Married?"

"No."

"Aha." Nita raised her eyebrows.

"What's that supposed to mean?"

"You just never know what God has in store." She put her hand on Joanne's shoulder. "You're too young to be alone the rest of your life."

"Thanks for the wisdom, Nita, but I can handle my life just fine." Even as she said the words, Joanne admitted to herself that her life was lacking. She'd made a valiant effort to move on in every area but relationships.

A movement in the doorway caught Joanne's eye. She followed Melissa Shafer's entrance into the office, noted the woman's eyes shifting from one side to the other. Joanne guessed her motive.

"Am I interrupting?" Melissa asked, giving Nita a look.

"Not at all. We were just talking," Joanne said.

"Just wanted to see what you did to the office." She wandered behind the desk and gazed out the large window overlooking the Detroit skyline. "It's nice to have real sunlight."

Joanne opened her mouth to apologize and then closed it. Recently, they had both been interviewed for the same position. Joanne had been given the promotion. "It's nice, but I'm not sure it's worth the added work and worry."

Melissa grinned. "You worry? Never.

You're too cool and collected, Joanne." She glided away from the window. "Well, congratulations. You made an impression and I didn't. No hard feelings."

"Thanks," Joanne said, amazed at Melissa's understanding.

Melissa strutted back to the doorway and paused. "You can get back to *business*." She wiggled her fingers in a wave and vanished into the hallway.

Nita's eyebrows arched. "I like the inflection. I suppose she assumed we were talking about her." Then she grinned. "I bet you did make a better impression during the interview."

Joanne shrugged, already wanting to forget the conversation. "By the way, here's the novel I said I'd loan you." She opened her desk drawer and pulled out the book she'd brought from home. "It's a good story, and a nice way to spend a quiet evening."

Nita skimmed the novel cover for a minute, then lowered the book and studied Joanne's face. "All joking aside, you look stressed. What happened? Did your friend have bad news?" She settled her hip against the edge of the desk and ran her finger along a picture frame propped beside Joanne's telephone.

Joanne's gaze rested on the photograph she'd taken of Greg and Mandy at the Detroit Zoo in front of the bear fountain. The sunlight played on Mandy's blond halo of curls, and Joanne felt a tug on her heart at the memory.

"It's a lot of things," she said, "but nothing that Benjamin said."

"Benjamin? He was your midnight visitor?" Nita sent her a perky smile.

"He left at nine."

Nita chuckled. "I'm only teasing."

Joanne drew in a long breath and tilted her head toward the frame. "Three years ago today the accident happened."

Nita's focus shifted to the photograph. She lifted it from the desk and studied the picture, then replaced it with sorrow in her eyes. "Oh, honey," she said, leaning over to give Joanne a hug, "I'm sorry. Here I am pulling your leg, and you're really upset."

Joanne wanted to tell her that her upset was about more than the anniversary date, but she hesitated. "Don't worry about it," she said finally. "I've had other things on my mind, too." Still, maybe Nita would understand. She looked into her friend's serious face. "Do you believe in—" She paused trying to find a word that made sense. "In premonition?"

Nita looked puzzled. "You mean like a sixth sense?"

"Sort of."

"Women's intuition?"

"A little more than that."

"A little more, how?" Nita rested her hands on the desk and leaned closer. "What's going on?"

"Voices?"

The word caused Nita to draw back. She straightened, as if she thought Joanne had lost her mind.

Joanne wondered herself. "Not really voices. A feeling. It's in here." She pressed her hand against her heart.

"You're hearing things?"

"I'm not crazy, Nita. The voice is like a child crying for help."

Nita's gaze didn't waver.

"It's Mandy's voice." Joanne heard Nita's sudden intake of air.

"Mandy's? Are you sure?"

"I'll never forget my child's cry. Never."

"But she's…"

"Dead, I know." Joanne's heart sank. "I

don't know what to make of it, but I'm hearing it. I keep asking myself what it means."

"I have no idea what it means, but I think you should get back into counseling. I'm sure these things happen. Hopefully it'll pass."

Joanne shrugged, feeling defeated. "Maybe." No one seemed to truly understand, not even Benjamin.

"Grief is a strange emotion," Nita said. "It manifests itself in so many ways, and just when you think it's conquered, it rises up again with a vengeance. You need to keep busy until the anniversary and the holidays pass. They're difficult times of the year."

"You're right. After the accident, I lost the joy of Christmas…and my life." Joanne tried to smile but her face felt frozen in a frown. "I need to get a new one."

Nita chuckled. "Sounds like you gave it a start last night. You had one pleasant distraction over for a visit."

"Don't start that again. *F-R-I-E-N-D.* Put those letters together." Joanne gave her a swat. "Get out of here. I have work to do."

Nita edged her hip off the desk. "I came in here for a reason. Feel like Christmas shopping tonight?"

"Not tonight. Benjamin called a few minutes ago, and I invited him over tonight. How about next week?"

"Certainly," Nita said with a grin. "I'd pass up shopping any day for that."

Joanne realized she would, too. A sweet sensation wove through her chest. Having Benjamin around made her feel comfortable. He reminded her of the good days when things were normal. No voices. No deaths. Tonight she was eager to have some laughs. If Benjamin did nothing more than give her a few hours of peace, she'd be eternally grateful.

After Nita waved and left, Joanne tried to pull her focus back to her work, but lost the battle. Her child's cries remained in her thoughts.

She angled her chair to face the computer screen and hit the e-mail button. A list of messages appeared. She saw one that made her smile and opened it.

Hi. Hope you slept well. It was so good to see you last night. Almost like old times. I'll be in touch. I'm looking forward to it. I hope you are.
Benjamin

The note warmed her heart, and she let her gaze linger on it for a moment before skimming the other addresses. Most of them were business e-mails but there was one she didn't recognize—Shadow@123go.com. Curious, she hit the read button.

YOU THINK YOU HAVE EVERY-THING.
WELL YOU DON'T.

The capital letters shouted at her, and she peered at the words again, not understanding the meaning. A strange feeling came over her again.

What did the warning mean? She didn't have everything. She'd lost everything she loved.

Chapter Three

Donna's hands perspired as she fumbled through the old photographs she'd found in the manila envelope in the basement. She knew so little about Carl. She'd never realized it before. She sensed he had two lives, one he allowed her to see and one he kept hidden. She didn't like either of them anymore.

"Mom."

Her heart jumped when she heard Connie's voice. "I'm down in the basement, sweetie. I'll be up in a minute." She glanced around the corner toward the staircase to make sure Connie hadn't come down.

Donna pushed the items back into the metal box she'd found in the closet under the stairs. Old newspaper clippings, photographs, things she didn't have time to scrutinize. She was ashamed of herself for being so suspicious, but the more Carl pushed her away and the more volatile he became, the more she wanted to know about him. Maybe if she learned something significant she could forgive him—or if not, have the power to escape.

A photograph fell to the floor, and Donna reached to retrieve it.

"Where are you?"

Donna's chest tightened at the sound of Connie's voice so near. She slipped the photo into her pants pocket, then snapped the lid on the box and slid it back into its hiding place.

"Right here, sweetie."

Donna came around the corner and met Connie head-on. "Oops. Let's get upstairs."

"Whatcha doing?"

Her mind scrambled. "I was looking for something I misplaced. It's not here."

Connie gave her a questioning look, then skipped up the stairs ahead of her, calling back, "Can I have a snack?"

"Fruit," Donna said, following her into the kitchen. "How was school?"

Donna rinsed off an apple and handed it to

Connie while she listened to her tales of the "bad boys" in her class, Connie's recess escapades and a star she had received for helping a girl with math.

As Donna began dinner, she watched the child—her animation, her blond ponytail swinging back and forth and her blue eyes wide with excitement. Donna sensed that Connie felt closer to her than to her father, and her heart swelled.

When Connie had finished her story and bounded off to change her school clothes, Donna slipped her hand into her pocket and pulled out the photo. She needed to get it back into the envelope before Carl found it and punished her for snooping—as he called it—but she believed a wife deserved to know something about her husband's past.

When she lowered her gaze to the photograph, Donna's heart stopped. Looking like he did before she married him, Carl stood outside a large brick home beside a dark-haired woman who held a toddler in her arms. Donna looked closer, trying to make sense out of the picture. If this was Carl's deceased wife and Connie, something was terribly wrong.

This child had dark hair like her parents. Connie was blond.

* * *

Benjamin came through the front door in the wake of a cold wind. Joanne struggled to push the door closed.

"I think that's what they mean by blowing into town," he said, sliding off his jacket.

Joanne laughed. "I should have told you not to come over tonight."

"No, I should have taken you out. There's a nice rhythm and blues group at the Java Café. You'd probably enjoy them."

"I might," she said, motioning him into the living room.

He went ahead of her and settled into a recliner, then clicked up the footrest while she sank into a comfy chair nearby. "I hope you wanted me to make myself at home."

She grinned again. Benjamin always seemed at home when he visited. He was the kind of easygoing guy she admired.

They sat in comfortable silence for a few minutes, eyes turned to the window.

"It's snowing again," she said finally. "The ski resorts must be thrilled."

"I'm sure."

Her gaze drifted to him, and she realized he was studying her. His look left her uneasy. "Is something wrong?"

He gave a quick nod. "I'm just thinking about you."

"Me?"

"You and the voice. How's it going?"

Again she didn't like the flippant way he asked, but she knew he hadn't meant it to sound callous. "I haven't called the shrink yet, if that's what you're asking."

"No, not that," he said, scrutinizing her, "but something else happened today."

"Yes, it did," she replied, wondering how he could tell. "This time at work."

"A phone call?"

"No. An e-mail. It was strange."

"Strange how?"

She told him about the message and how edgy it had made her.

"It's the same as a wrong telephone number. It's easy to mix up an e-mail address. I'd guess it wasn't meant for you."

"Probably." She pushed her uncomfortable thoughts aside.

"And it wasn't really a threat, but just in case, save it when you're at work tomorrow."

"Why, if it's nothing?"

"I'll mention it to my detective friend Hank Cortezi and see what he thinks."

"No. Don't." Panic settled in her chest.

"I've already made a fool of myself. Let's drop it. I'm sure it was sent to me by mistake."

Benjamin leaned closer, his face strained. "I'm worried about you, Joanne."

"I'm trying to reconcile myself to what it means, Benjamin. I know the snow, the holidays, make me nostalgic. It's happened every year since they've been gone. The year they died I'd gone Christmas shopping early, and I buried some of Mandy's Christmas presents in her casket." Sorrow weighed on her again. "Every year, I remember… I want to forget."

"It's natural. Each year will get better."

"That's what I thought, but this year is worse." She leaned toward him. "If I tell you something, you'll think I'm crazy."

"No, I won't."

"I think the voice is a warning of some kind."

His face twisted into a puzzled expression. "Like a premonition."

"Sort of, but more than that."

"You're sure it's Mandy's voice."

"Yes. A mother knows her child's voice, and she senses when her child is in danger."

"Yes, but—"

"Wait." She held up a finger and hurried

into her bedroom to find her Bible. Last night she'd been reading the Christmas story, and when she'd seen the Scripture, the message validated her previous thoughts and bolstered her sense of sanity. It had been a blessing. Clutching the Book, she returned to the living room and plunked herself into the chair.

"It's right here," she said, flipping through the pages. "It's in the Christmas story in 2 Luke. 'All who heard it were amazed at what the shepherds said to them. But Mary treasured up all these things and pondered them in her heart.' Mary knew Jesus would face trials. It reassured me. Mothers feel things about their kids. I sense my daughter needs me, Benjamin."

"I'm not going to disagree with you. I just don't want you to worry about what it means. I think it's the time of year. I truly think the voice will pass."

The dinner she'd eaten churned in her stomach, and Joanne could only shake her head. "I don't know," she said finally.

"You need to cheer up, Joanne. Let's do something different. Let's go…" He paused, thinking, then grinned. "How about shopping? Ladies love to shop."

"But men don't, and anyway, I promised to go Christmas shopping with Nita."

His face brightened as if relieved. "Okay, that saves me from a fate worse than..." He didn't finish but chuckled instead. "Let's decorate. It's almost Thanksgiving. It's never too early to put up a wreath and set out some holiday candles."

She opened her mouth to protest, but he'd already stood.

"Where do you keep all that stuff?"

"I haven't been doing much with that since—"

"Time you did," he said. He moved to face her and held out his hands.

Joanne couldn't bear to dampen his enthusiasm. She grasped his hands and let him pull her to her feet. "It's in the attic." She pointed upward.

"One of those holes in the ceiling?" His tone reflected his fading eagerness.

"This decorating business wasn't my idea," she said.

He grinned. "Where is it?" He grasped her shoulders and turned her to face the archway.

Joanne led him into her walk-in bedroom closet and pointed to the drop-down ladder.

"I'll go with you so you know what to bring down."

She snapped on the light from below while Benjamin climbed the ladder, then gave her a hand. At the top, she stood while he hunched to avoid the low ceiling.

She beckoned to him, and they moved across the plank floor to a pile of boxes. "It's all here. Some of it's labeled, but that's not always accurate."

In the gloomy light, they lifted lids and checked contents, and soon, they were lowering a few of the cartons to the floor below. Once the trap door was closed, Joanne piled three boxes into Benjamin's arms, then took one for herself, and they carried them into the living room.

Joanne sat on the floor and Benjamin joined her, and together they opened the boxes and checked the contents. Soon Christmas candles, window wreaths, and garland for the fireplace lined the floor around them.

"What's this?" Benjamin asked.

Joanne looked up and caught her breath. "It's Floppy." She reached out and grasped the plush, loopy-eared dog. "It was Mandy's favorite toy. She slept with him every night." Tears welled in her eyes as the scene rose before her—Mandy's blond hair pressed against the pillow and Floppy nestled beside her.

Benjamin shifted nearer and opened his arms to her. "I'm sorry. I thought doing this might be a way to—"

He stopped talking, and she rested her head against his strong shoulder, accepting his comforting arms. "It's not your fault," she said, once she'd regained control. She eased back and pressed the dog against her chest. "I'd forgotten I'd put him in with the Christmas stuff. We had the ornaments out to decorate, before I got the call that—" She stopped. Benjamin understood; she didn't need to explain.

She lowered the plush toy into her lap and brushed her fingers along its fake fur. "I'd planned to bury Floppy along with the Christmas toys, but… I couldn't."

"I understand."

"I couldn't, because I kept wanting to think it wasn't true, that they were wrong. I wanted the doorbell to ring and, when I answered, a police officer to be there with Mandy in his arms, but it didn't happen."

Benjamin only looked at her, his eyes so sad she wished she hadn't told him.

"Maybe this year will be a breakthrough," she said. "It could be."

"It could be," Benjamin said, rising.

"I feel something special. I believe this year will be different."

Benjamin's chest ached from the sadness he felt surrounding them both. He'd adored Mandy and couldn't imagine the pain Joanne felt as the child's mother.

He'd done a lot of thinking since they'd last talked, and had questions that he wanted to ask, but he knew she was too sensitive today. He watched her caressing the bedraggled, stuffed dog, his long ears soiled from Mandy's dragging him with her everywhere, and finally he had to look away or fall apart himself.

Then he mustered courage and spoke. "What makes you think this year is different? You don't really think Mandy will come through that door, do you?"

Her silence put him on edge.

"Joanne, please, don't—"

She held up her hand to stop him. "I don't know why I feel this way, but I've never felt that Mandy was totally gone. Gone from me, yes, but not gone. I hear that voice, and it's her, but she's not three anymore. She'd be almost six. Reality tells me she's dead, but I sense she's alive."

Benjamin's heart sank. "She is alive in heaven, Joanne."

"I know, but I mean…"

Her downcast look made him ache. Yet, common sense told him it could be no other way. He'd asked himself questions, too, about Mandy's death, but nothing made sense. His attorney's mind had sorted through the information and he had no doubt that a three-year-old couldn't have escaped.

The question came to his lips before he could stop himself. "How could Mandy have survived the freezing water of Lake St. Clair, Joanne? We're talking November."

Joanne turned toward him, her eyes searching his. "Maybe she wasn't in the car."

"She what?"

"I'm not sure she was in the car, Benjamin. That's the feeling I have."

He knelt beside her. "Joanne, I didn't like the details, either, and I know they never found her body, but what you're thinking is far-fetched."

"Far-fetched, but not impossible. In my heart, I knew that Greg would never let her in the car without her seat belt fastened."

"What if Mandy unhooked it? Did you think of that?"

"She'd never unfastened the belt before. I'm not sure she knew how. I think someone else unhooked it. I've been thinking about this for the past few days."

Her admission swam through his mind like a fish avoiding a baited hook. He couldn't imagine the possibility, but he'd found that fact of the case disturbing, including the child floating through the partially opened window.

"And the window," Joanne said, as if she had read his mind. "Why would Greg have the window open on a cold November night? The police speculated and dismissed that fact. It's lived inside me for too long. I think something else happened that night. Before the accident."

Donna sat on the edge of Connie's bed and brushed the child's soft cheek with the back of her hand. "You're a beautiful young lady— do you know that?"

"Uh-huh. You always tell me I am."

"Well, you are." The words almost caught in her throat. "Connie."

"What?" The girl peeked at her from beneath the blanket she'd drawn up to her nose.

"Do you remember your real mother?" Donna wanted to kick herself for asking, but she'd been plagued by questions and fears that she couldn't control.

"No."

Donna had figured the child wouldn't remember much at her age, but she'd hoped.

"Is Daddy coming home?"

Connie's voice wavered when she asked. Donna knew the child heard their arguments and her cries of pain when Carl knocked her around. She'd had to cover her bruises with makeup so that Connie wouldn't see them. "He's out of town tonight. On business."

"Good," she said, her pink lips turning up at the edges.

Connie's faint smile reflected Donna's sense of relief. The night alone would give her time to think—and to "snoop," as Carl called it.

"I love you," she said, bending over to kiss Connie's warm cheek before she stood.

"Love you, too."

Connie's sleepy voice touched Donna's ears as she slipped through the doorway.

Donna stood in the hallway to think. Tonight she had time to search for something that would help her learn more about Carl. Ever since she'd found the photo, she'd been sick with confusion and fear.

Carl had said he wouldn't be home until tomorrow, which would give her time to put the photograph back and see what else he'd hidden down there.

The bulb had always been dim in the closet beneath the stairs, so Donna located the flashlight and carried it with her. Her nerves stood on end like the hairs on a scared cat. Every sound caused her to jump.

At the bottom of the steps she headed back to the door beneath the staircase. She turned on the faint light, then stepped inside. The room appeared to have been a small pantry at one time, but now it held miscellaneous items—luggage, boxes of papers in manila folders and the metal box.

She opened the box again and pulled out more of the photographs. Tonight she had time to study them. The same dark-haired woman appeared in numerous shots. One showed Carl with his arm around her. She had to be his first wife. The child appeared again, and Donna knew she wasn't Connie. The features were wrong. She dropped the photos back into the envelope and set it on the floor.

Petrified by her thoughts, Donna delved into the metal box, rifling through old receipts, car registrations, and the restraining order envelope. Then she saw another legal-size envelope. She pulled out the document, and her heart stopped. *Stella Rose Angelo, Plaintiff. Peter Carl Angelo, Defendant.* Divorce papers. Peter again. She'd seen that name used in the restraining order. Donna skimmed the contents. His wife agreed to forgo some of her settlement in trade for his agreement to never see her or their daughter again.

And then she died?

Her hand shook as she stuffed the paper back into the envelope. Her mind spun with questions and fear swept over her. She knew Carl was abusive. He'd treated her badly, but so far, he hadn't hurt Connie. Would he?

As Donna lifted the documents to place them back in the metal file, she spotted a newspaper clipping near the bottom of the box. Her tremors grew as she reached in to pull out the paper. Fingers fumbling, she unfolded it, and the headline flared before her eyes: "Attorney and Daughter Drown in Lake St. Clair."

Below the article, Donna saw the grainy photographs—a man and a blond toddler. She gazed at the photo. Donna clasped her face, gasping for air. Black spots peppered her eyes, and an unbearable hum roared in her ears. She lowered her head and clung to the wall, fearing she would faint.

Donna stayed there until she regained control of herself. Then she inched upward, still grasping the closet wall for support. Her breath came in gasps as she scanned the text of the article.

Gregory Fuller and his three-year-old daughter Mandy drowned when Fuller's car accidentally skidded into Lake St. Clair last night during a snowstorm. Fuller works for the law firm of Saperstein, Fuller, Drake and Welsh.

Donna skimmed the rest of the article with disbelief. Fuller had left his wife, Joanne, behind. Gregory Fuller. The name rang in her ears. Where had she heard it? She lowered her gaze to the envelope at her feet and gaped at the return address: Saperstein, Fuller, Drake and Welsh, Attorneys at Law. The divorce papers.

She eyed the restraining order sent by the same firm, then unfolded the document. The truth struck her. The plaintiff's attorney was Gregory Fuller. Carl's wife had hired Fuller to represent her, and a year later he died.

Joanne Fuller? According to the article, she lived on the east side in Grosse Pointe, about twenty miles from Dearborn.

Donna returned her gaze to the photos beneath the article, studying Mandy Fuller. Her head swam. Could it be? She lifted her eyes toward the basement ceiling. Connie was sleeping upstairs—Connie with blond hair. It couldn't be. Donna loved Connie— she couldn't be someone else's child. Donna couldn't live without her.

But what if—

"What are you doing?" The voice bellowed from the staircase.

Carl. Donna jerked and dropped the restraining order, then spun around.

Carl loomed in the doorway. "I told you to stay out of there." He grabbed her arm and jerked her from the closet.

"What's wrong, Carl?" Donna panicked,

struggling to find an excuse. "I was looking for luggage to store some summer clothing."

Carl clung to her with one hand and leaned in to grab something from inside the closet. Then he stepped back, hurling a piece of luggage across the basement. It struck his tool bench, and metal tools clanged to the concrete floor. With a swift move, he grasped her by the throat and pinned her to the wall.

Donna felt her breath leave her. She tried to speak, but choked. Color drained from the room. *I have to get away. Connie must get away.* The hum filled her head as her knees buckled.

Chapter Four

Joanne pressed the telephone to her ear but heard only silence on the line.

"Hello," she said again.

Nothing. She lowered her gaze to the caller ID. Blocked. She hated crank calls, especially now that she'd become so nervous.

"Can I help you?" she asked, her voice rasping with irritation. She listened for a second more until a faint sound like a moan wavered along the wire, making her neck prickle. She closed her eyes, then dropped the phone onto the cradle and sank into a kitchen chair.

The desperate moan reverberated in her ears. Voices and silent callers. How much more could she take?

She let her frustration subside, then rose and headed for the coffeepot to make coffee for Benjamin. Joanne spooned in the grounds, added water, then wandered into the living room. The clock on her cable box showed 7:47. She had expected Benjamin earlier. Uneasiness filled her, but then she laughed at herself for being so jittery.

The phone rang again and for once she didn't jump. Joanne knew Benjamin well enough to realize he'd call if something was keeping him. She strode into the kitchen and grabbed the receiver.

"Hello," she said, expecting Benjamin's rich, baritone voice.

Distant unclear sounds drifted over the line, but no one spoke.

"Benjamin?"

Then she heard it again—the emptiness.

It grated on her senses like nails on a chalkboard. Her knuckles turned white against the dark beige of the phone. "Either say what you want or stop calling." Her own determined voice startled her. As she yanked the telephone from her ear, she finally heard something, and brought the receiver back to listen.

"I—I…" A woman's voice.

"What do you want?"

Only a sigh wrenched the silence.

Breath shot from Joanne's lungs like air

from a pricked balloon. Anger fired within her. "If you're not going to talk, then leave me alone."

She heard a *click,* then an empty line.

Joanne slammed the receiver onto the cradle.

Sick people. They had nothing better to do than harass people. Play the jokester. But it wasn't funny. Not at all. Then her thought shifted. She recalled the voice and the foreboding. The coincidence seemed too great.

Benjamin? Was he on the way? She called his numbers and got his answering machine. She hung up. The police. She needed someone. She grabbed the telephone book from a drawer, found the number and punched the buttons. Her body trembled as she waited.

"Grosse Pointe Department of Public Safety. Officer James. May I help you?"

Joanne opened her mouth and choked on the words. "I—I've received some strange telephone calls." She sounded foolish.

"What kind of calls?" the officer asked.

She gave her name and tried to explain, but the more she said, the more insane she sounded. The officer obviously didn't see the connection between her daughter's death three years ago and two anonymous calls. Right now, neither did she.

"Was the caller abusive or obscene? Or were you threatened in any way?"

"They were hang-ups," she said, realizing how trivial it sounded.

"Ma'am, two hang-ups doesn't really warrant police action. You're welcome to call your telephone company, but unless the calls are threatening or abusive, we can't take action. After three telephone calls from the same caller, you can contact the telephone company and then we'd be happy to take your report."

Frustration charged through Joanne. "Thank you for your time."

"If this continues, call your phone company and then give us a call."

"Thanks," she said again, and hung up feeling mortified. He'd explained twice, as if she were stupid.

Joanne eyed the clock again, wishing Benjamin were there. Her mind reeled as she wandered to the living room. She sank into a chair and her hands trembled as she ran them along the nape of her neck, thinking about the calls. Two hang-ups was nothing, just as the officer had said. So why was she distressed?

She needed Benjamin to tell her she wasn't losing her mind. Hearing Mandy's voice in her head had been bad enough. Now, on the anniversary of her death, anonymous calls struck her as a cruel coincidence.

She lowered her face into her hands. "Lord, why? If You love me, why are You tormenting me like this?" But beneath her frustration, she could hear Benjamin's voice: *You can't blame God for all the evil in the world.*

Joanne lowered her head to the table and wept while her prayer rose from her heart, asking the Lord to forgive her. *You've promised to be here when I call Your name. Here I am, Father, begging for mercy.*

Her mind whirring with questions, Joanne rose and dragged herself into the living room. Weariness had overcome her, and she wanted to sleep. She stood for a moment in the light of the living room and watched the snow drift to the ground—white, pure, fresh, like a baby, like Mandy had been once.

Tears pooled in Joanne's eyes, then rolled down her cheeks in rivulets. She'd felt sorry for herself for so long, and now this woman's voice had dragged her back into self-pity.

Joanne shook her head, trying to release her twisted thoughts. What did it matter?

God knew the caller's identity. It wasn't her place to sit in judgment. "Lord forgive this woman," she said aloud. "Forgive me for thinking the calls had any evil purpose. Help me find peace."

Gooseflesh rose on Joanne's arms as a Scripture came to her: "Peace I leave with you; my peace I give you." Then verses rolled through her mind: "Do not let your hearts be troubled and do not be afraid." She'd read similar words the other night in the Christmas story, when the angels told the shepherds not to be afraid. The words settled over her like rays of the sun. She needed peace, too. "Thank you, Lord."

She forced herself from the window as the snow blew into drifts, preparing the earth for everyone's dream—a white Christmas. It hadn't been her dream, but since Benjamin had returned, he'd brought a little light into her spirit. She wanted to talk with Benjamin and hear his calm, reassuring voice.

The sound of a car caught Joanne's attention. She rose and went to the window. Benjamin at last. She opened the door and waited.

When he saw Joanne, Benjamin knew immediately that she was distraught. "I'm so sorry I'm late," he said as he stepped inside. "I couldn't get out of the dinner, and it went on forever. You remember Greg's long evenings. It hasn't changed."

"I'm just glad you came," she said, beckoning him into the living room.

He followed her through the archway. "What's happened? More voices?" He sank onto the sofa as she paced in front of him.

"A voice, but this time a real one."

"A real one? What do you mean?"

"Telephone calls. I had two tonight." She finally settled into a chair.

Benjamin winced, knowing he should have been there earlier. His chest tightened. "What kind of calls?"

"Anonymous. Nothing, but they upset me. I called the police, but they can't do anything. I made a fool of myself."

"No you didn't. You felt threatened. So tell me exactly what happened."

He listened as she detailed the incident. His mind tried to make sense of it. He understood why the police had passed it off. Two calls—hang-ups really. What could they do? "What's going on at Solutions? Is someone frustrated with your status with the company?"

She shook her head. "I can't imagine it

being anyone from there. Certainly there's tension at times, particularly in the powwow sessions when everyone has competing ideas, but no. No one would do that."

"What about your promotion?"

"No. It's no one from Solutions. I'm positive."

"You never know." He didn't want to remind her that most crimes involved people who were family or friends.

"When Greg was alive, I learned to tolerate such calls. I'm sure you've had them. They were rare. Angry defendants usually blame the prosecuting attorney." She looked at him as if seeking validation. "But why me, and why now? It's morbid and awful."

"It was a wrong number or a crank call. The world has some sick people."

"I know, but..." She rose again to gaze out the window. "I'd probably blow if off if I weren't so jittery already." She turned and gave him a telling look. "I'm infuriated at myself for letting it upset me."

"You have every right to be, but don't be angry at yourself." He stretched his arm toward her. "Come here."

Her look softened as she walked across the room, then sank beside him on the sofa.

"Don't forget, if it continues you can do something," he said. "You can change your telephone number. Have it unlisted." A new thought struck him. "You have caller ID, right? Did you notice—"

"It was blocked. Both times. I looked."

"It's frustrating." He shifted his hand and rested it on hers. Her fingers felt as cold as his had been when he arrived. Benjamin pressed his warm palm against them. "I wish I had better news, but unless you're threatened or continue to be harassed, like the officer said, you can't do much about it. It's one of those things."

Joanne gave a faint nod. "I know that now."

"People call wrong numbers all the time, and then they're careless enough to try the same number again. Not bright, but not uncommon. I'm sure there's a reasonable explanation."

"I hope so," she said, but her voice didn't sound convincing.

"Have faith, Joanne."

On Sunday morning, Joanne slipped into Benjamin's car.

"Feeling better?" he asked.

"Not much, but let's not talk about it now," she said.

He gave her one of those looks that let her know if she were a witness in court he wouldn't let her get away with it, but today he would. He backed out of the driveway and headed toward the church, talking about the weather and any mundane thing that came to mind.

"How's work?" he asked.

"It's suffering. I'm the head of a think tank, and I doubt that I could find the solution to punch my way out of a paper sack. My co-workers are giving me strange looks."

Benjamin didn't respond as he nosed the car into the church parking lot. He supported her elbow as they ascended the church steps, and she gave him the best smile she could muster to reassure him that her mood had nothing to do with him. Joanne wasn't even sure what bothered her. The woman hadn't called since Friday night. She should be pleased, but she wasn't.

Joanne had a difficult time thinking the woman's calls had been a wrong number. She sensed that, like the voice, the calls meant something, but church wasn't the place to dwell on it. Today, she needed strength and rejuvenation.

As they settled into their seats, the service began. Music rose and the congregation lifted their voices in praise. Benjamin smiled as if he was glad he came. He'd mentioned he hadn't been to church since he'd moved back from Seattle.

Church had become a difficult place for Joanne after the funeral. Joanne knew that might sound strange to most Christians, but she and Greg had shared so much there. They'd been married and had had Mandy baptized at the same church. They had been at worship each Sunday. After he was gone, she felt abandoned by Greg and by God. Now, with Benjamin beside her, she felt complete again.

When the sermon began, the message startled Joanne. As if the pastor knew her need, he spoke about evil attacks on God's children. "It's like a war, a battle of good and evil. God cries to us in one ear while the sin beguiles us in the other. We need selective hearing when it comes to good and evil.

"But those who are victims of evil, remember this from Deuteronomy 23: 'For the Lord your God moves about in your camp to protect you and to deliver your enemies to you.' God's children are never alone in the fight. Though all seems lost, keep your eyes pointed to heaven and your ears tuned to God's Word. He might speak to you in a whisper, but His power is almighty. Let these words from Psalms be your prayer as you face the powers of evil. 'God is our refuge and strength, an ever-present help in trouble.' Amen."

As she rose for the prayers and final hymn, Benjamin glanced at her as if wondering if she'd been listening. She would assure him that she had. Having heard the message, Joanne knew she had to let God be her strength and refuge. *Thank you, Lord,* she said in silent prayer.

The last hymn began, and Joanne was surprised to hear Benjamin's rich baritone voice as he belted out the last verse of "Stand Up, Stand Up for Jesus."

"I needed that," Joanne said minutes later as she slipped from her pew into the aisle.

"I did, too," he said, sending her a tender smile.

He walked beside her into the cold, and she shuddered as they turned into the wintery wind.

"Want to stop for coffee?" Benjamin asked,

slipping his arm around her shoulders as if to ward off the cold.

"That would be nice." She glanced at him, afraid to gaze too intently. His closeness affected her in a way she hadn't expected. She felt a familiarity she hadn't felt since Greg died.

Benjamin nosed the car onto the highway and soon a small coffee shop appeared on the right. He pulled into the parking lot. "Is this okay?"

"Anything's fine," she said as she opened the door.

They hurried inside, and a waitress waved them toward a table. They ordered mugs of coffee, which were brought to their table immediately. Benjamin sipped the hot brew and Joanne lifted the cup and let the aroma surround her.

"Thanks for coming to worship with me today. I felt less lonely than I have in a long, long time." She paused, then decided to continue. "I like the feeling."

"So do I," he said.

"I was thinking that you're a glutton for punishment, though. I'm not the greatest company lately."

She took a sip of the coffee and looked at him over the edge of the cup.

"You've always been good company, Joanne. You and Greg."

"Thanks," she said.

He set the mug on the table and leaned forward. "I think we're avoiding something, Joanne. What's on your mind?"

"It's the same." She gave a shrug. "I'm worried about the calls, yet disappointed she hasn't called again. I need three, remember."

He seemed to study the murky pattern in his mug.

"If I only knew what she wanted."

He looked up. "It might have been a wrong number, and you can't assume it's a she, Joanne. People sometimes change their voices for crank calls."

She saw the flicker of frustration in his eyes and felt the same emotion.

"Remember the sermon today," he said. "God is in your camp. The Lord is your ever-present help in trouble."

"I heard the sermon." She immediately regretted the edge in her voice.

"I know, but believe it."

Her terse comment hadn't swayed him, and she felt good knowing he cared that much.

She'd hurt him with her abruptness, and she longed to smooth the concerned look from his face.

"I'm so afraid when it all pans out to be nothing that you're going to be hurt," he said.

His hand slid over hers, and the warmth rolled up her arm. She sat a moment in silence, then drew back her shoulders and sent him a brave smile. "I'm making a big deal out of two calls. Maybe wrong numbers. Forget it. I will, too." She rested her free hand on his shoulder. "I should have listened to you. You said tomorrow will be better. Maybe it will."

Hearing her sound more positive lifted Benjamin's spirits. "Good for you," he said, tapping his index finger against her hand, hoping she'd smile. "You need a break from all of this tension. "Let's do something fun, Joanne. Let's be kids again and enjoy one day without thinking about all of this."

Her brow wrinkled and her eyes narrowed, but he didn't let the look stop him. "I'm not kidding. It's Thanksgiving. Let's go downtown to the Thanksgiving Day Parade."

She gave him a disbelieving grin. "Are you sure you're not kidding?"

"I'm not. How long has it been since you went?"

"Four years, I guess. We took Mandy when she was nearly two, but she was too young to enjoy it."

"But did you?"

"Enjoy it? Sure. Who doesn't love a huge parade like that one."

"Then it's time to go again—giant helium balloons, marching bands, floats, clowns. What do you say?"

"I say you're ridiculous. Two adults going to a kids' parade?"

"Let's be kids for a day. Come on." He chucked her under the chin, and she laughed.

"Okay, but if it's freezing cold you'd better bring along a thermos of hot chocolate."

"I'll do better than that."

Donna sat in the living room and watched Connie concentrate on her toy house. Sometimes she was amazed at the depth of love she felt for the child. She'd been her stepmother for less than three years, but time didn't matter. Connie fulfilled her longing to be a mother, a pleasure her body would never allow her.

She remembered that when she met Carl, one of the draws for her was the child. Connie seemed so lost and so in need of a woman's touch. Carl said he'd hired sitters to care for her, but that wasn't a mother's love. Donna had opened her heart to Connie.

"Can we go to the parade?" Connie asked, looking up from her playhouse. Plastic furniture and plump, molded characters were strewn across the floor.

"You mean the Thanksgiving parade?"

Connie nodded. "My friend Sarah is going. Can we go?"

Donna had never taken Connie to the parade. Carl wouldn't take the time or effort to fight the Detroit traffic, then stand out in the cold to see the gigantic helium balloons and the floats or listen to the bands. "I'll ask your daddy."

Connie hung her head.

Donna realized the child knew her father too well.

"Could *we* go?" Connie asked.

"You mean just you and me?"

Her face brightened and she nodded.

Donna knew there were shuttle buses. Maybe if they went to Fairlane Town Center they could take public transportation. "Let me think about it, okay?"

"Please." Her blue eyes shone with excitement.

"I'll do my best. That's all I can do."

Connie accepted her offer and went back to her play, while Donna closed her eyes to think. Every child deserved to see the Michigan Thanksgiving Day Parade. It was televised in cities across the U.S. It seemed unfair for Connie not to go. But Carl? He wanted his Thanksgiving turkey.

Carl wanted a lot of things—and gave so little.

Donna's thoughts slipped again into escape mode. She had made two calls to Joanne Fuller, but she'd lost her nerve. When she'd opened her mouth, her voice froze. She'd been disheartened by her actions. Donna needed to know if Connie was truly Joanne Fuller's daughter.

She sensed Carl was having business trouble. Or *he* was in trouble. He would never tell her, but she'd seen his behavior change for the worse these past few months. She was certain he'd gotten into some kind of racket and that it had backfired. When Carl had problems, Donna had greater ones.

Escaping had preoccupied her mind because she feared for her life. It seemed as if Carl took out his anger and frustrations on her. Now she feared for Connie, too, and she needed to make sure she'd found Connie's real mother. It was beyond her comprehension how Carl came to have Connie, but she felt certain she had deduced correctly. After she made sure, she would devise a plan—a plan to escape.

Wouldn't a mother pay a great deal of money to know her daughter was alive? Money would mean nothing with a child at stake. If Donna had cash, she could get away. She could even take Connie with her. Her love for the little girl had grown as deep as if the child were her own, and she couldn't bear the thought of losing her.

If she made Joanne Fuller believe she would lead her to her daughter, the woman might be willing to pay her, but instead of leading her to Connie, Donna could take Connie and leave the U.S. She could go to Canada or Mexico—anywhere to be free of Carl's cruelty.

She had to think her plan through carefully. One mistake and she could scare off Joanne or get the police involved. Or worse, Carl could find out and she'd be a dead woman.

Chapter Five

Joanne sat beside Benjamin as he drove down
the side street off Woodward Avenue and took
the ramp into the underground Cultural Center garage adjacent to the Detroit Institute of
Arts. Traffic had bogged down as soon as
they reached the downtown area as nearly a
million people crowded into the area.

"Are you sure this is worth it?" she asked,
as Benjamin pulled into a parking spot stories below the city.

He gave her a smile and turned off the ignition. "You tell me once we're there."

She swung open her door, and he met her
as she stepped out. As they passed the trunk,
he lifted the lid and pulled out two seat cushions with handles, and a car blanket.

"This won't keep us warm, but it might help."

His thoughtfulness impressed her, but she teased him anyway. "You forgot the thermos."

"I told you I'd do better than that. Remember?"

He'd piqued her curiosity. She waited with him for the elevator to street level, and when they saw daylight, she realized they were at the front of the parade. The wind struck them as they exited, and she tugged on her gloves, then adjusted her scarf, wishing she'd worn a cap.

Benjamin motioned her to follow and they struggled through the crowd along the sidewalk. She wondered how they would see anything with such a bustle of humanity.

To her surprise, Benjamin reached a roped-off area near the grandstands and handed passes to a ticket-taker.

"Grandstand seats?" she asked, amazed he had such pull.

He gave her a wink. "I told you."

She gazed in delight at the bleacher seating that would raise them above the crowd for a full view. As she headed up, her focus settled on the stage where Santa would speak with the children. Santa. Her heart gave a kick as her thoughts flew to Mandy. She'd never had a real kid's chance to enjoy the bounty of Santa's gift bag.

But Joanne had told her little daughter about Jesus. Joanne had sung her children's hymns and told her stories about the Savior. Joanne had always been confident that Mandy was in heaven—

Her thoughts stumbled. No. Joanne didn't know that for sure anymore—not since the voice. She tugged her heavy coat around her more tightly.

Benjamin gave her a questioning look, and she realized she'd fallen silent. "I was thinking," she said without any more explanation.

Benjamin seemed to understand. The Thanksgiving parade was for children more than adults. It was natural her thoughts would be of Mandy. Filled with a sudden melancholy she climbed the stairs.

When they'd found a good spot about halfway up, Benjamin dropped their gear and glanced at his watch. "Let's leave the blanket and cushions here to hold our spots. We have time to go inside."

"Inside what?" She didn't let him answer because she had another question. "How did we get grandstand seats?"

"I know people." He grinned.

"So do I, but I guess it's *who* you know."

He put his hand on her back as they descended to the ground again. "I have a client who's a sponsor. He gets sets of tickets and can use them as he wants."

"And you're one of the recipients," she said over her shoulder.

He chuckled. "Along with the real bonus we're about to enjoy." He motioned for her toward the Detroit Institute of Arts sidewalk.

"We're going to an art show?"

"No, but they have free coffee and muffins inside. We can come into the building to get warm and to use the rest room. Plus it's much nicer than standing on the street, craning our necks."

"I won't argue that," she said.

They ascended the broad stairway into the museum and warmth greeted Joanne when she stepped inside. The scent of fragrant coffee filled the air and a bounty of pastries were spread out for the guests. Benjamin guided her forward, and after they'd filled their cups and grabbed a pastry, he pointed her toward a table for two.

She set down her cup and shifted a chair. Before sitting, she slipped off her gloves and loosened her scarf and coat. She took a sip of the warm drink. "Yummy. This makes up for having to get ready so early."

He grinned and took a bite of a Danish pastry, then followed it with a swig of coffee. His eyes smiled, and she couldn't help but smile back. Today Benjamin, the respected attorney, had become a child. His cheeks glowed from the cold wind or, even more, his excitement being here.

Outside, her heart had melted when he'd pointed to the children's gleeful faces as they waited for the parade. Little tots bundled up in outerwear doubling their size— boots, snowpants, jackets, caps, mittens, and scarves wound around their noses.

"You like kids," she said.

"I do. Very much."

The question she'd longed to ask made its way to her lips. "Why haven't you married, Benjamin? You'd make a wonderful father."

The glow in his cheeks deepened, and Joanne realized she'd asked a sensitive question. She held her breath, fearing she'd put a damper on their morning.

After a moment he gave her a crooked grin. "You've never asked that before."

Her pulse skipped. "You're right. I hadn't

thought of it until recently, and then I figured it was none of my business."

He chuckled. "But it is today?"

"My business?" she asked, catching his little dig. "Not really, but we're friends, so I'm asking."

"Fair enough."

She waited, but he seemed to drift away in thought. Finally he looked her in the eyes. "I fell in love once, and since that time no other woman could compare."

The candid statement answered her question, but again she couldn't stop herself. "Did she die?"

He lowered his gaze and shook his head. "No. It was one of those impossible things."

His face looked strained, and she knew she should stop. "She didn't love you?"

"She did, I think, but not the kind of love I wanted." He lifted his cup and drained it. "Are you ready? We don't want to miss the parade."

Joanne looked down at her barely nibbled pastry and realized she'd forgotten to eat. "Sure," she said, taking another sip of coffee before rising.

Benjamin didn't say any more, and Joanne realized she'd asked too much.

By the time they climbed back into the stands, the bleachers were filled. As a marching band blared on the street, they settled onto the planks. A cold wind swirled upward beneath their feet and Joanne adjusted the seat cushion while Benjamin tucked the blanket around their legs.

Drifting above their heads was a huge helium elephant balloon, tethered to the ground by a host of volunteer clowns who tugged on the lines to keep it from flying away. Children clapped their hands and the crowd roared in her ears.

"Remember when the penguin balloon, Chilly Willy, broke loose years ago? It floated miles away."

He grinned. "They found it in Canada just off Walpole Island, if I remember right."

She grinned at the memory. Then a passing float drew applause—a bright spectacle with toy soldiers surrounding a large drum caricature whose arms stuck out from its sides forming drumsticks that beat a rhythm. Joanne loved the fun, yet she had a difficult time concentrating on the passing parade. Her mind fought between her conversation with Benjamin and her longing to have Mandy by her side.

A cheer rose, and Joanne turned to see the float of Santa's sleigh, the highlight of the parade for the children. As she gazed into the crowd of sweet upturned faces, her stomach knotted. Standing below her near the street were a woman and child—a child with blond hair and oval face with features that matched her own.

Mandy? Her awareness sharpened and she felt a driving panic. She stood, her legs moving without her command.

"Joanne," Benjamin called behind her.

She bounded down the bleacher steps into the crowd. Humanity surrounded her now, and she'd lost the child and woman. She searched the crowd for a hooded azure jacket, but the faces blurred and colors ran together.

"Mandy!" she heard herself cry, and people turned in her direction. She wavered, then stopped. Her heart thundered in her throat as hopelessness assailed her.

"Joanne." Benjamin appeared behind her and drew her into his arms. "What are you doing? What's wrong?"

She lifted her tear-filled eyes. What *was* she doing?

The shuttle bus swayed and bounced as it traveled along I-94 to Oakwood Boulevard.

Donna brushed her hand across Connie's hair. The hood of her blue jacket lay twisted around her shoulders as she nestled in the corner of the bus seat with her head resting against the window. The parade had tired her. They'd had to get up early to reach the shuttle and arrive downtown in time for the parade.

Donna had hoped to find a place at Grand Circus Park, but the bus had dropped them at the head of the parade. Once she realized that's where Santa left the sleigh to speak to the children from the special stage, she had been pleased, but the crowd there had been fierce. Connie had had to squeeze through the mob lining the curb so that she could see.

The bus hit a pothole, and Connie's head bounced against the window. She opened her eyes and gave Donna a sleepy smile.

"Tired?"

Connie grinned. "Nope."

"Not anymore maybe."

The child giggled. "I loved the balloons and the clowns best."

"Really?"

Then she wrinkled her nose. "Best after Santa."

"I thought so," Donna said, holding out her arm for the child to cuddle against her.

Connie shifted and rested her head against Donna's frame. Love filled Donna's heart, and a deep ache pulsed in the pit of her stomach. She'd already taken too many chances. From now on, she had to be careful. She'd let her plan mull in her head. She'd never done anything illegal before, but now it was different. Donna needed to assure her own safety and most of all, that of Connie.

Carl seemed to be losing it. Donna envisioned one of his recent violent outbursts, and her stomach lurched at the memory. He'd called her names, threatened her and hinted that he'd rather see her dead.

She couldn't blame his reaction on her questions about the past. Her interest had been motivated by his daily tirades. Donna needed to understand. More and more she gathered pieces of information from his late-night phone calls. He'd been involved in a car ring of some kind. His trucking company, apparently, was a cover for a car-theft business. She had no details, but she'd put two and two together.

Carl-Peter-whatever-his-name-was thought she was stupid, but Donna had more brains than he did. She'd cooked up a plan that would help her escape and take Connie with her, but first she had to make sure she had things right. She had to prove for certain that Connie and Mandy were the same child. If so, Donna knew a mother's love would prompt the Fuller woman to take chances, and follow Donna's instructions. She *had* to.

Donna had never imagined extorting anyone or hurting anyone, but to get away and to keep Connie in her life, she had no choice.

She felt a twinge of regret. Her friend's message about Jesus had affected her. With Jesus in her life things could be different, but the Lord would have to be in Carl's life, too, and she couldn't imagine that.

No one was in Carl's life—not Connie, not her. Carl's focus was on Carl.

Joanne pulled a round steak from the refrigerator. After church that morning, when Benjamin had invited her out to dinner, she'd said, "Sounds good, but tonight, the treat's on me."

She knew he thought she would take him out to dinner, but she had decided that Benjamin would probably enjoy a home-cooked meal better than fine dining. She hadn't made beef stroganoff since Greg died and today she would see if she still had the talent to make the tender morsels of steak swimming in a sour cream sauce so full of calories she should feel ashamed.

Ashamed. The word triggered thoughts. Joanne regretted her over-the-top behavior during the past week. Not only had she jumped too quickly to make something sinister out of the telephone calls, but now she'd reacted like a madwoman at the parade, chasing after a mother and child. What had gotten into her? With her jangled nerves and sense of foreboding, she needed help.

Pushing her worries aside, Joanne tackled the dinner. She pulled a knife from the cabinet drawer and began the ritual of cutting the steak into long thin slices. That was part of her secret. She liked beef so tender she could cut it with a fork.

As she wielded the knife, making the final slice, the telephone rang—and when she jumped, the knife slashed her index finger. She jerked her hand away from the cutting board. Blood oozed from the wound, and she held her hand over the sink while she grabbed paper towel.

After wrapping her finger, she picked up the receiver and said hello. That ominous silence ran through the wire. Bitterness, yet victory filled her as she eyed the blood seeping through the toweling. She needed this third call for the police.

"Hello," she said again. It was the same pattern. She talked. The caller didn't.

"I—I shouldn't have called," a woman whispered.

"Who are you?" Her mind spun.

The woman didn't answer, and Joanne waited for the hang-up. She heard an intake of breath and then a whisper.

"Was your daughter's body found after the accident?"

Your daughter's body. Joanne heard a moan, but this time it came from her.

She grasped the wall to support herself. "No," she said. "Please leave me alone." She slammed down the phone without waiting for a response, then gasped, realizing she'd made a profound mistake. She snatched the receiver from the cradle—only to hear a dial tone.

Heart hammering against her chest, she wondered if the woman might have said more. Joanne's eyes burned with hot tears as she retreated to the sink, and her hands trembled as she pulled off the stained paper and placed her finger beneath the cold tap water. She watched the blood swirl down the drain…

like the hope that had dissipated with that telephone call.

When the stinging sensation stopped, Joanne grasped a clean sheet of toweling, blotted her finger and headed for the bathroom to find a bandage. As she pulled the adhesive strip from its container, the doorbell rang. She glanced at the mirror, startled by her pale reflection. Carrying the bandage into the living room she opened the door.

Benjamin stood behind the storm door cradling a bouquet of flowers, but his smile faded when he saw her face. He grasped the door handle and stepped inside. "What happened?"

"I cut myself," she said, holding up the strip.

He placed the flowers on a lamp table and pulled away the toweling. "You might need stitches."

"Just a bandage. Okay?"

He held her hand in his palm. "Then at least put an antiseptic on it. You don't want to get bacteria in the wound."

She agreed and followed him into the bathroom, where she pointed out the cream. He spread the ointment on her cut, then covered it with the adhesive bandage. When he finished, he raised her finger to his lips and kissed the spot.

She smiled while her heart ached. How many times had she kissed Mandy's boo-boos?

"How'd you cut yourself?" Benjamin asked, grabbing the flowers and following her into the kitchen.

"Thanks for the bouquet," she said, wishing she could forget the wretched phone call. She located a vase in the cabinet and filled it with water, then added the flowers. "It's beautiful."

He touched her arm, and when she turned toward him, he looked into her eyes and shook his head. "Another call?"

She nodded. Benjamin seemed to read her expression. "This one was worse."

"Worse?"

"She asked me if Mandy's body had been found."

"What?" His face blanched.

"I hung up, and then I panicked. What if she knows something about the accident? I didn't give her a chance to say anything else."

"Oh, Joanne," he said through a deep sigh.

He drew her against his chest and held her there while she breathed in his familiar scent. His arms gave her comfort, and pressed against him, she let her emotions flow freely while he swayed and caressed her back in small circles.

Her tears soaked his jacket. Too much, she thought. Too much for one person. Yet she knew God promised not to give her more than she could handle. Finally she eased away, embarrassed that she'd allowed herself to give in to sorrow.

"God gives me a lot more credit for strength and courage than I have." She tried to smile—anything to break the gloom that seemed to follow her.

He didn't speak, but slipped his arm around her shoulders and led her to the sofa. "Here's the good news," he said drawing her closer. "You've had the third call."

"That was the victory," she said. "I know what I should do now. Report it to the phone company and then call the police."

"What else would you do, Joanne? This is what you've waited for."

She held up her hand. "But wait. I'm confused. I'm terribly mixed up."

"We both are, and that's why we need to report this."

Fear filled her. "No, Benjamin. I don't want

to scare her away. I need to know more. What if she knows something about Mandy. What if I do something that frightens her enough that she never calls back?"

"Why is she calling? Let's make some sense out of this. If this truly has to do with Mandy and this woman doesn't want to be caught, then why is she calling? What's her motive?"

She pressed her face into her hands. "I don't know."

"Joanne, look at me."

She ignored him and kept her face hidden.

He slid his fingers beneath her chin and urged her to raise her head. "Look. You can't solve this by yourself. We can ask to have the telephone tapped. That will tell us where the calls originate."

"They've been blocked."

"That doesn't matter. Even blocked calls can be identified by authorities from the telephone switching facility."

Her gaze searched his. "I don't know."

"I do know."

"I'm not doubting your word. I'm afraid. What if Mandy is alive? What if she's in danger?"

Benjamin's face twisted. "You don't know

that Mandy is alive. This woman might know something, or she could have another purpose in mind. You don't know anything. If Mandy *is* alive, time is of the essence. We'll call the police. I have a detective friend who might help us." He eased her onto the sofa. "Stay there, and let me call."

"I have a powerful feeling, Benjamin."

"Please don't get your hopes too high. Crackpots roam the earth. They get their kicks from hurting people."

"I know, but I feel it in here." She pushed her hand against her chest where her heart ached.

He gave her a gentle look that brought tears to her eyes. Benjamin truly cared, and she thanked the Lord he'd come back into her life. So many people had fled from her after Greg died, but he'd returned. She rose. "I'll come with you. I have meat on the counter."

"Meat? I thought we were going out."

"It was my surprise."

His gaze was tender. "Thanks, but right now, it can wait. Let me call and find out when Hank can see you." He lifted his finger as a gentle warning and vanished through the doorway.

Joanne leaned back against the cushion,

feeling drained of energy. Benjamin's kindness wrapped around her. His thoughtfulness went beyond the call of friendship, and she knew a home-cooked dinner or a night on the town could never repay him for just being there, especially now. She sensed she was on the brink of something, yet anxiety coursed through her. She feared Benjamin was right. Her hopes set her up for deeper hurt.

She longed to disobey Benjamin's finger-shake and follow him to find out what the detective would say. Instead she rested her hand in her lap, feeling the throb of the recent wound that matched the ache in her heart.

Chapter Six

Benjamin stood in the kitchen with his teeth clenched so tightly his jaw ached. Who would do this to Joanne? He closed his eyes, grasping for unimaginable answers. Joanne didn't deserve harassment. She'd been through enough for a lifetime.

He glanced at the beef on the counter, and her efforts touched him. A home-cooked meal. What could be nicer for a man who thought a can of spaghetti was home cooking? So many times he'd sat at the kitchen table talking with Greg while Mandy played beneath his feet. Joanne, always the gracious hostess, would come into the kitchen with her warm smile and offer him a snack or something to drink.

Benjamin propelled his legs to the telephone and pulled a list of telephone numbers from his wallet, then punched in the detective's. "Is Hank Cortezi available?" he asked when an officer answered. Benjamin prayed Cortezi was on duty. He glanced at his watch, suddenly realizing the time.

"Cortezi." A raspy bass voice boomed through the receiver.

"Hank, this is Benjamin Drake."

The detective listened while Benjamin told him the details.

"We can put a trace on her line. That's about it. Have her come in tomorrow morning. I'll tell her how to get it set up. We'll go from there and hope it helps. The calls probably mean nothing, but I'll check out the reports we have here. When did her husband's accident happen?"

Benjamin gave him the date. The memory ate at his stomach as he relived the night in his mind.

"I'll let you know if I spot anything unusual in the report."

"Thanks, Hank. I'll have Joanne there in the morning." He lowered the telephone, then heard Cortezi's voice again.

"Drake?"

Benjamin brought the receiver to his ear. "Yes."

"Tell her to think. She's probably offended someone, or see if anyone's paying unusual attention to her. You know, anything out of the ordinary."

"I'll do that."

He lowered the receiver while his mind swam with questions. He knew little about Joanne really. He didn't know her friends or co-workers. She hadn't mentioned any friends since he'd returned, except the woman she worked with. Who would play such a cruel joke? Joke? The word made him cringe. He turned away from the telephone. He and Joanne had to talk.

Benjamin returned to the living room and eyed Joanne's curious face.

"What did he say?" she asked.

"You can have a trace on your phone. He'll explain it tomorrow when you go in to see him, but for now he suggests we talk."

"Talk about what?"

"Talk it through. He wants you to review the details of the calls. Come up with possible suspects."

"Suspects?" A puzzled look settled on her

face. "Did he believe you? Did he think I'm crazy?"

Benjamin strode to her side and rested his hands on her shoulders. "He believes you're being harassed. That's what's important. You'll go in and give them the statement, then find out about the phone trace." He tilted her chin up. "Now you have to think."

"I've given it thought. It's useless." She placed her hands on his and grasped them. "Let me up and I'll do something with that beef."

"Beef?"

"In the kitchen." She gave a head toss in that direction. "We can discuss it there. I'm sure you're hungry."

He didn't think so. Not after all the confusion, but he gave up fighting her. He realized Joanne needed something to do to keep her busy. Nervous energy sparked in her eyes.

He followed her, knowing she didn't want food any more than he did. In the kitchen, she headed for the counter while he strode to the telephone and hit the caller ID log.

"Blocked call."

"I told you. It's always blocked."

He ambled back to the table and sank into a kitchen chair, watching her sauté the beef and slice onions. After she added water and covered it, Joanne joined him at the table.

"If I hadn't hung up, she might have said more."

Tears welled again in her eyes, and Benjamin reached across the table, capturing her hand. "If it's important, she'll call again. Something is obviously keeping her from talking."

"She's afraid. I can hear it in her voice, her breathing."

Benjamin glanced away for a moment so he could think. When he looked at Joanne, all he could see was her desperate expression, and his reason faded. "She's frightened of...?" He faltered. "She could be worried you'd recognize her voice."

Joanne lifted her shoulders. "Or she could be scared someone will hear the call."

"Maybe someone told her not to get involved." His legal mind kicked in, questioning the caller's motivation. No matter what it had been, the woman's question was a strange one—a sick one.

Joanne looked at him with sad, searching eyes as if she hoped he had an answer. He didn't.

"Who else knew Greg's accident happened

this time of year? Did you mention the date of the accident at work?"

"I never talk about it there." She paused. "I did mention it to Nita. She said I looked stressed out, and I told her."

"About the date?"

"Yes, and the voice I heard. Nothing else." She shifted and lowered her head. "I told Nita. No one else."

He pondered how to ask the next question. "Would she... Is she the kind of—?"

"Nita? She would never do anything like you're thinking. She's always been a good friend. She's very caring. It's not her. I know. I'd bet my life on it."

Being a lawyer, Benjamin couldn't be so certain. Many psychotics hid their disorders for years. However, Joanne's determined look halted further comment. He'd let it slide for now.

"No one else?"

"No one. I'm positive."

"A church friend? An acquaintance?"

Her brows lifted as her eyes widened. "No, absolutely not. I've never mentioned it, and I can't believe anyone I know would want to hurt me like this."

"Okay," he said, realizing he was getting

nowhere. Joanne would defend a seasoned criminal. It was her gentle nature. "What about friends? Other people in your life."

She looked away, and he saw a look of pain spread across her face.

"What other people?"

"Friends. Who do you hang out with?"

"No one since Greg died. I'm like the plague. People just vanished. No couple wants to hang out with a widow."

Benjamin's chest tightened. "I'm sorry, Joanne. I'm shocked."

Her brows knit. "Maybe the women think I'll try to steal their husbands. I don't know."

Gazing at her beautiful face, Benjamin realized that to an insecure woman, Joanne might seem like a threat.

"It's not just friends. My family turned their backs on me. I've had no one but Nita and a few co-workers, but I don't see them socially. I don't know—maybe there's something wrong with me."

"There's nothing wrong with you. People don't handle tragedy well." He longed to hold her in his arms, but he fought the urge. "We'll have to wait for another call."

"I can't believe I have to wait for something so awful," she said, rising to stir the simmering meat, "but this time the police will know who's calling."

"You'll know for sure who it is, and hopefully why she's calling."

"The caller knows something about the accident, I'm sure of it. Maybe she knows where Mandy's body is."

Benjamin's heart rose to his throat. It didn't take an attorney's mind to question that idea. "Joanne, it's been three years. Why would she call after all this time?"

Joanne's head drooped and she covered her face. "I don't know how she'd know, Benjamin, but I feel it inside me. She knows something about my daughter."

Joanne shifted the papers on her desk, fighting to stay focused. If she messed up, Melissa Shafer or another candidate could walk away with her job. They all probably knew she was serving as an intern for a six-month period before she'd be handed the position permanently.

"Ready for shopping tonight?"

Joanne lifted her head and managed to smile at Nita. "I wore my walking shoes." She swung her foot above her desk and pointed to her comfy footwear.

"Good for you." She gave her a thumbs-up and took a step, then leaned back into the doorway. "We have a meeting at ten, right?"

"That's what I hear," Joanne said.

Nita gave a nod and continued down the hallway.

Joanne slipped her notes into the manila folder, then turned to her computer and opened her e-mail program. Her eyes scanned the list of messages. Nothing from Benjamin. A wave of disappointment rolled over her.

Then she saw it. Shadow@123go.com.

She hesitated, then moved her cursor to delete, but she couldn't bring herself to do it. Instead she clicked "read."

WATCH YOUR STEP.
I HAVE MY EYES ON YOU.

A chill rolled down her back as she hit delete.

While sitting at the mall café, Joanne struggled to make conversation. "It's a relief to get this much shopping finished. I have packages to ship out of state." She lifted the frothy coffee and took a sip. Her thoughts shifted from the phone calls to the holidays. Her only joy this year would be Benjamin.

"Are you visiting your folks this year for Christmas?" asked Nita.

Memories of her unhappy Christmas visits home raced across her mind. Her pulse gave a little kick. "I'm staying in town."

"If you're alone for Christmas dinner, you're welcome to join us—"

"Thanks, but I'm planning to do something with Benjamin." She spotted the look on Nita's face and stopped her. "We're friends. Do I have to spell it out? It's as far from romance as…well, as far from romance as you can get."

"Methinks the woman doth protest—"

"Nita. Stop. He's worried about me as a friend and it's nice to have someone I can trust drop by for a visit. I don't have to play games with Benjamin."

"Why's he worried?"

Joanne felt her chest tighten. She wanted to avoid the details but how could she keep all of this from Nita? She took a minute to gather her courage. "For one, calls. Anonymous telephone calls."

Nita wrinkled her nose. "Here or at home?"

"Home. Over a week ago. Occasionally it

happened with one of Greg's publicized trials or when a plaintiff didn't like the court's ruling. Lawyers take the brunt of a lot of anger as well as jokes."

Joanne shook her head. "I didn't know, Nita." She wondered how much to tell her. Benjamin seemed to think saying too much could cause more problems.

"What did he say to you? Those perverts are sick."

"It's not a man. It's a woman. Until last Sunday she didn't speak. She just hung up."

"Hung up?" Nita arched a brow and tilted her head. "Any idea who it could be?"

Joanne wished she could say yes. "None at all. She spoke the first time last Sunday, but I didn't recognize her voice. She whispered."

Nita's face was filled with concern. "That's weird."

"Benjamin asked about someone from Solutions, but who and why?" Joanne lifted her paper cup, then set it down again.

"How about Bambi?" Nita's mouth twisted to a faint grin.

"Bambi?"

Nita chuckled. "In the office next to yours. Melissa."

Joanne looked surprised. "I realize she

didn't get the promotion, but I don't think she'd go that far."

"What about Daryl?"

"Daryl?"

"From the mail room."

"He's a guy." Joanne eyed Nita to see if she was joking.

"I think he has a thing for you. Maybe he wants to ask you out, but he's afraid. Perhaps every time he calls he loses his nerve. That makes sense."

"It's a woman."

Nita grinned. "Have you ever listened to Daryl when he gets nervous? His pitch goes up an octave."

Joanne gave her a halfhearted smile. She hated being evasive and realized she should open up and tell her the whole thing. "Last Sunday the caller asked me if Mandy's body had been found."

"Oh, no."

Joanne realized she'd shocked her. "I'm sorry. I hate to talk about it."

"Here I'm being silly again, and you're hurting and sick over this. I'm so sorry, Joanne."

"It's okay, Nita. I should have been up front from the beginning."

She held up her hand. "No apologies necessary. This is traumatic for you."

"I sense she knows something, Nita. She opened a wound that was nearly healed, and now I'm bleeding again." Joanne glanced down at the bandage still covering her wound. The pain had gone— Only the sensitivity remained.

Nita's gaze followed hers. "What happened to your hand?"

"I cut myself."

Nita seemed to accept her response without explanation, and sent her a look of sympathy. "What do you do now?" She shook her head as she lifted the latte to her lips.

"I've called the police."

"You did?"

She told Nita the details of her first visit. "When she called Sunday, Benjamin phoned a detective friend for me. I went in Monday morning."

"That's why you were late for work," Nita said.

Joanne nodded, wishing she hadn't kept her troubles so quiet. "I didn't want to worry you."

Nita's eyebrows rose.

"I know. It was silly."

Nita shifted her hand to Joanne's arm, and gave it a pat. "You shouldn't have to go through this alone without support or prayer."

"I've had Benjamin's support." She realized how cutting the comment was. "But you're a good friend, too, and I should have told you. I really need your prayers."

"You have them. You know that." Nita squeezed her arm, then shifted her hand back to her cup handle. "So what is the detective doing?"

"He asked a million questions about everyone I know or ever knew. Then he wanted every detail about the caller. The sound of her voice, background sounds, the time she usually called and the dates. Then he asked me about that night—the night they died."

"Really? Why?"

Joanne gave a perplexed shrug. "I suppose trying to connect it to something tangible besides my crazy suspicions."

"They're not crazy."

"Thanks." She managed a smile. "The phone company put a trace on the phone line. They do it all electronically now. Even blocked calls can be traced to the telephone used for the call. It's not like the old movies and they don't really listen anymore. I have to keep a log of the call, and then the phone company checks it out." Joanne rubbed her neck, feeling the tension building. "It's all too confusing and horrible."

"I know, but I feel better hearing you've taken this to the police. Pray she calls again soon."

Joanne nodded, then took the final sip of her latte. "I never thought I'd pray anything so horrible, but that's exactly what I'm doing."

Nita frowned. "You said for one. Is there a for two?"

"What?"

"I asked what your friend was worried about, and you said, for one, calls. What's the other problem?"

"E-mails."

"At work?"

Joanne nodded.

Nita slid her cup to the side and leaned closer. "Do you think the e-mails are connected to the phone calls?"

"I don't know." She tried to remember the content of the messages as clearly as she could. "They don't make sense, but it's obvious someone is trying to frighten me."

Nita shook her head.

"And it's working," Joanne said.

Chapter Seven

Joanne balanced the packages from Christmas shopping between her knee and the door frame, then turned the key in the lock. The bags rustled against the molding until the door opened and she carried them inside.

She'd purchased most of the gifts to be mailed, and felt good about her accomplishment. Though she'd been tense the past few weeks, today she'd almost been touched by Christmas spirit with the help of Nita and the shopping spree. For the past three years she had forced herself to pull out some ornaments, then wept and put them back. Christmas had seemed lost to her. But this year she'd already made progress, with Benjamin's encouragement. Perhaps this year she'd have the strength to use the decorations.

As she carried the gift bags into her room, thoughts of Benjamin filled her mind. He'd been tied up with a court case, and though he'd called, she didn't think he'd have time for her today. But the e-mail had set her on edge and she missed him more than she could imagine. Two weeks ago, he'd been only a memory. Now he'd become the backbone of her existence.

Joanne recognized that Benjamin thought of her as Greg's wife—just a friend—and she'd always felt the same about him, until lately. Now her heart gave a skip when she saw his generous mouth curve into a playful smile. The sensation nudged her with an uncomfortable guilt, as if she were cheating on Greg, but she knew her husband was gone. She'd meet Greg again in heaven, but while here on earth, life seemed lonely without a partner.

Joanne knew that she should move on. She was free to experience romance and to find love again. The idea washed over her in waves of mixed emotion. Loss and newness warped into one emotional experience.

After searching her closet, Joanne selected something to wear, then slipped off her office clothes. She stepped into a pair of pants, and then, feeling a chill, she gave her arms a brisk rub before pulling a bulky sweater over her head. She disposed of her work outfit, then headed for the kitchen.

As she came through the doorway she eyed the telephone and her stomach knotted. The answering machine gave off a steady blink: she had a message.

Apprehension crept over her. She drew up her shoulders and hit the play button. *"You have three messages. Message one, Monday, November twenty-eighth. Five-thirty."*

Joanne held her breath.

"Hi, Joanne."

She smiled hearing Benjamin's voice.

"I guess you're not in. Give me a call when you get home."

Sweet Benjamin. Despite his busy day, he'd called. Always thinking of her....

"Message two," the mechanical voice said, *"Monday, November twenty-eighth. Five-forty-nine."*

Joanne tilted her ear closer to the speaker. She heard the hiss of an open line, then a hang-up. Her stomach twisted. It was the woman again, she felt certain. She slammed her hand against the telephone. If she'd been home, the caller might have spoken.

The machine indicated that the third message had occurred at six-fourteen. She listened with her heart in her throat. Another hang-up.

Hands trembling, she crossed the room and sank into a chair. She covered her face with her hands, knowing she should be relieved that the woman had called again, but instead, she felt weak and tired. Frustration overwhelmed her. Her chest ached from her pounding heart, and all she wanted to do was sleep.

She hoisted herself from the chair and walked back to the telephone to phone Benjamin. When she heard his voice, she burst out with the news.

"She called again. Twice, I think, but I wasn't here," Joanne said. "It was on my answering machine."

"What did she say?"

"Nothing. I can't stand this anymore." Her fingers ached from her death grip on the phone.

"She spoke to you once, Joanne. She'll talk again, and this time the phone company will have her. I don't think she would leave a message."

"If I hadn't gone shopping I would have been home."

"Stop. You can't live your life waiting for the phone to ring. You're there now, and I'll be over later."

After he disconnected, Joanne felt lonelier than she had in years. She turned from the telephone and pulled the teapot and tea from the cabinet. In a daze, she put water on to boil. As she worked, she tried to put herself in the stranger's shoes, to understand why she continued to call. Did she really have anything to say? Joanne banged into a mental wall every way she turned.

When the tea was ready, she carried it into the living room, then paced in front of the picture window, not knowing what to do with herself. She finally settled into a chair and waited for Benjamin.

Eventually, headlights reflected off the snow and turned into the driveway. Joanne's heart thumped as she rose and headed for the door. She'd begun to equate comfort and security with Benjamin.

Joanne watched him slip from the car and walk up the sidewalk, and felt a smile relax her face. When he reached the porch, she pushed back the storm door.

"Hi," he said, bringing in the crisp smell of new snow. Flakes drifted to the floor from his jacket as he pulled it from his shoulders.

"Hi." Joanne gazed at him, fighting the urge to kiss him hello. The vision heated her cheeks and she turned away, fearing he'd notice.

He slipped off his coat, which she hung in the closet. She held back the emotion that rattled her from the phone calls and from the unexpected sensation when she'd seen him.

"I've just made some tea." She motioned him toward the living room. "Have a seat. I'll bring it in."

But he didn't. Instead, he grasped her arms and closed the distance between them. "Are you okay? You sounded upset on the phone."

"I'm fine now." *Now that you're here,* she added to herself.

Instead of releasing her, he drew her closer, and she felt his lips press against her hair. Her heart hammered at the nearness. He'd held her before to soothe her tears. Today was different. When he stepped back, his expression looked as surprised as she felt.

Neither spoke a word, and she turned away. What was happening? "Go ahead." She motioned toward the living room. "I'll bring it in."

This time he listened and vanished through the archway, while Joanne stood a moment in the foyer to catch her breath.

"Mind if I put on a CD?" Benjamin called from the living room.

"Go ahead," she said, glad to have something break the silence. She returned to the kitchen and finished pouring the tea, then grasped both cups and followed the music back into the room.

He'd selected a Michael W. Smith CD. The instrumental music drifted through the doorway, filled with faith and the power of God's love. Benjamin knew what she needed.

"Here," she said, handing him a mug. She settled near him in the same chairs they'd used on his previous visit.

"Tell me what happened," he said.

"I told you about the calls today—the hangups."

"And you suspect they're her again."

"Yes, but—" She hesitated to tell him, but she knew she must.

"But? There's more?"

"I opened another e-mail today. The same sender as last time."

His expression knitted to a scowl. "What did this one say?"

She repeated the message. "What do you think?"

He shook his head. "That's threatening, Joanne. The two e-mails and the hang-ups could be connected. I don't think we should fool around with this. I'll call the station and see if Hank's in. If not, I'll talk with someone else." He rose and headed for the telephone.

A shudder shook Joanne. Threats, but why? She sat riveted to the chair, waiting and wondering. The night sky loomed outside the window, and for the first time, Joanne felt truly frightened.

"Did you print a copy of the message?" Benjamin asked as he came into the room. "He wants to see both of them."

"I think I deleted them. I'll have to check tomorrow."

"Go to the mail drop-down menu and see if you can recover them. The e-mails might have been sent in error, but that seems too coincidental to me."

"Okay," she said, wanting to change the subject. She sipped her tea, letting the music fill her ears.

Benjamin's eyes seemed focused on the window. He sat deep in thought with his hands folded, his elbows braced on his knees.

Joanne finally stirred. "I've been thinking about Christmas."

He looked surprised, probably having expected her to talk more about the situation.

"You mean, because of all the decorations at the mall? I noticed the city has the streets trimmed already."

"True. The wreaths, the garland, the music all make me nostalgic." She longed to admit her feelings. "But this year is different."

"Different? In what way?" He lifted a brow as if he didn't understand.

"I'm looking forward to the holidays for the first time since the accident." She wished she hadn't mentioned it. Benjamin gave her a curious look, and she feared he would misunderstand what she wanted to say.

"That's good. Time makes a difference. You'll never forget, but time wears away the rough edges. Instead of the sands of time, it's the sandpaper of time." He gave her a tender smile.

She grinned back, appreciating his attempt to lighten the mood.

"It's you that's made the difference," she said, deciding to open up.

"Me? Mr. Scrooge?"

The glint in his eye played games with her

pulse. "You'd never be a Scrooge. You're too kind, and yes, it is because of you. I've lived behind these walls without thinking about me for a long time. Now you're here and I can remember what life used to be like before…before the accident. We used to have so much fun."

"We did. Greg was a great friend."

"And I was your great friend's wife?"

His gaze left a soft feeling in her stomach. "No. I considered you a special friend. I've always admired you, Joanne. I'm not sure you realized how much. I never told you."

"Admired me? Why? I can't even imagine."

"You'd get a swelled head if I told you." He looked into the mug as if searching for tea leaves. "It's because you're you. Charming, warm, talented and beautiful."

Her focus lingered on his generous mouth. She forced her gaze away. "Maybe you need glasses."

"Me? Have you ever looked in a mirror?"

She recalled looking at herself after one of the phone calls and seeing a death-white face gaping back at her. "Thanks for the flattery. I'm not used to it anymore."

"It's the truth, not just flattery." He leaned back, stretching his shoulders and looking a little tense. "So what are you planning for the holidays? Anything special?"

"I thought I might have a tree this year."

His eyes widened. "You mean you haven't had a Christmas tree since—"

She nodded. "I will this year if you promise to come over to admire it."

"I'll do more than that. I'll help you buy it and decorate—"

The telephone's ring jarred them. Joanne gasped, and Benjamin reached across to calm her.

"Don't panic. Answer it," he said.

She rose, her legs already like gelatin. Benjamin followed her into the kitchen. She glanced at the caller ID.

"It's my folks' number," she said.

He backed away as she lifted the receiver.

"Hi, Mom," she said, after hearing her mother's greeting.

"Are you coming home for Christmas?" her mom asked.

Her parents' house hadn't been her home for years. This was her home, where she and her husband and daughter had lived, where her life had been filled with joy. "Not this year," she said.

"Is something wrong, Joanne?"

A blast of air shot from her lungs. "No, I have company."

"Really? Is it...?" Her voice faded.

"It's Greg's old friend Benjamin. You remember him."

"Not really."

Joanne stared at the receiver, wondering what to say next. "I have some things going on here, so I'm staying home for the holidays. Sorry if I disappointed you."

"Your sister and her family are coming. I thought maybe... Are you sure you're okay?"

"I'm fine."

The strained conversation lasted a few more sentences before they said goodbye. Joanne heard the *click* and lowered the telephone. When she turned, Benjamin was watching her from across the room, his shoulder resting against the door jamb.

"She asked me about Christmas. I'm staying home."

He only looked at her, then took a step closer. "You'll never heal without opening your heart."

"What does that mean?"

"You know what it means."

"I don't have it in me, Benjamin. I—"

The telephone rang again, and Benjamin

darted forward and pointed to the caller ID. She followed the direction of his finger, already knowing what he'd seen. *Blocked.* He stood nearby as she picked up the receiver.

Joanne said hello, then held her breath.

The line remained silent, and Joanne had to harness the impulse to scream, to threaten, but she clamped her jaw and waited. Her instinct was to hang up, but she couldn't. The woman would talk. She sensed it, and best of all, the police would be able to locate her.

Finally, Joanne heard an intake of breath.

"Did your daughter have a birthmark?"

The whisper slithered down Joanne's spine. Control. She needed control. "Yes," she murmured as she looked at Benjamin for help.

"What?" he whispered, grasping her arm.

Joanne held up her hand.

"A small heart shape on her upper thigh?" The woman's voice was so faint Joanne barely heard her.

She couldn't breathe, and her control shattered into shards of anguish. "I don't believe you," she screamed into the phone. "You can't know that. Who are you?"

The telephone went dead and Joanne crumpled to the floor.

Chapter Eight

Benjamin crouched, clutching her against him. He trembled, knowing something horrible had happened yet not knowing what. He waited for her sobs to subside before helping her to her feet and guiding her back into the living room. He eased her onto the sofa and sat beside her, steadying her against his shoulder.

"She knows about Mandy's birthmark," she said, her voice a whisper.

Mandy's birthmark. "I didn't know she had one." He grasped for an explanation. Who would know that? Friends? Even he hadn't realized Mandy had a birthmark. A doctor? Nurse? His mind spun with empty responses.

A tremor rolled through her as she drew fresh air into her lungs. "She described it perfectly—a small heart-shaped mark on her upper thigh. How could she know that unless—?"

"Think logically, Joanne. Relatives, Mandy's doctor, a nurse, a baby-sitter, a friend—"

"You're my friend, one of the best, and even you didn't know. She's alive, Benjamin. Somehow Mandy's alive."

The panic in Joanne's face wrenched his heart. She had hopes that seemed far-fetched, unbelievable. "I'll call Hank back. This is what you've been waiting for. Now they can trace the number."

Greater hope shone in her eyes, but logic told him Joanne had set herself up for deeper wounds, greater sorrow than she already had experienced. The calls and e-mails could lead to nothing but a warped mind.

"This could be it, Joanne. We'll have the answer soon."

Donna filled the bowl with cereal. She slipped the box back into the cabinet before heading for the refrigerator for milk. "Connie, are you ready?" she called over her shoulder. She glanced at the clock, then walked to the kitchen doorway. "You'll be late for school if you don't hurry."

"I'm coming."

She heard the *thump-thump* of Connie's footsteps along the bare wood hallway, and poured the milk into the bowl, then added some to a tumbler. "Want some raisins in your cereal?"

Connie came through the doorway looking grumpy. "No."

"No, *thank you*."

Connie gave Donna a nod. "No, thank you," she repeated, and slipped onto the chair. She dug her spoon into the bowl and lifted it to her mouth. When she pulled it away, milk dripped from the edge of her lip to her chin.

Donna grabbed a napkin to catch it. "You'll be a mess before you get to school." She patted Connie's head. "Are you feeling okay?" The child usually came to the kitchen with a bounce in her step.

The child gave a faint shrug. "I had bad dreams."

"I'm sorry," Donna said, squeezing her shoulder. More and more, Connie complained of nightmares and Donna feared it was because of Carl's booming voice when he came home angry, which happened too often lately.

Then again, Donna wondered if the child sensed her stepmother's confusion and rising fear. She sat across the table and looked at the six-year-old, morphing her image back three years. She couldn't believe it could be true, but since she'd seen the newspaper photo of Mandy Fuller, Donna had been driven to learn if Connie was in fact Mandy. Now she was sure.

Donna had become a sleuth on her own. Yesterday, she'd dropped Connie off at school, then driven across town to the Fuller house. She'd seen Joanne Fuller and had been overcome by the resemblance of Connie to her birth mother. Later, when Connie visited with a school friend, Donna had followed Joanne home.

She'd longed to speak to Joanne, to tell her about Connie—how sweet she was and how much she loved the child, to prove she's been a good mother, but reality swept over Donna. She'd been rash coming here. Contact with Joanne would foil her escape plan. Connie might not be her birth daughter, but she was the daughter of her heart. Donna would never give her up.

Realizing the truth, that Carl had abducted the Fuller child before her father's accident, another thought blasted through her mind.

Had Carl been responsible for Greg Fuller's death?

Carl's raging moods made no sense to Donna. She had done all she could for the past week to keep him calm. Ever since the night he'd found her in the basement, he hadn't trusted her. He popped into the house at unexpected times, as if checking. For the past month, Donna felt relieved when he didn't come home at night.

Something horrible had happened in Carl's life. His hatred for women seemed delusional and he'd begun to rant about his mother. Donna didn't want to imagine what had happened in his life to create such a monster.

Donna slipped beside Connie and knelt. "What's bothering you, sweetheart?"

The child didn't answer, but stared at her cereal and stirred it with her spoon. Her face pulled with emotion, and Donna's heart ached.

"Are you afraid of something?" Donna asked.

Connie nodded without lifting her head.

"What are you afraid of, sweetie?"

Her slender shoulder lifted in a shrug, and then Donna noticed tears rolling down her cheeks. "Are you afraid of your daddy?"

Her downcast eyes closed until finally she gave a slight nod.

"What has he done, Connie?" Donna's chest tightened with fear.

"He comes in my room at night when he thinks I'm sleeping and says mean things."

Donna could only imagine the horrible words Carl uttered to the child. He hated them both, and he'd become a madman as a result of whatever problems and pressures had pressed on his life.

"Wouldn't it be fun if you and I could go away?"

"Just me and you?" A hopeful look spread across Connie's face.

"Just me and you. Would you like that?"

"On vacation? We could go to Florida and—"

"Longer than a vacation. Would that be better?"

Connie let the spoon fall against the bowl, then reached up to curl her arms around Donna's neck. Tears welled in Donna's eyes, and she knew she needed to make a move now to save them from Carl's violence before… The possibilities stunned her, and she held Connie closer.

She needed to act before it was too late.

* * *

The next afternoon, Joanne sat in a wooden chair, watching Hank Cortezi thumb through a manila folder. Benjamin sat beside her, his hands folded in his lap as if he'd sat through many sessions like this one. Outside the private office, which she suspected was used for a variety of purposes, Joanne could hear the buzz of conversation and the ring of telephones.

"I have to make this fast," Hank said, finally lifting his head to look at them. "I have bad news."

Joanne's hopes dwindled. "What do you mean bad news?"

Benjamin shifted his hand to the arm of her chair and rested his fingers over hers.

"The call was from a pay phone outside a pharmacy in Dearborn."

"A pay phone?" The last fragments of hope took a nosedive.

Cortezi tapped his knuckles against the file folder. "She's smart enough to cover her tracks."

"But why the blocked call, then?" Joanne asked.

"If you'd noticed the exchange, you could pinpoint the location from which the call was made. Like I said, she's using her head, covering her tracks."

Hank looked at her with tired eyes, and at that moment, Joanne felt as exhausted as he looked. Benjamin gave her fingers a squeeze and shifted his hands back to his lap.

"What now?" Benjamin asked Cortezi.

Hank shrugged. "We can keep the trace on another week and see if she slips up and calls from home. We can't do much more about those, but we have the e-mail now, and we can check on that. Let's see if she does this again." He glanced at his watch as if he had someplace to go.

"What about the phone booth?" Joanne asked, dismayed that he sounded so uninterested. "Can't someone keep an eye on that location. Maybe—"

"Ma'am, I realize you think your daughter might be alive, but let's get practical. It's been three years since the accident. You have no evidence except some crackpot phone calls, an e-mail, and a feeling in your gut. We don't even know if the calls and e-mails are connected."

He stopped and ran his fingers through his hair. Joanne felt her frustration mounting. She could barely keep from running from the room.

Hank continued. "The Detroit area has hundreds of crimes a day—robbery, shootings, murders, muggings, car-jackings. You name it, we got it. We're working with Dearborn on a stolen car racket right now. We don't have enough officers to do surveillance on a telephone booth for a crime we're not even sure was committed."

"But—"

"We've taken up enough of your time," Benjamin said, rising. He extended his hand toward Hank. "Thanks. We appreciate all you've done."

Cortezi accepted his handshake, then closed the file folder with the flip of his fingers. "Sorry, but if we get something solid on the calls, I can have an officer look into it. As of now, speculation isn't evidence. I take the e-mails seriously. That sounds like a threat. The birthmark comment—I don't know what it means."

"Thank you," Joanne said, trying to look appreciative when she actually felt naive, stupid and overcome with disappointment.

Benjamin grasped her arm as they headed for the station door. The wind gusted as they exited, and she gulped in the cold air to cool her fiery thoughts.

"They don't care," she said to Benjamin as they trudged down the sidewalk to the parking lot. "How will we ever know anything now?"

He didn't respond.

When they reached the car, he opened the door and she settled inside, then he rounded the front and climbed into the driver side. The keys jingled in his hand, but he hesitated. "I know you're disappointed," he said finally.

His words opened a floodgate to her welling tears. She lowered her face to her hands and wept, feeling overwhelmed with discouragement and humiliation.

Benjamin reached over the space between the bucket seats and drew her closer. "I wish I could do something for you. I'd do anything, Joanne, but I'm lost. We need to think. We're missing something."

Missing something. She lifted her head, then brushed her tears away with her gloves. "I don't know what we're missing. I've gone over and over each nuance of her voice and her meaning. I'm lost, and I'm so depressed. So sad."

"I know. I know." He tilted her chin upward and brushed his cheek against hers.

Joanne felt the beginning stubble after his early morning shave. She drew in the faint aroma of aftershave blended with his familiar masculine scent. She hadn't touched a man's face like this since Greg died and an impulse rose in her. She raised her hand and drew it along his jaw, feeling the hint of prickles.

Benjamin captured her hand against his cheek and held it there, his eyes drawing her in. She felt breathless, startled by the depth of her feeling.

Could this be real, or was it only her need for a friend? Benjamin—her friend, Greg's friend, yet now so much more than that. She was ashamed of her thoughts. Benjamin had stepped in and given her company and concern at a time when she needed it, and now she was losing control. She'd become a teenager, imagining romance and wondering what it could mean.

"How about some distraction?"

Benjamin's question surprised her, and she pulled her mind from her dilemma. "Distraction? What do you mean?"

"I can't bear to see you so depressed. I've told you over and over that you were opening yourself to all kinds of misery. I know you couldn't stop yourself, but this is what I feared."

"I tried to stop. I kept telling myself I'd be devastated, but I couldn't control it." No more than she could control her feelings at this moment, looking into his eyes. His full lips looked soft in the dusky light ebbing through the window. Shadows deepened the lines in his face, giving him character and strength, like a man who'd lived through a war and came home a hero. Benjamin had become a hero in her eyes.

Joanne witnessed his concern and forced herself to let go of the doldrums that weighed on her. "I'm ready. Distract me."

Her sudden outburst made him chuckle, and the sound surrounded her like a warm bath. A grin relaxed her tense face, and the feeling lightened her spirit. She wasn't giving up. With God on her side, all things were possible. She just needed to believe it.

Benjamin put the key into the ignition and the motor came to life. Immediately the heater's air came through the vents and began to warm her. "Where are we going?"

"First," he said, glancing over his shoulder as he backed from the spot, "we're going to buy a Christmas tree."

* * *

"Is it straight?"

Joanne stood back and eyed the tree. Benjamin's body stuck out below the branches as he turned the eye bolts on the tree stand. "It looks good."

He grunted with the last twist, then squirmed from beneath the limbs on his belly. When he'd cleared the boughs, Benjamin stood and brushed his hands on his pants.

"I probably have sap all over me now. Can you see anything?"

She studied his broad chest and lean waist. Her gaze drifted down his long legs to his loafers. "You look very good," she said, amazed she had the nerve to speak her thoughts aloud.

A frown flickered on his face, then it eased as he moved back to where she was standing. "It's straight as a plumb line."

"Did you doubt me?"

He looked as if he'd planned to make a comment and then stopped himself. "Where's the Christmas music? We need carols."

She gestured toward her CD rack. "Look near the bottom and pick out something while I make hot chocolate."

Joanne watched him for a moment as he

strode across the room and crouched beside the CD pillar. His good looks sent her pulse on a gallop, and she realized that by adding thoughtfulness, kindness, faithfulness and generosity to a set of broad shoulders and a mesmerizing smile Benjamin had unlocked her longing and had given her the urge to live again.

She pulled her gaze away and hurried into the kitchen. Her feelings had blossomed with such speed that she felt lost as to how to handle them. Never would she want to scare Benjamin away with her overzealous behavior. She needed to calm herself and realize the feeling might stem from her needs.

Joanne put on the teakettle and pulled out two mugs and the hot chocolate powder. She watched the flame beneath the pot as her thoughts flickered as brightly as the burner. She knew she'd always love Benjamin as her dearest friend, but the feelings that consumed her now were far from friendship. Her mind played games with her imagination. She had to get a grip.

A shrill whistle signaled the water was hot. The sound blended with the music filling the air. Joanne made quick work of the cocoa, then carried the mugs into the living room.

Benjamin had knelt near the fireplace and was adding a final log. Joanne crossed the room and set his mug on a nearby table.

"I haven't made a fire since—"

"Hot chocolate, Christmas carols and a flickering fire. What could be better than that?"

Her heart skipped.

He struck a long match and bent to light the scented fire starter that she kept near the kindling. The cup of wax and straw glowed, and soon the small sticks burst into flame that caught in the large branches.

Benjamin stood and set the package of matches back on the hearth. They stood side by side, listening to the instrumental carols of the Mannheim Steamrollers and the *snap* and *pop* of the blaze.

"Pretty," Joanne said, wanting her heartbeat to slow and her thinking to clear.

"Not as pretty as you," Benjamin murmured.

His comment caught her, but she clamped her jaw without comment.

After a moment, Benjamin stepped away. "We'd better get those lights strung, don't you think?"

"Tonight?"

"Sure. Why do you think we set up the tree?"

She hadn't thought. Her mind had been tangled in the detective's comments and her dizzying awareness of Benjamin. "Christmas is three weeks away."

"I believe in being prepared."

She knew it was a ploy to distract her, so instead of dissuading him, she agreed.

A few minutes passed while they carried boxes down from the attic. When Joanne located the Christmas lights, she untangled the strings while he tested them. When they finished, they'd located five long strands that worked.

Her on one side and Benjamin on the other, they passed the strings back and forth, looping them around the limbs while the rich pine scent wafted around them. His hand brushed hers each time, and a tingle rolled up her arm. Each pass renewed the sensation, and her emotions jogged through her limbs like a marathon runner.

When the last strand was in place, Joanne stepped back and Benjamin secured the plug in the socket. The white lights danced across the limbs like stars. "It's beautiful. Thank you."

He strode across the room and stood beside

her again. The CD player shuffled, and Mel Torme's smoky voice filled the room.

Joanne struggled to keep her tears in check. The feeling of loss rippled through her, followed by a rich, sweet sensation.

Benjamin rested his hand on her shoulder, conveying gentle heat. Her knees felt rubbery and a faint tremor shook her body. When she found the courage to look up, his eyes were fixed on her.

She felt it coming, like a light illuminating a dark room—the feeling of coming home. His hand shifted from her shoulder and brushed along her neck to her cheek. The caress fluttered like the wings of a moth above a candle, translucent and airy.

Shifting her weight, Joanne let her heart replace reason as Benjamin's mouth neared hers. The touch caressed her lips with the gentleness of a breeze. She reveled in the exquisite feeling—strange yet familiar, urgent yet tender.

She accepted the delight like a hungry bird, returning his kiss.

Benjamin eased away, his hand still caressing the nape of her neck. Surprise brightened his eyes, then was replaced by something different. Perhaps guilt or sadness. "I'm sorry. I—"

"It's okay," Joanne said, hoping to soothe. "We got caught up in the moment."

His gaze searched hers as his hand slipped down to her shoulder, almost as if he were holding her away. "I hadn't expected that to happen."

She hadn't, either, but it had happened, and she didn't want to dismiss it. "Friends," she said, captured by his darker look.

"Always," he whispered.

Chapter Nine

The morning sunlight stretched across the sand-hued carpet of Benjamin's office. He swiveled his chair and gazed out the window offering a view of the Detroit River, and beyond it, Canada. He'd slept badly. Joanne's image clung to his thoughts and no tossing or turning would dispel the longing that wound through him. He'd kissed her, and it was too late to take it back.

The memory of the kiss was like a wonderful dream. He'd controlled his yearning for too long, and last night, he'd lost control. Joanne had stood across the room, her face bright and smiling as she gazed at the Christmas tree. Her long golden hair had cascaded around her lovely face and spread across her shoulders like molten gold.

Her beauty had swept over him like an avalanche, unexpected and unrestrained. Benjamin had always admired her lovely features—her large sultry eyes the color of a summer sky, a mouth that curved to a gentle smile, but greater still, her sweet nature, her love of life, her mothering skills, her joy of family. Those were the qualities that made her unique.

And now he'd ruined it. Their relationship would be strained. He had seen it in her face. Her eyes had widened in surprise, and her comment had sent him to the depths. *We got caught up in the moment,* she'd said, as if she'd already dismissed what had happened.

What could he do now?

Benjamin struggled to focus on his work. His last assignment had left him empty— a business merger. Dry, dull facts, financial figures, clauses and addendums marched through his head. He shifted the file and opened the folder, then grabbed his small digital voice recorder and pressed the record button. He begun to spew out notes for the secretary.

When his thoughts drifted, he hit the stop switch and leaned back again. He should have specialized in personal injury, or criminal defense—anything but contracts, arbitration and business litigation. Working with people rather than corporations would give him a greater sense of purpose. Though he was good at it, corporate law had been a mistake.

Greg had worked with people. His cases had weighed on him and had taken a toll on his emotions at times, but when he'd finished a case, he knew he'd changed someone's life, hopefully for the better. All Benjamin felt he'd done was solve a problem for a conglomerate.

Mental images of Greg triggered a thought. Joanne's phone calls seemed connected to Greg's and Mandy's deaths. Why? And as Joanne said, why *now?* After three years, what would cause a woman to ask questions about Mandy? Did she suspect Mandy was alive? What evidence did she have? Was it only speculation? And now Joanne had received those odd e-mails. He needed to know more.

Joanne's startling comment had struck him. *Maybe she wasn't in the car.* That hadn't made sense at the time, unless—

She'd been taken out by someone. Her seat belt had been unlatched, Benjamin recalled. That fact had bothered Joanne. He'd wondered if Mandy knew how to unhook her belt. She had been a bright child, but she had also been well-behaved and had minded her parents. He didn't believe the child would un-latch her seat belt.

So where did that leave him? The impact had undone the buckle or someone had un-latched it. Perhaps Greg had reached over the seat to— No, that wasn't possible. Greg's belt had been fastened when the divers found him. He couldn't have leaned over to release it.

Another thought nudged itself free. Greg's death had been deemed accidental, but what if…? Benjamin shook his head. He'd seen too many movies. He pushed the thought aside. Yet it hung on the fringes of his concentra-tion. What if Greg's death hadn't been acci-dental? What if a case he'd been working on had set off a madman who wanted revenge?

Foolish. He'd gotten as bad as Joanne with that kind of thinking. Anyway, if Greg had been worried or threatened, he would have mentioned it. Or maybe not. Benjamin had already moved to Seattle. Why would Greg spend valuable telephone time discussing a speculative fear? Greg had never exhibited fear. He'd charged into his cases like a man on a mission. Fearless.

No. It couldn't be.

Benjamin longed to have the problem-solving ability of a detective. For now, he would wait. If Joanne received a more telling e-mail or if the woman called Joanne again, perhaps something would click. Once the cops had more to go on, they'd take action.

Joanne leaned against the door frame and gazed at the Christmas lights strung on the tree. She and Benjamin had gotten no further the night before. Her heart skipped thinking of what had distracted them—the unexpected kiss that she'd accepted with every fiber of her being. The sensation had startled her, and now guilt rippled at the edges of her reasoning.

Greg had been gone three years, and she'd remained faithful to the love they'd shared despite her anguish and pain. She'd leaned on no one but herself and, finally, on the Lord. But the sorrow had put a wedge between her and God. She had tried to trust and to be assured that all things happened for a purpose, but the loss seemed too great, the hurt too deep, the sorrow too overwhelming.

Along with Greg and Mandy, she'd watched friends walk away. Her family acted tense when she visited and they never came to Grosse Pointe. This had caused her sorrow to turn to bitterness. Her heart had turned as cold as the December wind.

Tears burned in her eyes now and the tree lights became prisms. The one joy she'd experienced these past few weeks had been Benjamin's return, and now she feared the kiss would strain their relationship.

He'd apologized, and she'd passed the beautiful experience off as a frivolous moment, a meaningless event. The kiss had been so far from meaningless that Joanne couldn't even think after it happened. Her rash response knifed through her as the words left her lips. Why hadn't she admitted she'd enjoyed the moment, that Benjamin had become her mainstay since he'd come back into her life and that she'd always admired him as a person and respected him as a dear friend.

Didn't friendship make the best base for romantic relationships?

She brushed the tears from her eyes. Preparing a lonely dinner no longer appealed to her. Instead Joanne crossed the room, drawn by the heady scent of pine and the twinkle of the lights.

Boxes beside the tree were filled with ornaments she'd normally have shoved back into the carton. Today she opened a lid and pulled out a clear ball with the manger inside. Looking closely at the loving scene, Joanne felt her heart twist in sorrow. "Round yon virgin, mother and child…" The Christmas story filled her mind. When Mary looked at her newborn Son, she knew the truth, but until she experienced it, Mary had no concept of the pain and grief her mother's love would endure.

Joanne could never compare herself to that kind of sorrow, but she had known the grief of losing a child, and now new hope had wiggled its way out from the hidden places in her mind.

As she pulled out each ornament and gazed at it, her mind shifted from Mandy to Benjamin, a rapture of sweet and sorrowful thoughts, leaving her yearning for a distraction.

As she hung a pink and gold angel on an upper branch, the telephone rang. She hoped the caller would be Benjamin, with something to take her mind off her heavy thoughts.

But on reaching the phone, she glanced at the caller ID and her heart stopped. *Blocked*.

She gathered courage, noting the time, then picked up and said hello.

This time the silence lasted only moments. "I'm afraid for my life."

The statement nailed her to the floor.

"Who *are* you?" Joanne asked, keeping her voice as steady as her pounding heart would allow.

"That's not important. I am positive your daughter is alive."

Your daughter is alive. The words caught her and wrapped with such strength around her chest, Joanne couldn't breathe. Before she could speak, the woman continued.

"I have to get away. All I need is enough money to get far away from here so he'll never find me."

"Who? Get away from who?"

"If you can give me the fifty-thousand dollars I need, I'll tell you where to find your daughter."

"What?" Sobs ripped from Joanne's chest. Mandy. Alive. Could it be? She'd sensed it. She'd felt it in her heart. She'd heard the whispers of her daughter's cry. But—

"I'm sorry," the woman said. "I must do it this way for our safety."

Her safety and who else's? Did she mean

Mandy? "How do I know you're telling me the truth? I don't know you. You're a voice." Her legs quaked and she grasped the wall to stay upright. *Be strong,* she told herself. Extortion. People will say anything.

She gathered her courage. "I have no proof you truly know where my daughter is. Prove it to me, then talk to me about money."

"I don't have much time. He'll find me."

The line clicked and went dead.

"Who are you?" Joanne cried, pressing the telephone against her ear as if the contact would keep the line open.

A mechanical voice broke in. *"If you are trying to make a call, please hang up and try again."*

The telephone slipped from Joanne's hand and bounced on the end of the cord like a yo-yo until it spiraled to a stop.

Disbelief flooded her, drowning her reason and hope to the depths of despair. She knew she should call the detective. Her sensible mind told her it was the only thing to do, but her heart told her otherwise. The woman might tell her where to find Mandy, but if Joanne called the police, she might lose the chance forever.

Fear rose in her as she grappled for logic.

Ransom. Her daughter was worth more than all the money in the world, but what if the woman was lying? She should call the detective.

Joanne stared at the dial pad, her finger poised over the buttons.

Donna's hand felt riveted to the receiver. Her palms were damp with perspiration, and she glanced through the telephone booth's dirty windows, fearing she'd be traced. She always blocked the calls, but she knew that technology today could probably locate her anyway.

At least she'd been smart enough to change phone booths. A chill ran through her from the winter wind that slid through the small structure's gaps. Donna slid open the door and stepped into the bitter air. She eyed her watch and realized she'd better hurry to the neighbor's for Connie. The woman never asked questions, and Connie didn't, either, because she loved to visit the neighbor's daughter.

She slipped into her car and started the motor, her mind flying in crazy directions. She had to prove to Joanne Fuller that her child was alive. But how? A recent photo-graph came to mind. Any mother should recognize her child even three years later. But how could she give Mrs. Fuller the photograph? She'd thought about writing to the mother, but tracing a letter seemed too easy. She couldn't use the mail.

When she had learned where Joanne worked, she'd thought about contacting her there. One day she'd stood outside her office building after dropping Connie at school, thinking she'd say something and then make her escape, but that had been the dumbest idea she'd ever had. She'd seen those police artists, the ones who sketched faces so close to the real features that anyone could identify the criminal. She couldn't take a chance.

But she'd find a way.

Donna headed home on Telegraph Road through the heavy Dearborn traffic, then turned onto Cherryhill. She made a left, pulled up in front of the neighbor's house and gave a toot. The woman opened the door, and in minutes, Connie dashed toward the car, a sweet smile on her face.

A blast of cold rushed into the car when Connie opened the door. She slammed it shut and gave Donna a hug.

"Did you have fun?"

"Yep. We played with games and colored.

I colored you a picture." She giggled and reached into her coat pocket, pulling out a ragged sheet torn from the coloring book.

Donna took the paper in her hand and her tension faded. A colorful butterfly sat on top of a flower. Connie had used every crayon imaginable to create the bright kaleidoscope of the bloom. "It's beautiful."

"It's for you."

"Thank you," she said, bending down to kiss the girl's cheek. The touch of her soft, icy skin against Donna's lips brought home a truth. She'd just talked with Connie's real mother—asking for money. She felt sick over her actions, but things could be no other way. She couldn't walk away from Connie, and for all the child knew, Donna was the best and only mother she had. Her stepdaughter loved her, and she loved the girl more than life itself.

Donna tucked the torn sheet onto the dashboard and pulled away from the neighbor's house, but as she neared her own, icy fear gripped her. Carl's car stood in the driveway. He'd come home early.

Where had she gone? She needed an excuse, some logical reason. She grasped at possibilities. It was too late to turn back and pick up groceries from the store. He'd probably been watching her from the window. He had become suspicious, and his unexpected appearances sent her bones rattling in her body.

"Daddy's home," Connie said, but her voice had lost its lilt.

"I see," Donna said, trying to sound noncommittal. "You run right upstairs and change your clothes, okay?"

"Okay," she said, concern in her soft voice.

Donna eased her car around Carl's in the driveway and pulled to the back. He'd parked closer to the road, and Donna wondered if he planned to leave again. Maybe he'd dropped home to pick up something he'd forgot.

As soon as the door opened, Donna knew she'd been wrong. Carl glowered at her from the kitchen table, his hand clenching a beer bottle. She pushed Connie behind her.

"Where have you been?" he growled.

"I ran an errand."

"You've got your nose stuck into things that don't involve you, don't you." He jumped up, flipping the table on its side, and shot toward her with such speed that she couldn't duck.

"I don't know what you mean," she said, pushing Connie toward the hallway door.

"Where are you going?" he bellowed at the child as she tried to escape his wrath. He caught Connie's arm and pulled her around to face him. "What are you two up to?"

Connie's face twisted as sobs ripped from her throat. "Nothing," she said. "I was coloring."

The child was innocent and Donna had dragged her into her scheme without realizing the consequences. "She's done nothing, Carl. Let her alone."

"Tell me what you're up to, and I'll let her go."

Donna reeled. What could she say that would stop him from hurting her or Connie? "It's someone's birthday coming up, Carl." She motioned with her head toward Connie.

His face twitched as he thought, then he released Connie's arm and gave her a shove. The child fell to the floor, tears rolling down her face. When he turned back to Donna, Connie bounded up and scampered out of the room.

"I'm not sure about you," Carl said. "You're sneaky." He circled the table and came toward her. "You've been snooping and sneaking around here. I don't trust you anymore. You're a stupid woman. That's why I married you. Don't try to get smart on me, Dumb Donna."

"I'm not smart, Carl. I'm dumb, and I know it, but it's Connie's birthday in a few days, and I wanted to price some toys and then talk with you."

Her legs trembled as she stood near him with nothing to cling to but her determination to get free of his bondage. Carl was cruel, and as far as she could figure, a murderer. He could as easily kill her as Connie.

"Get out of my sight," he said, giving Donna a shove.

She hurried from the room and into their bedroom, closing the door and sinking onto the bed. She tried to control the spasms of fear that gripped her.

Donna knew she could call the police, but she had no idea whether Carl had them on the take or if they'd laugh at her. Domestic violence—so common, so ignored. He'd be released in an hour, and she would pay for it. Donna knew she'd be left in a worse situation than now.

Her best plan was to escape. All she needed was the money from the Fuller woman, then she'd take Connie to Canada or Mexico. Maybe California. Someplace he'd never find them.

But she needed to prove to Joanne Fuller that Connie—Mandy—was alive. She sensed that the mother's love would come through, and then Donna would make her escape with Connie.

Chapter Ten

Joanne's fingers hovered over the telephone buttons. Then she let her hand drop to her side and hung up the receiver. If she called the police, she could scare the woman away. She'd already heard fear in the caller's voice, and any other action might mean she'd lose Mandy.

And Benjamin? He rose in her thoughts like a beacon, but the light dimmed. She couldn't tell Benjamin, either. He'd stop her from being extorted. He loved Mandy, but he didn't understand the desperation she felt, the longing, the feeling that God had opened a door to help her find her daughter.

She sank into a kitchen chair and bowed her head. If she were to succeed, it would only happen with God's help and blessing.

Her prayer flowed heavenward as fervently as tears that rolled down her cheeks. The emotion had become overwhelming. She couldn't bear the anxiety, the fear, the doubt, the hope that roiled through her body and heart. She'd thought herself a strong woman. Now the chaos had about undone her.

She took a calming breath. What would the caller do now?

The doorbell chimed, and Joanne pulled herself together, grabbed a napkin and wiped her eyes. She knew she looked a mess. The bell rang again. She drew back her shoulders as she walked through the kitchen doorway into the hall.

At the front door, she glanced through the security peephole. When she saw Benjamin on the other side, guilt skipped through her. She needed strength to keep the truth from him.

"Hi," she said, opening the door. "I wasn't expecting you." When his eyes met hers, she saw concern.

"I usually call, but I was on my way home and had the urge to drop by."

"I'm glad you did," she said, more anxious than glad.

"Something's wrong," he said, pushing the

door closed before he turned to face her. He touched her cheek. "You've been crying. She called again."

Joanne's mind searched for a response. "I've been looking at the ornaments," she said. Not a lie, she'd been doing that. The Christmas balls had brought back memories.

"Oh, Joanne," he said, drawing her into his arms. "I'm sorry. You shouldn't do that alone. I'd like to help."

"You always help me, Benjamin. I suppose I should learn how to deal with things by myself one of these days." She drew in the winter scent of his jacket mixed with the familiar aroma of his aftershave.

"You've done it alone all this time," he said.

His voice whispered against her hair and sent a chill down her back. The sensation stirred her emotions, and she longed to feel his mouth on hers. The recollection of his tender kiss filtered from her mind to her limbs, and she felt weak with the memory. Fighting the feelings, Joanne drew back and invited him into the living room.

Benjamin slipped off his jacket and hung it on the closet doorknob, then followed her. He wandered to the tree and touched a limb, then drew his hand away to smell the fragrance on his fingers. "We need to keep this watered. Do you have a watering can?"

Joanne backed away, smiling at the word *we*. She headed for the kitchen and lifted a plastic container from beneath the sink. After filling it with water she carried it back.

Benjamin had just loaded a disk into the CD player. The Christmas music wrapped around her as she crossed the room. She felt her courage fade, knowing she was keeping something so important from him, but she believed she had no choice.

Benjamin took the container from her hand and knelt beside the tree, filling the stand with water. "There," he said, rising. He set the can near the archway, then returned to her side. "How can I help?"

She shrugged. "How are you at cookie baking?"

He sent her that crooked smile that brightened her spirit. "What about hanging the ornaments?"

"That can wait another week. I'm enjoying the lights, but I need the cookies for the church's Advent midweek service."

"Then we'll make cookies." His voice was matter-of-fact as his hand slipped behind her back. They stood listening to the instrumental melody of "What Child Is This?"

Joanne felt him inhale, then exhale, his feet shifting as they stood. His hand stirred on her arm, sending her pulse skittering. And as the scent of pine and Benjamin wrapped around her, she wished she could define their relationship. What was he now? Friend or more than friend?

"I'm concerned about you," he murmured.

"I'm okay, Benjamin. Really. It's the season, I think."

"Christmas."

"And all this confusion. The phone calls. The e-mails. The hopes that may never come to fruition."

"I know," he said, his look so tender it made her weak.

She gave his shoulder a squeeze and eased away. He didn't release her immediately, and she loved the feeling of being held by someone unwilling to let her go.

Melancholy overtook her mood. The woman caller had opened doors—doors of hope. Joanne had no idea if the woman had been telling the truth or lying, but her heart said it was true.

Now what? She'd demanded proof. What

would the woman do to prove Mandy was alive? Could Joanne trust her to follow through, or had she destroyed her only chance of finding her daughter?

Joanne gestured toward the archway as she turned to the kitchen, hoping the cookies would distract her from the phone call and the emotion that gnawed at her.

"Do you have any apple juice? I make a mean mulled cider." Benjamin's voice shot into her thoughts.

Joanne glanced at him. His smile warmed her heart and melted the icy feelings she'd had. "I might just have some."

She entered the kitchen with Benjamin on her heels. Inside her pantry cabinet she found the juice, and while he warmed it along with some orange slices and a tea ball with cinnamon and cloves, she began gathering the ingredients for her cookie recipe.

"This has to simmer," he said, moving to her side. "What can I do?"

She slid him a large bowl and measuring cups. "I'll get the sugar and shortening ready while you handle the dry ingredients."

He studied the recipe and went to work like a man who knew what he was doing. Joanne grinned at the precision with which he measured the floor and baking soda. Seeing him in the kitchen lightened her mood and she realized her disturbing thoughts had drifted away for a moment. When he moved back to her side with the flour mixture, her heart sped up at his nearness.

"If that's finished," she said, "you can grind the pecans for me. It's part of the filling."

She formed the dough, then rolled it out, cut it in squares and sprinkled in the nut and sugar-cinnamon mixture, then formed it into crescents. Benjamin shifted them to a cookie sheet and soon she slid the first batch into the oven.

"While you're finishing," he said, tilting his head toward the next tin, "I'll make a fire."

"Good idea," she said, happy to be alone for a moment. Joanne realized she needed to get her thoughts in order. She had so many things to say and ask, but the phone call had filled her mind. Pushing it aside, she focused on the night before, and their kiss.

While she cleaned the kitchen, she pulled out the first batch of cookies and slid them onto a cooling rack. The cider's spicy fragrance rose from the pan and mixed with the nutty cinnamon aroma. By the time the next batch came out, she had slid a few that had cooled onto a plate. She carried them into the living room.

Benjamin had tossed a couple of logs on the fire and was watching the glow of the kindling beneath. He turned when she entered the room, and pointed to the sofa. "I'll get the cider." Benjamin stood back a moment, then set down the matches and headed for the room.

Joanne settled onto the cushion, propping a pillow behind her back so she could face him, then lifted her legs and curled them beneath her. Having a man in the house had become a treat. She never used the fireplace anymore. Once she had loved sitting on the carpet in front of the logs, listening to the crackle of the flames and watching the sparks spiral up the flue.

She watched now as the fire left the kindling and licked up the bark, gaining speed as the red glow turned yellow with flickers of blue. Her feelings for Benjamin had grown in the same way.

Benjamin followed the scent of the cinnamon and cloves as he made his way into the kitchen. He pulled two mugs from the cabinet and turned off the burner. His mind felt weighed down with Joanne's problems.

She'd said her tears had been because of the ornaments, and perhaps that had been it, but his gut told him they had been motivated by something else. Why wouldn't she admit that the woman had called again if that was the case? He couldn't believe Joanne would keep things from him or do something foolish.

Why not? He'd been foolish the night before when he kissed her. Tonight his concern revolved around that incident, as well. Had he upset her? Did she feel betrayed or disappointed? He'd come to her as a friend and now he'd let his emotions loose.

Benjamin longed to tell her how he felt, longed to tell her that the kiss hadn't just happened, but that he'd cared about her for years when he had no right. He could only thank God that he'd been a gentleman and had never deceived or misbehaved in any way when it came to Joanne.

So what would happen now?

He ladled the spicy mixture into the mugs and carried them back into the living room. When he saw Joanne nestled on the sofa, his stomach coiled. He was about to have another fight with his heart.

After he handed her the mug, he sat beside her, gazing at the flickering flames and longing to talk about the things that burned inside him. Nothing was more important than knowing what was on Joanne's mind.

"You're quiet," she said.

"Thinking," he said.

"About the kiss?" she asked.

Her question startled him, and he gave her question thought before answering yes.

"Me, too," she said.

Seeing her frown, he said, "I hope you're not upset. I never meant—"

"Upset? No."

"Disappointed?"

"No." She gave her head a strong shake.

He searched her face for the answer. "Then what?"

"Wondering what it meant. I was surprised."

So had he been, not only at his action, but at her eager response. Yet she'd dismissed it, when it had meant so much to him.

"What did it mean to you, Joanne?"

She looked away and gazed at the sparking flames, then at the Christmas tree. "I'm not sure. I—I know what it did."

"What it did?"

"It made me feel alive. It's the first time I've kissed a man since Greg."

"I didn't mean to offend you. It seemed right. It seemed natural."

"We've been friends a long time," she said swiveling to face him. "It did seem natural... and right."

"But strange?"

She gave him a faint smile. "Yes, strange, but nicely so."

That broke the tension and he chuckled. "So where are we now?"

She lifted her shoulders. "Together in the living room. Alive. Feeling."

"And thinking."

"And thinking," she agreed. "Right now, I'm caught up in these telephone calls and in praying Mandy's out there somewhere. I don't have a lot of room to think about—"

She faltered, and he watched an uneasy look spread across her face. "About the future?" he asked.

"The future. But I want to, Benjamin. I truly want to live again, and you're one of the finest men I know. I don't know what I would do without you."

He let the words settle over him, trying to decide if her comment should give him hope or remind him that he'd always been just a friend. For now, he could live with the latter, but for how long, he didn't know.

Donna stared into the dress-shop window, watching Joanne Fuller's movements. She'd never followed anyone before, but today she'd become an expert. The idea had come to her out of desperation. Joanne Fuller wanted proof of Connie's existence, and Donna had tossed out the idea of sending a traceable letter or sliding something inside her storm door. Those methods were all too dangerous.

Instead, she'd located where Joanne worked and had hired a sitter for Connie so she could find some way to give Joanne the proof. Today had finally worked to her advantage. The busy mall filled with Christmas shoppers kept her undercover and still could afford her the opportunity she needed.

Joanne Fuller wandered away from the men's shop window and headed into an open café. Donna shifted from her location and wandered nearer. The woman headed for a small table, dropped her packages on the floor beside a chair, then slipped off her coat and left it there before she moved to the counter and focused on the menu.

Donna slipped past her and heard her order a skinny latte. The familiarity of the woman's voice caused Donna to jerk as she moved away. How many times had she heard the woman's panicked voice ask for information? Donna had struggled to speak that first time. Finally after the third, she'd found courage to open her mouth. Now she hoped the calls could soon end, so she and Connie would be safe.

With Joanne Fuller occupied, Donna passed the small table and made her move.

The rich coffee aroma hung on the air as Joanne waited for her drink. She loved the little café, a place to rest and regroup in the midst of the Friday after-work shoppers. Realizing a busy mall could be filled with shoplifters, she glanced toward the table where she'd left her packages. No one seemed to have noticed them.

But as she watched, a harried-looking woman scooted past her table, and Joanne noticed her car keys slip from her hand. The woman faltered, then glanced down. As she bent over to retrieve her keys, the clerk's voice drew Joanne's attention.

"That'll be three dollars and seventeen cents," she said, sliding the drink in front of Joanne.

Joanne slipped her hand into her bag and pulled out her wallet. She counted out the change, slipped the billfold into her purse and grasped her latte. When she turned back, the woman and her keys were gone.

Joanne returned to her table and eyed her packages. They were all there and she felt ashamed for wondering if the woman or someone else might have stolen her Christmas gifts.

As she sipped the fragrant coffee mixture, Joanne's thoughts settled on the anonymous caller's recent request for money. The fearful sound of the woman's voice and her comment about safety filled Joanne with deep concern. If Mandy were alive she could be in danger. But why and from whom? She'd hoped to hear from the woman again, but days had passed with no more contact, and that made her fearful.

Joanne still hadn't mentioned the incident to Benjamin, though her good sense told her more than once that she should. But she knew Benjamin too well. He'd insist on contacting the detectives, and if the caller found out, she'd back away. Joanne felt as certain of that as of the fact Mandy was alive.

Dear Benjamin. More and more he filled Joanne's thoughts. She'd never met a kinder, gentler man—he was known to be a powerhouse in a court room and at a bargaining table, yet he touched her life with a tenderness beyond compare. He'd brought her around.

Lately her thoughts had drifted back to times they had spent together when Greg was alive. She recalled how he'd always shown genuine interest in her. He'd been complimentary and thoughtful even then. Greg always chuckled that Benjamin had never married and figured he'd kill a wife with kindness.

That memory triggered a renewed thought in Joanne's mind. Benjamin's unfulfilled love. Since he'd told her that he'd been in love once, she'd longed to find out more about the woman. What would keep a woman away when a man like Benjamin loved her?

The only thing that seemed possible also seemed *impossible*. He had said the woman loved him, but not in the same way he loved her. Had the woman been engaged to someone else? Married? Had she loved him like a brother? Joanne had no idea, and wished the question didn't come to mind so often.

Joanne pulled her thoughts away from Benjamin's past and to the present. He'd suggested they do something tomorrow evening—a surprise, he'd said. He knew how the chaos and the holidays had affected her. She'd become teary too often. Last year Joanne remembered she'd gotten through the holidays with only the feeling of melancholy. Visiting her parents' home left her feeling out of place and unwanted. Had her sense been true or only her own warped view?

Her mother's phone call... Joanne was sorry Benjamin had overheard it. She'd been taken aback when he'd said she sounded hard. Maybe that had been true. She didn't want her family's interference now, with so much going on, but she should call back. Her mother deserved the courtesy.

With the added stress of the anonymous phone calls, she could barely contain her emotions. Tonight Joanne had no idea how Benjamin planned to surprise her, but it didn't matter. Just being with him would be enough.

She took a sip of the latte and let her mind return to her task as she reviewed her purchases. She'd found a great Christmas tray for Nita who loved to entertain, but she still wanted to find something special for Benjamin. She'd looked at scarves and found them too boring. Then she'd thought a leather belt might be nice, but she didn't know his size.

She took another drink of coffee and let it glide down her throat. Other gifts popped into her mind—a shaving kit, though she hoped his travels had ended. Then a new attaché case struck her as a good idea, but she'd seen his recently and it looked fairly new.

A tie? Boring. Handkerchiefs? Really boring. Pajamas? Too personal. Some things wouldn't work. A sweater? Joanne figured she could guess his size even if— She faltered as an eerie sensation washed over her. Joanne had the unpleasant feeling she was being watched.

As her gaze swept the patrons, a woman in a dark coat turned away and rounded the corner of the food court. Joanne scanned the crowd again. A man's gaze caught hers, and he winked. She frowned back.

Then Joanne glanced behind her. The woman who'd dropped the keys seemed focused on her from across the mall, and when she made eye contact, the stranger turned away. Feeling uneasy, Joanne rose. She gathered her packages and clutched them against her. Was she being ridiculous, or was she being followed?

Chapter Eleven

"Ready?"

"I think so." Joanne's hand brushed along the skirt of her silver-blue dress. "Where are we going?"

Benjamin grinned at the curious expression on her face. "It's a surprise."

"Am I dressed okay?"

His gaze drifted down the soft suede fabric that followed her slender form to the top of her knees. She'd cinched a thin woven belt at the waist and topped the dress with a matching jacket that touched her rounded hips. He'd never seen anyone so lovely. "Perfect," he said, unable to pull his gaze from her amber hair curving in soft waves along her face.

She smiled at him with eyes the color of

her attire, an amazing sky blue that stirred his longing.

"If you're sure," she said.

"I'm positive."

When Joanne pulled her coat from the closet, Benjamin took it from her and held it out as she slipped in her arms. She gave him another puzzled glance over her shoulder, but he only smiled, anxious to surprise her.

Once they were in the car and the motor kicked in, warm air rose from the heater. He'd longed to ask her about the calls, but he hadn't, afraid he'd rile her again. She'd been quiet, and he'd wondered if that meant the calls had ended.

Benjamin could feel Joanne's gaze on his face, and he glanced at her. She looked expectant, as if waiting for him to say something.

"Are you okay?" he asked.

"I'm fine. Just wondering where we're headed."

"To downtown Detroit."

She lifted an eyebrow and asked no more. He guessed she'd figured out that he wasn't talking. Joanne eased back against the seat and gazed out the window.

Maybe he was being silly not telling her,

but he knew she would love the evening and he'd hoped it would relieve the stress she'd been under.

"You're quiet. What's up?" He sensed she had something on her mind.

"Nothing much. I'm trying to keep the problems at bay. I'm thinking Christmas thoughts," she said.

He slid his hand across the empty space and touched her arm. "You're worried?"

She nodded. "I haven't heard anything since—" She faltered. "I don't know. It's been a while. I don't know what to think."

If the woman had stopped calling, Joanne would soon realize it had been a hoax. "Be patient. God's in charge, Joanne. I know that's difficult to remember. We all want things to happen on our time, but that's not how it always is."

She looked at him as if she understood but didn't like the situation.

He let his hand slide over hers. Her skin felt soft and warm to his touch, and he brushed his fingers along hers, enjoying the sensation and the closeness.

Joanne's hand shifted, and she rolled it beneath his so the palm was up, then wove her fingers through his. Her action settled in his gut and stirred his longing to take her in his arms. He'd kissed her only once. Tonight he yearned to kiss her again.

He drove with one hand on the wheel until he had to turn the car onto Woodward. The loss of her hand against his left him feeling lonely, and Benjamin realized his life was tangled with Joanne's more tightly than their fingers had been.

When the building came into view, he pulled into the right lane, then turned into the parking lot. Joanne craned her neck to read the sign.

"Detroit Symphony Orchestra Hall?" She eyed him as he followed the parking attendant's instructions. "Is that where we're going?"

"You've always talked about this, and I thought it would be fun."

"The Nutcracker." She shook her head as she gazed at him. "That's the nicest gift in the world. You know I love this ballet. I can't believe you're willing to sit through it for me."

"I like the music." He grinned at her astonishment. "I can handle the dancing, too, I think."

He pulled into the designated parking spot and turned off the engine. Before he opened the door, Joanne leaned over and captured his face in her hands. Her eyes searched his, then she gave him a gentle kiss. His heart skipped at the touch and the emotion startled him—embarrassed him, really. How could a grown man be so overwhelmed by a woman's brief caress?

Joanne had been surprised by her own forwardness, but she'd enjoyed it, and it had taken her mind off what she'd almost done— she'd almost mentioned the recent call from the woman.

Forcing the worry from her mind she gazed ahead at their destination. When they reached the sidewalk, she watched the downtown traffic zip past—horns honking, motors revving, tires screeching—until the light changed to red. Benjamin took her arm as they crossed Woodward Avenue. Orchestra Hall stood close to the sidewalk, a magnificent edifice in an unlikely part of town.

The crowd shoved inside to escape the cold, and as she and Benjamin stepped into the warmth, the usher steered them to the right and midway down the main floor seating.

Joanne felt Benjamin's hand against her

arm, and she was filled with pleasure. When they were seated, she opened the program, then glanced at him. "You're amazing."

"You think so?"

"I know so. Thank you so much for doing this."

"It's for me, too," he said.

His look swept over her, making her limbs feel like jelly. She'd grown too close to him, was too captivated by his attention and his manners. But though they'd kissed, she feared their relationship, formed as a deep friendship, could never change. Greg would always stand between them.

The hall lights dimmed and the orchestra opened with the great Tchaikovsky Overture. As the familiar melodies rippled through her—"Waltz of the Flowers," "Dance of the Sugarplum Fairies," "March of the Toy Soldiers"—her mind shifted to Mandy.

Mandy would have turned six a couple of months ago, and Joanne knew she would have brought her daughter to see this wonderful program that captured the playful view of Christmas. Next she would have taken Mandy to see the Rockettes' Christmas program that depicted the nativity story with live animals. A child needed both at Christmas—the magic and the truth. Nothing could outshine Christ's birth.

Joanne realized her mind had taken a dour turn. It had slipped back to the time she'd finally accepted that Mandy had died in the icy waters. Her hope had begun to fade after she hadn't heard anything more from the woman caller. Three days had passed. Joanne had been certain the caller would have done something by now to prove Mandy was living. The woman had sounded so sincere and so desperate. Joanne wondered if her demand had frightened her away.

What had she expected the caller to produce? What kind of proof would make her certain? Joanne only knew that her mother's heart had not been the same for the past two months. Something had settled there, whether intuition or premonition. It had been something unreal, yet tangible. Something bizarre, yet so believable she couldn't let it go.

Pulling her thoughts back to the orchestra and the stage, Joanne focused on the colorful dancers, the toy-soldier mice who marched across the stage. Though the bright melodies filled her head, sadness settled on her heart.

When her sigh escaped, she caught Benjamin's worried look. He shifted and placed his hand on hers. The warmth rushed through her, and his touch reminded her of their conversation. She bowed her head and prayed. If ever she needed God, it was now.

"Happy birthday, dear Connie. Happy birthday to you." Donna's lone voice sang the little song as Connie grinned at her above her cake. "Make a wish, sweetie."

Connie lowered her head, then puffed out her cheeks and blew out the six candles. "Will it come true?"

"I hope so." Donna hoped for so much these past weeks, but the rays of hope seemed to be dimming.

"Can I tell you my wish?" Connie whispered, although she didn't need to because they were alone.

"It's supposed to be your secret," Donna said, grinning at the child's eager face.

"It can be *our* secret."

"Okay, tell me," Donna said, knowing no matter what the child wished for, it would probably not come true.

"I wished we could go away forever. Just you and me."

Donna's heart lurched. She bent down and

nestled the child's head against her chest, then kissed her soft hair. "I wish the same."

But Donna's hopes were fading. She'd tried to get the courage to call Joanne Fuller back the evening after she'd followed her after work, but fear had stopped her—fear of Carl's wrath and fear of being caught by the police. She could never allow Carl to be alone with Connie. His hatred had grown in the past month to the point of psychosis.

Donna had done everything to keep her whereabouts secret. She'd blocked calls and phoned from telephone booths, even changing location with each call. But getting away seemed more and more impossible.

Still, waiting for Donna to call again would give Joanne Fuller time to find the photo and accept the truth that her daughter was alive, and then come up with the money.

Donna had always phoned after Joanne arrived home from work, but calling during the day seemed easier while Connie was in school. Until recently Donna hadn't known where Joanne worked, but now that she did, calling her at work, where the lines weren't tapped, might be wise, and getting away during the day would be easier.

The new idea gave her hope. Today was

Saturday. Sunday wouldn't work, but Monday would. She smiled at the thought of her plan. When she glanced at Connie, the child's face looked puzzled.

"I bet you're waiting for your present," Donna said.

"Do we have to wait for—?"

"No, let's open it now."

Connie hugged her around the neck, and Donna fought the tears that rose in her eyes.

Joanne pulled into the driveway and turned off her car. Worship had felt lonely without Benjamin at her side. He'd been exhausted from his busy week and worrying about her, she knew, and last night after their wonderful evening at *The Nutcracker,* he'd complained of a sore throat. She had insisted he stay home and get some rest.

The lesson for the day stayed with her. God knew what she needed to hear, and perhaps it was best she was alone. When the pastor began 1 Corinthians 13:1, Joanne knew she had to listen, because the message of love had been clinging to her thoughts since her mother had called. "If I speak in the tongues of men and of angels, but have not love, I am only a resounding gong or a clanging cymbal."

She'd been a clanging cymbal, she feared. She thought about the cold treatment she'd given her mother. Joanne realized she had closed the door to healing just as Benjamin had said. By the time the pastor had gotten to the eleventh verse, the truth hit home. "When I was a child, I talked like a child, I thought like a child, I reasoned like a child. When I became a man, I put childish ways behind me."

Joanne had been unable to give up childish things. She knew her family. She knew their ways, so why had she allowed their behavior to pull her from what she knew was right? Jesus said to turn the other cheek. She'd followed the Old Testament—an eye for an eye.

Joanne looked up at the winter sun streaming down from the sky and melting the hard mounds of snow. Her heart had experienced the same with the warmth of God's Word.

She unlocked the front door and pushed it open, feeling the rush of heat from inside, but it was no stronger than the heat she felt from her resolution. Healing needed time, but she would begin today. Benjamin had roused her thoughts and she didn't want to disappoint him.

She hung up her coat and headed straight

for the kitchen. After having a bite to eat, she resolved, she would call her parents—but as she came through the doorway she saw the light blinking on her answering machine.

She checked the caller ID and smiled. *Benjamin.* She pressed the button.

"Hi, I'll be over shortly," he said.

She heard him fumble for a second.

"It's ten-thirty, and you should be home soon. I'll be bringing fresh bagels!"

Joanne grinned as she deleted the message, but refused to be swayed from her decision. She put on some coffee, then called her parents. Talking to them was a struggle, but she mentally reviewed the verses she'd heard in church and prayed she had left her clanging-cymbal days behind her.

The adult Joanne put her childish ways aside as she spoke and shared the problems she'd been facing.

"Oh, no," her mother said. "Who would do that?"

"I don't know, Mom, but the police are on it." Were they?

"Do you need me?"

How often she'd needed her mother, but not today. She had the authorities and she had Benjamin. "I'm fine, really," she said, allowing the truth to set in. She had God on her side and He was her greatest ally.

"I'd be happy to come," her mother said.

"No. Really. I'm fine."

The doorbell rang, and she ended her call, feeling she'd made some progress. At least she'd been honest with her mother, and she had heard a sincere reaction to news of her recent trials.

Benjamin stood on the porch with a grin on his face and a bag of bagels in his hand. As Joanne opened the door he breathed in the aroma of freshly brewed coffee. He gazed at her and noticed a brighter look on her face.

"You look smiley today," he said.

"I feel good. Great sermon. Too bad you missed it."

His grin widened. "Did I need to hear it?" He stepped inside and headed for the kitchen.

She shook her head. "No, I did."

He chuckled as he sat the bag on the table. He put out the cream cheese with chives as Joanne got plates and knives and poured the coffee.

"What's up? No calls? E-mails?"

"None." She looked away, then turned back. "I called my mom."

"Really."

"You got me thinking."

"I did?"

Her gaze drifted away from him. He missed looking into her eyes.

"About my hard-heartedness," she said.

"I didn't mean to confront you."

"No. I needed to hear it." She lifted the knife and scooped up some cream cheese. "The sermon focused on the same thing. I knew it was something I had to do." She shifted toward him. "I've looked at this totally from my point of view, not theirs. I've always known my family was a little self-centered. I have been, too, I suppose."

He'd never seen Joanne act self-centered, but maybe he was prejudiced. "So what happened with the call?"

"I decided to tell her about the things going on here. That way she'd understand why I decided not to visit for Christmas."

"And?" He lifted a bagel, then paused. "What did she say?"

"She wanted to come here. I told her no."

That confused him. "Why did you do that?"

"I figured it would save embarrassment. If I encouraged her to come, she'd have to find an excuse why she couldn't make it. This way it saves her the trouble."

Benjamin felt his jaw sag. "You really feel that way?"

Joanne shrugged. "If she came, what could she do? The police haven't done anything."

"You don't know that."

"I'm confused. I don't know what I think."

"Joanne, let's not argue. You're exhausted. Too much has happened and you're over-whelmed. I'm a mess. Let's try to keep our spirits up." He slid his hand across the table and grasped her free hand. "Will you pray with me?"

Her eyes glazed with tears. "Please, Benjamin."

She bowed her head while Benjamin took their concerns to the Lord.

"Where did you go Saturday night?" Nita propped her hip against Joanne's desk. "I'm telling you, Benjamin is so romantic. I don't care what you say."

Joanne had grown tired of denying her feelings, and today she spoke her heart without a qualm. "He is, but I don't think he knows it."

Nita snorted a laugh. "You don't think he knows it? How can that be?"

"I truly believe he's being a friend."

Nita leaned closer. "What about you?"

Joanne shook her head at Nita's persistence. "I admit—it used to be just friendship, but now I'm really crazy about him."

"Finally!" Nita's face glowed.

"I can't fight city hall."

"Or your heart." Nita gave her a hug. "I'm thrilled for you. I really am. You've been a faithful wife to Greg, but the marriage vows say 'as long as you both shall live.' It's time to let go, Joanne."

"I think I have, Nita, but I'm not sure about him."

"Can't you ask him? Just tell him how you feel."

Joanne's pulse fluttered at the idea. "I don't think I can. Pride or fear. I don't want to lose his friendship. It's too precious to me. We've been so careful, but things are starting to change naturally. I think I'll just pray God opens the door."

"You can't go wrong with that." Then she laughed. "And if Benjamin tries to lock the door, maybe you can give him a little help. You know."

Joanne chuckled at her friend's eagerness for her to find love. "You're a dear friend."

As the words left her mouth, the telephone rang. Joanne lifted her index finger to halt the conversation and grabbed the receiver. "Solutions. Joanne Fuller speaking."

"Do we have a deal?"

The hushed voice wheeled over her like a steamroller. Her heart skipped, and her eyes shifted toward Nita. She couldn't let on. "One moment, please." She covered the mouthpiece with her hand. "This will take a while."

"I'll talk to you later," Nita said with a nod.

Once Nita left the room, Joanne pulled her hand from the mouthpiece. "What deal?" she asked, praying the woman hadn't hung up. "I asked for proof. I haven't seen any."

"I gave you the photo."

"What photo?"

"The photograph I put in your shopping bag."

The woman's breathing sounded labored, and her voice trembled. Joanne feared she wouldn't stay on the line long. "I don't know what you're talking about."

"At the café at the mall. I slipped a photo of your daughter into your shopping bag."

Joanne's chest burned as each breath left her. "I didn't find it. I'm sorry."

As she opened her mouth to ask more, the telephone clicked, then disconnected.

Tears pooled in Joanne's eyes. Her last visit to the mall dashed through her thoughts. Was it the woman with the keys? Joanne had left her packages and had been distracted only for a moment. How had she missed seeing someone near her bags? She tried to recapture the face of the woman—harried, Joanne remembered, and with eyes that had watched her from the other side of the mall.

Could it be?

She tensed as she thought of the packages tucked in her closet, waiting to be wrapped. Every time the woman called, Joanne heard greater desperation in her voice. And now she might have scared the caller off with the delay.

Joanne placed her hand on the telephone, longing to call Benjamin, but she stopped herself. She couldn't. He'd stop her if he knew. Loneliness surrounded her. Her hand twitched as she pulled it away and turned to the computer. Instead, she'd write him an e-mail about nothing, so she could feel connected to him without his seeing her face. Benjamin always knew when something had gone wrong.

She clicked on the e-mail icon, and her mail opened. Glaring back at her was Shadow@123go.com. She gaped at the message.

YOU'RE ABOUT TO LOSE WHAT YOU WANT.
YOU'RE GETTING CARELESS.

The words raked over her. *Lose what you want.* Her daughter was what she wanted.

She hit the print icon, then deleted the e-mail. Her chest ached with desperation.

Dear Lord, please, don't let it be too late. If Mandy is alive, Father, lead me to her. Give me the strength I need, and forgive me for my doubts.

Her amen whispered through her mind and into her heart.

Chapter Twelve

Joanne raced into the house, threw her coat over the chair and darted down the hall to her bedroom closet. Like a madwoman, she tore into the pile of shopping bags and dragged them onto her bed.

Sitting on the edge of the mattress, she ripped the gifts and boxes from the tissue and spread the items across the quilt. When she pulled out Nita's tray, something fell to the bed. Her hand trembled as she lifted the white rectangle and turned it over.

A child's face looked back at her. A blond child with pale blue eyes and Mandy's features—more mature, sadder, but Mandy's. A sob rent Joanne's chest and she clutched the photograph to her chest, her body shaking with uncontrollable tremors.

She had no doubt, not one question. The child in the photograph was Mandy. She would stake her life on it. Joanne recalled school pictures of herself at age six. She and Mandy looked like twins, except that Mandy had her father's mouth, the generous smile with a hint of dimples.

Pushing the gifts and packages aside, Joanne fell back onto the bed, the photograph clutched against her chest. She struggled to breathe, to believe what she had seen with her own eyes. The truth wrapped around her, strangling her with the amazing occurrence. Mandy was alive. How? Why? She had no answers, and now she didn't care.

Mandy lived and breathed somewhere. "Oh, Lord," Joanne cried aloud. "Help me find my daughter."

Joanne awakened still holding the photograph. Darkness pressed against the windows, and she was startled to think she'd fallen asleep. She pulled her body upward and slid her legs over the edge of the bed, then glanced at the clock. She'd been there for two hours.

She knew Benjamin would call and want to drop by, and she needed to get a grip on herself. Her focus returned to the photograph, and her heart knocked double time while she struggled to breathe. What should she do? Now she had proof, but if she told Benjamin he'd insist on telling the police, and Joanne sensed she'd lose her caller. The woman was already afraid—petrified was more like it, judging by her tone—and if she panicked and ran, then Joanne would be the loser.

She couldn't lose her daughter again.

Her pulse riffled through her body as reality engulfed her. She had to follow the woman's wishes. Money was nothing compared to having her daughter back in her arms. Greg had left Joanne well off. She had her job. She had investments. She could get her hands on the sum easily—and she would. She had no choice.

Joanne crossed the room and slipped the photograph into her jewelry box. She couldn't chance anyone seeing it. Not now. Not until she'd had time to organize her finances and make her move.

She had the third e-mail, too, and she needed to tell Benjamin about that. She should have dropped it off at the police department, but she'd been too frantic to get home.

The doorbell rang, and Joanne answered

it, confident it was Benjamin. He'd become a daily part of her life, so much so that she felt lost without him. Yet now, seeing him caused her grief because of the secret she would keep from him.

"Hi," she said as she opened the door.

His smile lit the room as he entered, and he slid his arm around her waist and gave her a brief hug. "I've stopped calling before I visit. Did you notice?"

She managed to grin back. "It just means we're best friends. No pretenses—" Her heart surged with the reminder. "No need to impress. What you see is what you get."

A flicker of concern whisked across his face and caused Joanne to wonder. In a heartbeat his smile returned, and he slipped off his jacket, then hung it on the doorknob.

"What are you up to?" he asked.

The question sent a slither of guilt down her spine. "Nothing much." She walked ahead of him to the kitchen. "To be honest, I fell asleep for a few minutes."

"I'm sorry. Did I wake you?" His voice came from behind her.

"No." She turned to face him. "I woke up a while ago. I'm surprised I fell asleep. I never do that."

He reached her and rested his hand on her shoulder. "You're exhausted with everything going on, Joanne. Emotion is the worst for sapping people's strength."

She nodded, realizing she hadn't eaten and knowing she didn't want to. "I got another e-mail today."

"No." He searched her face. "Do you have it here?"

She nodded and headed for her handbag where she'd placed it before she left Solutions. She opened her purse and pulled out the paper, then returned to Benjamin. "Here."

He unfolded the note and skimmed it. "I don't like this. 'You're about to lose what you want.' That sounds like a reference to Mandy."

"I know." She slid a chair from under the table and sat.

"We have to call Cortezi." His eyes caught and held hers. "You should have dropped this off at the public safety building."

"I know, but…" She heard her voice fade. What could she tell him? "I just didn't."

"You think it's a waste of time?"

She shrugged. "I know they're doing what they can."

"We can't overlook these e-mails. I'm going to call Hank now."

He rose and strode to the telephone. Joanne watched him punch in the numbers from memory. Her mind drifted as she heard his voice. She gathered from the conversation that Cortezi was there. Finally, she heard Benjamin disconnect.

"They're already on it."

"What does that mean?"

"He said they've already contacted the e-mail server to trace the address owner."

She felt tears growing in her eyes. "It'll be a relief when this is over."

Yet panic set in. If the person who e-mailed and the caller were the same, the police's inquiries could scare her away. Joanne would never find Mandy. Now she wished she hadn't told Benjamin about the e-mail.

He stood behind her and rested his hand on her shoulder. "Let's go sit where we're comfortable."

She agreed, and rose as he pulled out her chair. They walked side by side into the living room. She felt heavy with tension, and she knew he'd noticed when he lifted his hand and massaged the nape of her neck.

"Feeling better now?" he asked.

"I'm fine," she said, enjoying the feeling. But he stopped too soon and crossed the room.

"I hate to bring this up," Benjamin said, plopping into a chair.

She stiffened. "Bring what up?"

"Things we need to talk about." His intense gaze shifted, and he focused on the darkness through the window.

She squirmed, wondering if it was about their relationship. She'd been a mess since he'd come back to Michigan. She couldn't blame him for needing a break.

His attention left the window and returned to her. "I'd like to go back over that night."

"That night?"

"The night they died."

Her other concern faded. "We've already gone over it."

"I know, but you've suspected all along that something happened, and now I'm beginning to wonder, too." His lips tightened with his frown. "I admit I doubted your feelings about Mandy for a while, but I was wrong."

"I can't be angry at you for doubting, Benjamin. I know I must have sounded like a woman who'd lost her senses." She placed her hand against her heart. "But it happened in here. I heard her voice as certain as the sun rises. I know it's off the wall, but it's what I believe."

"So let's go back to that night." His eyes searched hers.

"If you think it's important."

"Can you tell me what you remember?"

Joanne forced her mind back to that horrifying night. "We'd gone out to dinner and a movie. The teen I usually had come to sit had a date, so we asked a lady from the church. She has kids of her own so we dropped Mandy there. She lives off of Moross, not too far from the Coast Guard Pier."

"So you went to dinner and a movie. Why weren't you with Greg when he picked up Mandy?"

"It was late, and we passed the house on the way to the sitter's, so Greg suggested I go inside and he'd go alone." She felt her stomach churn. "It was the worse decision I ever made in my life."

"No, Joanne. It was a natural decision, and remember, you would have died, too, and if somehow Mandy is alive, you wouldn't be here for her. God has His reasons for things happening as they do."

Sadness darkened his face. "The car went off the road on Lakeshore Drive."

"Yes. Not too far from the War Memorial. It had been slippery that night. Black ice. It's dangerous along Lakeshore Drive. The wind comes off the lake and there's nothing to block it."

"And according to the police, Greg lost control and skidded off the road."

Joanne remembered asking them that question, over and over. "They said it wasn't uncommon. They've put up that low curb as a barricade, but it doesn't stop cars from losing control and going into the lake."

"No other car tracks?"

"By the time the police got there, a couple of cars had stopped because they saw the headlights reflecting through the water." The memory caught in Joanne's chest, and she couldn't speak. "The snow was falling heavy by then, and they found nothing unusual. The police called it an accident."

Benjamin stared downward, then raised his eyes to hers. "But you think differently?"

"I don't know anymore, Benjamin. I can't imagine how it would have happened otherwise, but I'm not willing to say for sure."

Benjamin rose and came to her side. He eased down on the chair arm beside her and took her hands. "You said a while ago that you wondered if Mandy had been in the car. Why did you say that?"

Again, she tensed. "I don't know. It's the whole situation. The seat belt unbuckled. I said it before—Greg wouldn't have let her ride without her seat belt, and I don't think Mandy would unhook it even if she knew how. We explained to her about safety. She was young, but she was—"

"A really good kid," Benjamin said.

The tremor in his voice took Joanne's breath away. "Why are you asking me all of this? You heard it all when it happened."

"But I don't remember. We were all in shock, Joanne. I don't think any one of us gave the details any consideration. We accepted what the police said without analyzing it. It seemed obvious, but now, I don't know. What bugs me the most is the open window."

"That never made sense to me." She felt the pressure of his hand against hers and she longed to be in his arms, to have him hold her and make her memories and fear go away.

Benjamin became thoughtful and Joanne struggled to hold back her secret. He would be angry to know she was considering giving the caller fifty-thousand dollars to find

Mandy. He'd tell her it was extortion and a scam—but the photograph made her believe it was real.

She studied his pensive face. If he'd just co-operate with her and not call the police, she could tell him, but she knew him too well. Benjamin was an attorney. He'd probably seen many cases of people being swindled.

Benjamin's grip tightened on her hand. "Let's say someone took Mandy from the car." He shook his head. "It's sick, but let's just say it was true. Why? And who?"

"If I knew that, I'd have her back, Benjamin. I have no idea."

"What about the woman who baby-sat that night?"

"Marti? Never. She had two little ones of her own. She and her family are still members of the church. She was heartbroken just like we were."

"I'm sorry. It was just a thought."

He released her hand and rose from the chair arm, then walked to the window. Standing in silence, he stared out at the moonless night. Joanne stood and followed him. She held his arm while resting her head on his shoulder.

"I have two other thoughts," Benjamin said. "First, that it might have been a random kidnapping, but again, how and why? The other idea is that it was someone who had an association with Greg—an angry defendant or a frustrated client—and if that person abducted Mandy, do you realize what that means?"

He turned toward her and the look in his eyes frightened her. She didn't want to think about what it meant.

"Someone wanted Mandy enough to kill Greg," he said.

"Or someone wanted Greg dead, and didn't have the heart to kill a child." The thought sent shivers down her spine.

Benjamin faced her and wrapped his arms around her. She nestled against him, drawing from his strength and accepting his comforting concern. Her heart pounded, and her lungs burned with the fiery fear.

"I didn't mean to frighten you, Joanne," Benjamin whispered into her hair. "But it's something that's been eating at me."

Tears welled in her eyes and she leaned away from his chest to look into his face. "But who would do that?" Beneath her hands, she felt him shudder.

"Greg was an attorney. We make enemies. People hold vendettas. We're the butt of society's jokes and the bane of criminals."

"Is it possible? Someone kidnapped Mandy and killed Greg to get even? It doesn't make sense."

He drew her closer again. "Not to us. We're sane people. We use common sense, and we have ethics and morals. A criminal doesn't think as we do. He wants vengeance." He released a ragged sigh. "I'm only thinking aloud, Joanne, but it's possible."

"It's a guessing game." She wanted to cry out. She wanted God to give her the answer. "Then what can we do? How will we ever know?"

As she asked the question, she thought of the woman and the photo. If she knew who the woman was, she might have her answers.

"Do you recall if Greg said anything about one of his cases?" Benjamin asked. "Anything that might give us some ideas? I was gone then or he'd have talked with me if he had a problem."

"He didn't talk much at home. I think he didn't want to worry me." At times, she had resented Greg's quiet way. She'd wanted to hear what bothered him, but he wouldn't talk about it. She'd asked sometimes, but Greg wouldn't respond so she did her best to respect his feelings. "I'll try to think back, but nothing strikes me. This is a completely new line of thought."

"We need to consider the possibility," he said. "I'll restudy his case notes. I looked through them, but this time I'll scrutinize them. It's a long process, but maybe it'll turn up something."

She felt his hand tenderly caressing her, moving in a steady, soothing rhythm along her spine. Her eyes grew heavy with the gentle motion, and she faced her growing feeling.

No other man had roused her feelings since Greg died. The thought had never entered her mind. That part of her life had died with him that night, but now something stirred inside her. Benjamin's touch, his scent, his caring ways had renewed the part of her that had shut down. She longed to know if he felt the same, but she feared he didn't.

Her thoughts turned to God's love and she prayed for Mandy's safety and her own. She ached. She needed wisdom and feared doing something foolhardy. Yet she felt compelled to search for her child.

Benjamin pressed her closer to his heart, and Joanne wondered if he'd somehow heard her prayer.

Chapter Thirteen

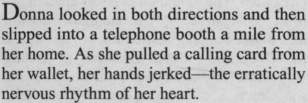

Donna looked in both directions and then slipped into a telephone booth a mile from her home. As she pulled a calling card from her wallet, her hands jerked—the erratically nervous rhythm of her heart.

She hadn't talked with Joanne Fuller since the day she'd called about the photograph. Disappointment had destroyed her confidence when the woman said she hadn't found the picture of Connie. Donna had thought for certain Joanne would see it when she stored her packages.

Gaining the courage to call again had taken effort. Donna knew extortion would mean prison. But she didn't fear for herself. Her life seemed like a prison with Carl, but she feared for Connie. The child needed a chance to live a normal life, and with some money to help them escape, Donna knew she could offer Connie all the love she had.

She reviewed her plan, then eyed her surroundings again. No one looked suspicious, but she was an amateur when it came to crime. She'd never been dishonest in her life. If there was a loving God like her friend had told her, Donna prayed He would forgive her and understand her motive. She couldn't leave the child. Ever.

Holding her breath, she dialed. When the voice gave instructions, she hit number one for English. The process seemed to take an eternity. She punched in the PIN, then Joanne's number and held her breath. The phone rang in her ear. Once. Twice. On the third ring, she heard the *click* and a hello.

"Did you find the photograph?" she asked in her hushed voice.

"Yes," the woman said.

"Is she your daughter?"

Donna heard only a pent-up breath.

"Yes."

The response tore through her. "If you want to find her, I need cash."

"Cash," Joanne Fuller said, her voice showing irritation. "It'll take me a day or two."

"I need to move fast. It must be tomorrow."

"Tomorrow? It can't be arranged that fast. Friday at the earliest."

"No. Thursday. Please." Donna's heart thundered. Why hadn't she realized the woman would need a couple of days? If she waited too long, Joanne Fuller could contact the police, and they'd be onto her. She'd acted stupid, just as Carl had always said she was. "Early tomorrow."

"I need more time. A few hours at least." The woman's voice sounded strained, and Donna feared she would panic.

"Okay. Eleven o'clock. That gives you two hours. I'm sorry, but it has to be this way."

"I'll try. Where?"

"In Mariner Park. By the lighthouse." Donna had scouted the location and hoped she could get out of the park quickly, pick up Connie at school and leave town—be far away from the Detroit area before anyone noticed. She would have their bags packed, and they could cross into Windsor from Detroit or maybe go into Canada via the Blue Water Bridge in Port Huron. That was even better. No one would be the wiser. She could stay in Canada for a while and then head for New York or anywhere.

"Cash?" the woman asked again.

"Cash in something I can carry, and no police. If I see anyone suspicious, I'll leave and you'll never hear from me again."

"You'll bring Mandy with you?"

Bile rose in Donna's throat. "I'll tell you where you can find her with no danger to you or her."

"I can't do that," Joanne Fuller said. "No. I want an even trade. Mandy for the cash."

"I'll be at the park tomorrow morning at eleven. If you want your daughter, be there."

Donna slammed the receiver onto the hook and grasped the wall of the phone booth to steady herself. What if—? She stopped herself. She'd taken every precaution. Yet fear assailed her. She had to get away from the phone booth for her own safety. Carl had been watching her, she was sure. She closed her eyes, drawing on her courage, and when she opened them she sensed someone stood outside the booth. She focused. A man watched her with narrowed eyes, and she felt her knees weaken.

He pushed against the door, and she gave the folding panels a jerk, flinging herself from the booth to make her escape.

"Hey, lady," he called, "are you all right?"

She didn't answer but darted past him without looking back.

* * *

Joanne hadn't been able to sleep. She'd tossed and turned trying to figure out how to come up with the cash. She had money in her safety deposit box. Not wise, but Greg had always said to keep some cash available. He'd stored most of his board of directors cash bonuses in the safety deposit box.

She had continued to stockpile cash for some time and she prayed she would find enough. Otherwise she would need a reason to withdraw a large amount from her account. Banks had limits.

What to do? Questions rattled in her head as she dressed. Her throat had knotted, making breakfast impossible. She made a cup of coffee and watched the clock. The bank opened at nine and she'd be waiting at the door.

Joanne hurried down the basement stairs to find something to hold the money. She looked inside the storage room and spotted an old briefcase. Grabbing it, she headed up again. Her legs weakened as she slipped on her coat. What was she doing?

As she gripped the doorknob on her way out, Joanne bowed her head, sending up a prayer for God's protection for Mandy and herself. Tears rolled down her cheeks as she prayed and her heart beat faster with a mixture of doubt and hope. Mandy alive. Could it be true?

It had to be. Joanne couldn't bear to be so close only to find out it wasn't the truth.

"Lord, give me strength," she murmured, then pulled open the door to the wintry wind.

In the car, she hesitated before turning the key in the ignition. A voice inside warned her to stop, but she had no choice. During the sleepless night, she'd devised her strategy.

She kept her eye on the time, fearing if she was delayed, the caller would become distrustful and leave.

Donna moved from the dresser to the bed in Connie's room, tossing clothes into her small suitcase. She grabbed a couple of her favorite books and a stuffed toy kitten the child always slept with. They could buy more once they got away.

Snapping the lid closed, she lifted the luggage from the bed. She took a last look, then hurried into the hallway where her case stood outside the door. She'd taken few of her belongings—only a few pieces to get her far enough away to be free again.

Donna hated what she was doing. Not so much taking the money from the Fuller woman, but promising to tell her Connie's whereabouts. She knew she would break the woman's heart—but better hers than Donna's. She'd had enough heartache.

Hoisting the two pieces of luggage, she moved down the hallway and through the doorway into the kitchen—

"Going somewhere?"

Carl's voice knifed her. Her legs turned to gelatin. Her breath failed and she dropped the cases at her sides.

Carl grasped her arm, his fingers digging into her flesh.

"Carl, please, you're hurting me," she cried.

"Oh, I'm sorry, Dumb Donna." He yanked her closer, his sour breath glazing her face. "Do you think *I'm* stupid?"

"No, Carl. Please."

"You planning a trip?"

"I—I…" What could she say? Fear knotted in her chest and words ran together like spilled paint.

"Thought you were pulling the wool over my eyes? Well, you haven't. I've been watching you." He jerked her against him. "Did you really think you were going somewhere?"

His free hand jutted upward and clutched her throat, his fingers pressing against her vocal cords.

She gagged. "Don't hurt me," she gasped as the pressure deepened.

"It won't hurt for long."

"No," she said, but the sound didn't come. Her own life was nothing, but Connie? As the darkness covered her, a prayer rose. *Lord, if you're really there, please take care of the child.*

Joanne made her way into the bank, signed her name and followed the clerk inside the locked room. The woman used the bank key and then Joanne inserted hers and gave it a turn. The box slid from its housing, and the clerk guided her to a private alcove whcre she left Joanne alone.

Her hands trembled as she lifted the lid of the large box. Her eyes settled on the velvet box holding her wedding and engagement rings. Memories washed over her of that loving day when her life had changed forever as Greg's wife. Such joy had been only a dream, but God had granted it for real. And now the joy had become just memories.

She gazed down at the neat stacks of one-hundred-dollar bills, bound in paper bands that Greg had used to keep the cash organized and accounted for. She removed five bound stacks and slipped them into the briefcase, surprised at the small amount of space fifty thousand dollars actually took up. Relief settled over her, now that she knew she had more than she needed. She gripped the edge of the table, waiting for the thundering in her temples to subside.

Joanne felt stifled in the small room. She closed the lid of the box and exited the gloomy interior, her briefcase held tight to her side. "I'm ready," she said to the clerk, trying to sound casual. The woman escorted her into the vault, and they returned the box to its place.

Taking a deep breath, Joanne left the building, knowing that she would have paid many times that much to find her daughter alive.

She slid into her car and placed the briefcase on the floor of the passenger side. Peering at her watch, she calculated the time she needed to get to Mariner's Park. She turned on the car motor and drove slowly. No need to rush and get a speeding ticket.

Her watch read 10:56 when she pulled into Mariner's Park. Two cars stood along the parking spaces closest to the green metal railing and parked in the row behind them. Joanne waited for a moment, steadying her nerves, then grasped the briefcase handle and slipped from the driver's seat. She stood there breathing in the crisp air and studying the other two cars. A couple sat in the front seat of one. The other appeared empty.

She walked to the railing, her gaze taking in the icy water of Lake St. Clair. Joanne held on to the cold railing for support. Her legs quaked from fear more than from the cold.

Letting her focus drift to the right, Joanne's pulse escalated as the lighthouse appeared in her peripheral vision. She lowered her gaze, looking for footsteps. She saw none. Was the woman in one of the cars? She turned again and peered at the two parked cars. As she watched the vehicle with the couple inside, the car motor turned over and they backed away, then headed toward the highway.

The lone car stood away from hers, and she eyed it again. Still no sign of life inside. She experienced a combination of fear, bewilderment and longing, but all her thoughts pointed to her purpose—to find her daughter.

Finally she found courage and turned to face the lighthouse. Perhaps the woman had come in from the other side of the lighthouse. Joanne held the briefcase handle tighter and forced herself to walk in the direction of the beacon.

Each step seemed weighed with fearfulness. Why hadn't she asked Benjamin for help? If she'd begged him, maybe he wouldn't have insisted she talk with the police. Joanne slid her free hand into her pocket and felt the edge of the photograph—the one showing the beautiful face of her daughter, she was certain. Sorrow coursed through her as she thought of all the missed years, all the agony. Now she had hope.

Her feet sank into the damp snow as she left the sidewalk and made her way around the structure. But when she reached the far side, she was disappointed. No footsteps. No woman. No car.

Warm tears rolled down her cheeks and heated her skin. She stood and listened to the only sound—the caw of a lone seagull reverberating from the water. *Dearest Lord, why? What do I do now?*

She felt her knees start to give way but she willed herself to remain standing. The briefcase felt increasingly heavy as she trudged back to the sidewalk and toward her car. The other vehicle had vanished, and Joanne's car stood alone in the snow-filled lot.

She climbed inside and turned on the engine. As warm air poured from the heater, she sat clutching the case against her chest, allowing the tears to drip onto its leather surface.

Time ticked past and her hope faded, but Joanne waited, watching the muted sun rise above her head, then shift to the west. Her despair turned to determination. She wouldn't give up. The woman had been delayed. She would be there soon.

She had to come.

Carl tapped his fingers against the steering wheel, waiting for Connie. He narrowed his eyes and stared at the school door. She should be there by now.

A long red scratch puckered on his right hand where Donna had tried to break his hold. She had been too scrawny to stop him. The poor dumb woman didn't know to leave well enough alone.

Eventually the door swung open, and Connie appeared beside another girl. She ambled down the sidewalk as if she had a lifetime. Carl tooted the horn, and Connie's smile faded when she saw him.

Donna had made the kid dislike him. He knew it. He pushed the window release button and the glass rolled down. "Hurry up. We don't have all day."

Connie left the other child and ran to the car. When she opened the door, concern plagued her face. "Where's Mom?"

"Get in," he said.

She climbed in, dropped her backpack by her feet and closed the door. "Where's Mom?" she repeated.

He bit the edge of his lip. "She went on a trip."

"No," Connie whined.

"Whatcha mean, no?"

"She promised to take *me* on a trip."

Carl knew she immediately had second thoughts about telling him, but it was too late. "Really," he said, "and where were you going?"

"Florida. To Disney—"

Carl let out a guffaw. "And I wasn't invited?"

"You have to work all the time," Connie said. She paused, then added, "Mom wouldn't go away without me."

"But she did."

He watched the child's face crumple, and tears edge her eyes.

"Stop whining. You're going on a trip, too. She even packed your clothes."

Connie's head jerked upward. "Going where?"

"It's a surprise."

Her eyes widened but they held a shadow of disbelief.

"I want to go with Mom."

Carl didn't bother to answer as his thoughts scuffled from one problem to another.

Chapter Fourteen

Joanne sat alone in her living room, watching the snow fall outside her window. The Christmas tree sat in darkness. She hadn't bothered to turn on the lights they'd strung along its branches, so only one ornament clung to a top branch. She hadn't had the strength to add the rest of the trimmings.

Tension pulled at every fiber of her being. She feared the woman had been frightened away, even though Joanne had hidden her actions from Benjamin and hadn't notified the police. She must have done something to cause the caller to renege on their agreement after they'd established the time and place.

Grief had returned. Mandy had seemed only an arm's length away, and now, after Joanne had returned home from her useless venture, hope had vanished like the snow-drifts that formed piles along the roadside one day and were gone the next with the sun.

Life sometimes seemed not worth the effort, and yet Joanne knew it was. She had a lifetime to live. She could even have another child. But the thought pressed against her as weighty as her grief. Now wasn't the time to think about another child. Joanne wanted the one she'd had six years ago.

Rising, she stood near the chair and gazed through the front window at the darkening sky, pondering what to do. Should she admit her actions to Benjamin? He would be upset, she realized, but how could she keep it from him? He read her behavior so easily.

The truth had to be told, she warned herself, and having made that decision, she left the window and crumpled into the chair, closing her eyes and giving way to exhaustion. She felt the dampness of tears pooling on her lashes. Her sorrow had returned with its relentless attack on her heart.

Joanne needed faith, and hers had dimmed like stars hidden behind the winter clouds. Her expectations sank into a dark abyss.

Now she pleaded with God. He'd promised her comfort? She had none. He had promised to lift her on eagles' wings? She felt abandoned. If she could only hear one word of assurance, one whisper of hope...

Joanne leaned back against the chair cushion. Behind her lids, the recent photograph of Mandy rose—the child's faint smile, sadness in her eyes.

"Why?" Joanne cried aloud. "Why did this happen?" She slammed her fist against the chair arm, then covered her face with her hands.

A *thud* came from outside—the closing of a car door. Benjamin. She'd come to know the sound that brought peace to her heart, but tonight she doubted anything could alleviate her sadness.

She heard his rap against the door—he never rang the bell anymore—and she rose to answer it. When she pulled open the door, she watched his smile fade. He stepped inside and paused, looking at her.

"Don't tell me nothing's wrong. I know something's going on."

As he slipped his arm around her shoulders, she fought the need to tell the truth, but she knew it wasn't worth the hurt to Benjamin and the pain she would suffer dealing with it alone.

"I've done something stupid," she said, moving away from him and reaching for his jacket.

He removed it, his eyes never leaving hers. "What have you done?"

She hung his jacket on the closet doorknob as he did so often, then went ahead of him into the living room and settled into a chair before speaking.

His eyes widened as she told him the story, and he shook his head.

"Never, ever do anything like that again, Joanne," he said, his volume rising with alarm. "You could have gotten yourself killed. Don't you realize that?"

"I didn't think." She wouldn't hold back anymore. "Sometimes I don't care, Benjamin. Sometimes life doesn't seem worth living."

He gripped her shoulders and leaned toward her. "Please, Joanne, don't say that. Do you hear me?"

She nodded, alarmed by his vehemence.

"I can't believe you would say such a thing," he said, his voice softening. "You're a Christian woman. You know you have a whole life ahead of you. This has been a fork in the road—perhaps one you shouldn't have followed. It's done nothing but open you up for disappointment and despair."

"I know, but what can I do. Mandy isn't your child. You have no idea how I feel—"

"Please, don't even go there." He backed away and caved into the sofa cushion. "No, Mandy isn't my child, nor could she ever be, but I loved her very much. I know it's different, but I loved her parents with every ounce of my being. I'd give my life to bring her back, Joanne."

His admission touched her.

"I would die to bring Mandy back, just to know it would make you smile the way you used to."

He'd knocked the wind from her, and like a pricked balloon, she suddenly felt empty and shallow.

"Life is difficult," he continued. "I said this before. God doesn't promise us moonlight and roses. He's given us free will to make choices. Some people choose evil, and some choose good. Sometimes good people are hurt while bad people go free. We're not puppets, bouncing around at God's whim. He's given us options to make what we can of our lives and to love Him without question."

He leaned forward and rested his elbows on his knees. "It's like marriage—for better or worse—a love that doesn't fail when hard times come."

Shame burned inside her. "I'm sorry, Benjamin. You're right."

"It's not right or wrong, Joanne. It's truth. Take God's gift of free will, but don't condemn Him for human failure. You have a life ahead of you if you'll only live it. Let go of the past. Not Mandy. Never let go of her memory, but you must face the truth. This whole thing is probably a hoax."

His words pierced her heart, but she knew he was being honest. "What I did was stupid, but I wanted to find her. That's all I could think of. I knew you'd stop me or the police would. I couldn't take that chance—" She faltered realizing what she had forgotten to tell him. "And now I have a photograph of Mandy."

His back stiffened. "You what?"

"The woman slipped it into my Christmas packages at the café at the mall."

A scowl crossed his face. "And you didn't tell me?"

She cringed, regretting that she'd kept it from him. "I didn't find the photo until last night and I knew you'd stop me."

"You've got that right." He gazed out the window, disappointment darkening his face. "If she's alive, we'll find her, but we need help—God's help and an authority who can act. We can do nothing on our own." He paused, his head hanging as if he suffered with her. "Do you still have the photograph?"

She nodded. "I think I left it in my coat pocket." She dragged herself out to the foyer and retrieved the photo from her coat pocket, then returned.

When she handed him the photo, she sank beside him on the sofa. She heard his intake of breath as he gazed at the child's image. He stared for a long time and didn't speak as he studied her face. Tears rimmed his lashes, and Joanne had to fight the urge to wrap her arms around him.

"She looks just like you, Joanne." His voice was a whisper. "This is Mandy—" He choked on the words. Then he turned and drew Joanne into his arms. "Dear Lord. This is in Your hands."

She felt him shudder, his strength seeming to flee as the truth set in. When he let her go, he turned again to the picture.

"I can't believe this. I can't. It's her. I have no doubt."

"Are you sure, Benjamin? I've questioned my judgment, but my heart tells me it's her."

"We must call Hank, Joanne. Please don't fight me on this."

Joanne raised her fingers and touched the

moisture below his eyes. Her lips tingled, and she wanted to kiss away his tears. "I shouldn't have doubted your wisdom. I'm sorry. I know you loved Mandy, and I know you would tell me to do only what's best. Why didn't I listen to you?"

"Listen now. That's all that matters." He brought her hand to his lips.

Her pulse fluttered as his warm mouth caressed her fingers. "I'm listening. Give him a call. See what he wants us to do."

He held her hand for a moment longer, then released it and rose. She saw his weariness, so like hers, as he headed for the kitchen phone. She didn't have the heart to follow. Benjamin had been right all along. She could ask God for help, but she had to listen to His instructions. Instead she'd fought what she needed to do. The authorities were trained to find a missing child. Too much was at stake for her to try to find Mandy herself.

When she heard Benjamin hang up the phone, Joanne rose and strode to the kitchen. He stood leaning back against the kitchen counter. His hand still gripping the telephone on the cradle.

"What did he say?"

"He's coming here. I hope that's okay."

She nodded. "It's fine. When?"

"Right away. I'm glad he's on tonight."

She was, too. Feeling that she was operating on automatic pilot, Joanne pulled coffee from the cabinet and spooned grounds into the coffeemaker. In the movies detectives always drank coffee.

"Did you eat?" Benjamin asked, pulling away from the cabinet. "You're looking more thin every day."

No, she hadn't eaten—the thought hadn't crossed her mind. She shrugged. "Food seems unimportant. My thoughts are filled with other things."

"But you need your strength. Should I order a pizza?"

Pizza? She usually loved it. Today the thought of it made her feel nauseated. "No. I have some ham and cheese. I can grill a sandwich."

"How about an omelette?" His smile was tender.

"That's fine. I'll make that."

"I will," he said. "Just rest."

He steered her toward a kitchen chair, and she sank into it without an argument.

Benjamin poured two coffees and added some milk to hers before setting a mug in front of her.

She watched him work, pulling out eggs, cracking them into a bowl and whisking them with a fork. His broad back rippled as he beat the eggs. He found the frying pan, dropped in a pat of butter and put the pan on the burner.

Her gaze didn't shift from him as he diced the ham and onions. When the butter had melted, Benjamin poured in the eggs, mixed them in the pan, then flipped them like a professional. He added the ham, onions and grated cheese from a package, and folded the omelette over.

"You know what you're doing," she said, admiring his skill. She also found herself appreciating his good looks. She'd taken his handsomeness for granted. He'd been in her life for so many years, and to her, his presence seemed natural and comfortable. But he was an attractive man.

The aroma drifting from the frying pan mingled with the scent of coffee, and her stomach rumbled. She was hungrier than she'd thought.

Benjamin pulled two plates from the cabinet and split the omelette, putting half on each plate. "We'd better eat this fast or we'll be sharing it with Hank. He likes his food."

He slid the plate in front of her along with a

fork and paper napkin. She grinned. She loved his taking charge. "It smells wonderful." She drew in the scent. "I even feel hungry now."

"Good," he said, sitting across from her. "May I say the blessing?"

She nodded, grateful that he'd asked. His voice sounded confident and in control as he asked God to bless the food.

"And Lord," he continued, "if it is Your will, help us to lean on You for our needs. You can do all things for the good of Your children. Father, be with us, and if Mandy is alive, we beg You to be with her. Spread Your mercy and love over her and us as we seek to do Your will. In Jesus' name, we pray."

"Amen," Joanne said. "Thank you so much. Please keep me focused, Benjamin. I count on you to keep my head straight."

He tilted his head in a silly way. "You need to do the same. I'm no better than you are."

She smiled, and for the first time that day, she let her fears slip from her mind as she nibbled on the eggs and enjoyed his company.

Minutes later, when they'd placed the plates in the dishwasher, the doorbell rang. Joanne let Benjamin answer while she poured a mug of coffee for the detective. She heard their voices coming from the living room and sensed that she'd made the right decision by allowing Benjamin to call him.

When she joined them and offered the coffee, Hank gave a chuckle. "You've seen too much TV," he said as he accepted the cup. "But you got it right. Black."

She settled into the chair across from him, and before long, she'd told him everything. He took careful notes. Finally, she showed him the photograph.

"You're certain this is your daughter?" He eyed her, then stared at the picture. "I can see a resemblance."

"I'd stake my life on it," Benjamin said. "I knew Mandy. This is her as sure as I'm sitting here."

"We need to get this photo on TV," Hank said. "I'm sure someone will recognize her."

Joanne's heart leaped. "Please, don't do that."

"Don't? Why not? We have the Amber Law. I thought you want to find your daughter."

"But I think she's in danger." She explained what she'd heard from the caller. "She said it more than once. She sounded desperate. I'm afraid that whoever has her will do something rash if they know you're on the trail. Can't you be covert? That's the word, isn't it?"

Hank didn't answer her but continued to study the photograph.

"*Covert* is the right word," Benjamin said in her ear. "I think Joanne's right, Hank. I trust what she's saying. Can we give it more time? Can we tap the phone? You know the calls are coming from Dearborn. Could we get a cop to patrol some of the phone booths in the area—to give it more time?"

"You think this woman will call again?"

Joanne brushed her hair away from her face. "Something scared her off today. But I think she'll call again. She's desperate for money to get away, and then she'll tell us where we can find Mandy."

Hank drew in a lengthy breath and shook his head. "I can't make the decision on my own. I'd get my neck in a rope. I'll have to talk with my supervisor. Maybe we can give you a couple days, but that's it. If you're right, we need to get on this or we'll lose her."

"Please, just give her a day or two. Once I know where Mandy is, then you can get involved."

"It's not wise, Mrs. Fuller. I think we'd be making a mistake."

A mistake? Joanne gaped at the detective. Could this be a mistake?

Chapter Fifteen

The next morning, Benjamin shoved his own work aside and carried a stack of Greg's files to his desk. He'd glanced over some of them earlier, after the idea had struck him that there might be a connection between one of Greg's cases and Joanne's calls. It was still a vague possibility, but Benjamin decided to pursue it.

He'd deliberated over the dates. Greg died in November 2002, so the case would have to have been shortly before that—or maybe not… Benjamin decided to work backward. He shuffled through Greg's folders beginning with the last ones he'd worked on.

Distractions kept pulling his mind from his task. For one, he'd begun to have second thoughts about Cortezi keeping Mandy's photo from the paper. Even if the detective's supervisor agreed to wait, Benjamin realized that if they lost the child because of their negligence he would never forgive himself, and he knew Joanne wouldn't forgive herself, either.

He sent up a praycr asking God to guide the detective's decision. If Hank's captain agreed, then it was God's will—at least Benjamin prayed it was. Still the thought niggled, and tonight when he saw Joanne he would ask her to think about it carefully. But she needed to make a quick decision.

Turning his thoughts back to the files, Benjamin plowed through the folders. Nothing struck him. Nothing looked serious enough to result in kidnapping and murder. He glanced at his watch, disheartened that he'd found nothing.

The next file he opened caught his interest—a restraining order case. Plaintiff Rose Stella Angelo. Daughter Connie Angelo, age two. Physical and mental abuse. Life-threatening actions. The names didn't ring a bell. Plaintiff won the case, and the defendant was jailed for a year in the county facility.

He continued, then found another file on Rose Stella Angelo, plaintiff. Divorce. Defendant Peter Carl Angelo. As Benjamin skimmed the disposition the hair rose on his arms. The plaintiff had forgone alimony and child support for a permanent restraining order against the defendant.

He calculated the dates. If Angelo spent one year in jail, his daughter and Mandy would have been three when he was released. Would a man be so sick as to murder in vengeance? He remembered the life-threatening abuse he'd read in the case notes and knew the answer. Yes. It happened too often. But could it be connected with Greg's case?

He couldn't let the possibility pass, and he wouldn't ask Joanne. She'd find some reason to keep the information quiet. He grasped the receiver and punched in the detective's number. To his disappointment, he got Cortezi's answering machine. Benjamin left his number and hung up. He'd try later.

He pushed the folder aside and opened the next file. He wouldn't stop now. Angelo might be a dead end but Benjamin didn't want to miss a possibility.

Joanne stood in the doorway of the sandwich shop, glad it was Friday. The tension had taken more of a toll than she could have imagined and part of her longed to go to bed and sleep forever.

The packed deli tables didn't look promising until she saw a hand waving at her. Melissa Shafer beckoned her over and Joanne waved and moved in her direction. Melissa wasn't her favorite co-worker, but Joanne needed to have a quick lunch and get back to work.

Lately she'd been buying a sandwich and eating at her desk. Today she wanted something warm. Soup sounded good. She felt chilled.

"Thanks," Joanne said to Melissa as she settled into the chair across from her. "I was ready to give up."

"No problem." Melissa slid her menu across the table. "You're just in time. The waitress hasn't taken my food order yet." She lifted her coffee mug and took a sip.

Joanne skimmed the menu and settled on cheese-broccoli soup. The waitress stepped up, and they placed their orders.

"I'll be right back with your tea," the young woman said, and hurried away.

"You look tired," Melissa said. "Are you feeling okay?"

"I'm fine. It's just the holiday rush."

Melissa nodded. "Baking, gift buying, wrapping. I know. At least you don't have a family."

Joanne tried to hide her shock at the thoughtless remark. "That's right. My husband and daughter died three years ago." She wanted to add a snide comment, but kept her thoughts private.

"I'm sorry," Melissa said. "I remember. That was a pity."

Then why bring it up? Joanne wondered. She studied the woman's face and remembered what Nita had suggested weeks earlier. Joanne had denied her caller could be "Bambi," as Nita called Melissa, but here she sat, saying she remembered Joanne's family and yet had sounded so callous.

Joanne quelled her thoughts. No matter how much Melissa irked her, the woman wouldn't have made the calls. It just wasn't in her.

"I hope the new job's not too much for you."

"No more than any new position. It takes time to adjust, but it's not that different from what I'd been doing. The only variation is the proverbial desk sign—The Buck Stops Here. I take all the flak for a bad job."

"But you got a raise…and an office with a window."

Joanne was tempted to give Melissa the office with the window just to get her to be quiet about it. Listening to her thoughts sent Joanne on a guilt trip. She halted her negativity and captured her Christian attitude.

She drew in a breath as she forced a pleasant expression onto her face. "I'm sure you're disappointed not getting the job, Melissa. I would have been, too. We don't know why one person's picked over the other. I like to think we all have a time when dreams come true."

"It's not set in stone," Melissa said. "I know you're an interim for six months. Who knows?"

Joanne's skin crawled. "True," she said, hoping the subject could now be dropped.

As the waitress arrived with her soup and Melissa's sandwich, someone turned up the volume on the TV attached to the wall above Melissa's head. Joanne let her soup sit while she watched the reporter on the noon news.

"Early this morning the body of an unidentified woman was found along the banks of the Rouge River in River Rouge Park in Dearborn. The woman appears to have been in her late thirties." The camera panned the brush-covered riverbank as medics lifted a stretcher and carried the body to the awaiting ambulance.

"That's terrible," Melissa said, craning her neck to see the television.

"Strangulation appears to be the cause of her death," the reporter continued, "and no witnesses have come forward. We'll have more details tonight on the ten o'clock news."

Dearborn. The city's name sent a chill down Joanne's spine.

"You look as white as a sheet," Melissa said, gaping at her.

Joanne let the spoon sink into her soup, her appetite gone. "I just hate hearing about death."

"Your family," Melissa said, nodding. "I suppose it does give you a jolt."

Joanne tried to pull herself together. She lifted the spoon and forced herself to swallow the rich soup, normally one of her favorites. It struck her that Melissa appeared to be looking for signs of weakness, and Joanne didn't plan to give any away.

Benjamin opened a computer search engine and looked for "Peter Angelo Trucking

Company." The case notes indicated Angelo owned a small trucking company in St. Clair Shores, but nothing appeared for St. Clair Shores. Benjamin went back to the search and put in "Angelo Trucking Company, Michigan." Then hit Go.

He waited until the list appeared, and saw Carl Angelo Trucking Company, *Dearborn.* His throat went dry. *Peter Carl Angelo.* He flipped open the file to make sure he'd remembered correctly. He had. Peter had probably begun to use his middle name.

Benjamin's attention returned to the company name. He grabbed a pen and jotted down the address. This time he put Carl Angelo's name into the search line, but before he hit Go, his telephone rang.

"Benjamin Drake's desk," he said into the receiver.

"This is Joanne."

He heard her frantic tone. "What is it?"

"I just saw a news bulletin at lunch. A woman's body was found along the banks of River Rouge in Dearborn." She gasped. "Benjamin, I'm so frightened."

"When did you hear this?"

"Just a few minutes ago. I went to the sandwich shop for lunch, and they had the TV on."

He gazed back at the computer screen, thinking twice about telling her what he'd learned. He decided it could wait.

"I'm really worried the woman is the caller. It's another of my gut feelings…"

"It could be anyone, Joanne. Don't get in a panic. Where along the river?"

"In the park in Dearborn. Should I call Cortezi?"

Her question gave him pause. He might have news of his own to tell Cortezi once he checked it out. "Let's wait until we hear more. If they identify her, then we'll have more to go on. I'm in the middle of something here but I'll drop by later."

"If you're sure."

"I'm sure," he said, praying he'd made the right decision. "Take it easy, and I'll see you after work as soon as I can get there."

"Okay, but I'm frightened."

He tried to soothe her, but he realized the conversation had done nothing for his own nerves. He'd become as jumpy as Joanne.

When she hung up, Benjamin hit Go on the computer. A Dearborn address popped up and he scribbled that down. He needed to make sure the two Carls were the same, and he figured he could get access to Wayne County Records at the City-County Building.

Benjamin left work early and headed to the county offices in downtown Detroit. He found parking off Woodward, then made his way into the building. Once he explained his mission and flashed his ID, the clerk agreed to cooperate.

"I'd like to check the address of the owner of Angelo Trucking Company," Benjamin said, sliding a piece of paper with the company name on it toward the clerk.

The young man gave him a know-it-all look. "A trucking business doesn't need a license. We only license trash dumping, vending businesses—"

"You mean you keep no records of businesses in the county?"

"Most people register the business, which protects the name from use by anyone else for five years."

"Then could you check that, please?"

"It'll take a few moments," he said, picking up the paper with the company name and shifting to a computer.

Benjamin watched the fellow type the information into the computer, and after a few minutes the clerk returned, verifying the address Benjamin had already found on the Internet. He could have saved himself five dollars for parking and a couple of hours' time had he been sure.

But another thought struck him before he stepped away. "While you're at the computer, is there a way you can check to see if this Carl Angelo—or perhaps a Peter Angelo— filed for a marriage license in the past three years?"

"I'll see what I can do for you." He arched a brow and looked curious, but returned to the computer. After a few minutes, he picked up a telephone and spoke so softly that Benjamin couldn't hear, but in a short time, he returned.

"Is this what you want?"

Benjamin stared down at nearly illegible penmanship: "Donna Nickels and Carl Angelo married on March 15, 2003." "Yes, thanks."

Benjamin hurried from the office, clutching the paper. He gave it another look as he waited for the elevator to the first floor, amazed he'd gotten everything he needed in one location. He reached the lobby, then raced to his car and paid the parking attendant. When he pulled onto Woodward, he drove a short distance, then turned left onto Jefferson Avenue.

Benjamin gazed at the elegant estates that stood behind high fences as he headed north—these were homes of the automotive moguls and the wealthy of Detroit. What people did for the almighty dollar made him sick. Too many people connived, twisted business ethics and loosened their morals for money, and they missed out on the joy of true happiness. He suspected this was the problem for Peter Carl Angelo—a man with no strength of character and no respect for human life.

Benjamin had no proof that Angelo had committed a crime. Still, Benjamin had a strong feeling that Angelo had been involved in Joanne's calls.

Jefferson Avenue changed to Lakeshore Drive and Benjamin veered over to Kercheval and then to Maumee. He pulled into the small parking lot of the Department of Public Safety and went inside. A counter and a door separated him from the offices inside.

When he reached the counter, a clerk looked up. "Can I help you?"

"I'm Benjamin Drake. An attorney. I'd like to speak to Detective Hank Cortezi if he's available."

"Let me check," she said, stepping away.

As he waited, he stared at the bare walls and the nondescript entry. Soon the inner door opened and Hank stood there.

"You just caught me," Cortezi said. "What's up?"

Benjamin gestured to the cramped lobby. "Should we talk here?"

Hank gestured Benjamin inside and pushed the door open farther.

Benjamin followed the detective's lead to his office, where they were alone.

Hank rested his hip against his desk and nodded to the chair. "Got something new?"

"A couple of things. I found an old case of Greg Fuller's. It involved a Peter Angelo, now known as Carl Angelo who owns—"

Cortezi's eyes widened. "Carl Angelo?"

"Right. Do you know him?"

"The Dearborn police have been working on a trucking company providing a cover for stolen cars."

"Owner Carl Angelo?"

He nodded. "They pretty much have it nailed. They found a connection on this side of town, so we're involved."

"I'm thinking he's involved in more than that." Benjamin detailed his suspicions about

Angelo. "And Joanne is afraid the woman they just found strangled by the Rouge River may be Angelo's second wife, Donna, and the woman who has been calling her."

Cortezi frowned. "You know her?"

"No, I just checked out their marriage license while I was at the County."

Hank gave a chuckle. "Should I ask if you're after my job?"

Benjamin laughed. "No, just worried about Joanne."

"Listen, we have no arrest yet, but tell her we think we know the source of the e-mails. We need to talk with the suspect before we do anything else."

If they knew the person who sent the e-mails and it wasn't Donna Angelo, then who was the dead woman? "Any theories on the murdered woman?" he asked Cortezi.

Hank held up his hand. "Don't ask me. I've told you too much already. I don't want to lose my job." He pointed to the scrap of paper Benjamin had given him. "I'll keep this, if you don't mind."

"That's fine." Benjamin patted his pocket, where he had another copy of Angelo's address. "Here's something else you could check. If Angelo's first wife died, then he might have his own child, and if that's the case we could be looking at the wrong man. His ex-wife's name is Rose Stella Angelo. If alive, she may have remarried by now. Their daughter's name is Connie. Can you check on that?"

He gave Benjamin a wry look. "Sure you don't want to?"

"No, I'll let you take the glory." He grinned.

"Listen," Cortezi said, taking a step toward the doorway. "I'll get back to you as soon as we have something solid."

Benjamin realized the action was Cortezi's tactful way of getting him out the door. "Thanks," he said, rising to go.

"And Drake?"

Benjamin turned back to face him.

"Don't do my job. Let the investigators do the work. You could get yourself killed."

"Thanks for the tip," Benjamin said, giving him a salute as he headed out.

Chapter Sixteen

Saturday morning Joanne lay in bed and thought about her conversation with Benjamin the night before. He'd been bursting with news from Cortezi and she'd been amazed at what he'd found out on his own.

Joanne vaguely recalled the case—not the family name, but that Greg had been disturbed by it, probably because of having a child the same age. Her mind spun with too many unanswered questions. She knew the police had other cases, some more dire than hers, she supposed, but to her, finding Mandy took precedence over breathing.

Was the dead woman who'd been found in River Rouge Park the woman Benjamin called Donna? Now Benjamin said the police had identified the person who'd e-mailed her. How did that fit in?

And then Benjamin added another question. Had Angelo's first wife really died? If Angelo had his birth child, then that meant his daughter wasn't Mandy, and if that was so, who was the child in the photograph? Joanne was certain the girl was Mandy. Joanne's eyes, mind and heart had been positive—and so had Benjamin.

Benjamin had shown her Angelo's address in Dearborn. He'd kept the paper, but Joanne had memorized it. She longed to drive there and see for herself. If only she would see the child in person.

Let the police handle the matter, she told herself. As Benjamin said, she could endanger her life by meddling. Yet her heart yearned to do just that.

Joanne swung her legs from the bed and headed for the shower. The hot water washed over her, swirling around her feet and vanishing down the drain—just like her mind had been doing. Ideas came and went, vanishing into dead-end thoughts.

She turned off the tap, dried her body and toweled her hair. She was relieved that steam covered the mirror. Lately she looked pale and aged.

In her bedroom, Joanne slipped into a pair of jeans and felt the loose waist—she had lost weight. She added a coral tunic top, hoping her clothing would help add color to her death-white complexion. She pulled her hair back and attached a clip, then padded down the stairs in her socks.

Coffee had become her usual breakfast. She sat at the table with a cup, wondering what to do with her day. Though she'd mailed the packages home, she still had gifts to wrap, a tree to decorate and numerous holiday tasks, but her heart wasn't in it. Since her clothes hung on her like someone else's garments, she needed to go shopping. She liked the trimmer look and feel, but hated the reason for the weight loss.

The telephone's ring jarred her and her stomach knotted. She responded to her first instinct and looked at the caller ID. A cellphone number. She picked up the receiver.

"Bagels or muffins?" Benjamin said.

She didn't want to let him know how much the phone's ring had frightened her. "What kind of muffins?"

"Let's see…"

She figured he was standing in front of a bakery case eyeing the goods.

"How about almond poppy-seed?"

She grinned for the first time in a couple of days. "How did you know?"

"That you love them?"

"Yes," she said.

"Lucky guess. I'll be there in a minute."

His bright voice warmed her heart. She needed Benjamin so badly to make her life full again. He'd become precious to her in such a short time.

She carried her mug into the living room and stood by the large front window. Today the snow on the ground glistened in the morning sun. Along the road's edge the white crystals had become tinted gray.

Her life had seemed like that. The pressures of her immediate life had dulled, yet beyond the fringe, God's goodness glistened in all its purity. Sin corrupted, and she'd been trudging through the evils of the world for the past month.

Joanne knew she wasn't sinless. She'd made so many mistakes in her life. She'd hardened her heart to her family without trying to understand their ways. She'd closed herself off from people and then blamed them for not opening their arms to her.

Who would want to hang out with someone dour and unyielding? She'd become difficult to be with, she was sure. Even Benjamin deserved a medal. He'd gone beyond the call of duty with her. Blaming others was so easy, she realized, rather than take a deeper look at herself.

Benjamin had forced her to take that look. His strong faith and unwavering trust in God shone as an example. Benjamin wasn't perfect, she knew, but he was close, and what sins he had weren't evident to her eyes.

Love is blind.

She was startled by her admission. Love? Could it be? And would it ever be returned? She knew Benjamin's kindly ways, and she would expect him to be thoughtful to an old friend. Or had he begun to feel more, as she had?

Though he'd kissed her once, they'd agreed it had been a thing of the moment. She'd kissed him, too—a brief kiss that went without comment. What if she kissed him the way she wanted to? What would Benjamin do? She feared she might chase him away.

Was it worth the chance?

Benjamin's car turned into the driveway, and she tucked the question aside and headed for the door, excited to see him.

When he came in he grinned and held up the bakery bag. "Hot from the oven," he said. "Where do you want these?"

She indicated the living room. "I'll get the coffee and napkins."

He turned in that direction, and she headed for the kitchen where she added hot coffee to her cup, then carried everything in to him.

Once she freed herself of the mugs and napkins, Joanne dug her hand into the paper bag. The sweet scent of almond rose as she pulled one out, peeled back the paper covering its sides and sank her teeth into the crust. "I love these things, but they're too fattening."

"You should eat a few of them, then. You're too thin." His dark eyes reflected concern.

"I'm fine. You don't like the trimmer me?"

"I like you every way, but I just don't want you to vanish before my eyes."

"No fear of that," she said, feeling a smile lighten her face.

His gentle eyes searched hers. "You're too important to me."

The words settled over her like down—soft

and silky and tickling her heart. She wondered if he really meant it the way she did.

"What are you up to today?" he asked.

"I've been thinking about everything you said last night. I would really like to know if the dead woman in Dearborn is the same woman I saw at the café."

"The police are doing what they can. Maybe—"

The shrill of the telephone cut him off, and as always in the past weeks, Joanne's heart flew to her throat. She flashed Benjamin a concerned look, then rose and headed for the kitchen. After checking the caller ID, Joanne answered and heard Cortezi's voice.

"I spoke with Benjamin yesterday about a few things, but I wanted to let you know that we've hit a couple of walls."

She'd glanced behind her when she heard Benjamin enter the room. "Would you like to talk with him? He's here."

"Either of you is fine," Cortezi said.

"Okay, I'm ready."

"As I said, we've hit a couple of walls, but we haven't given up. We've been unable to locate Rose Stella Angelo. We found no death records. She appears to be alive, but we realize she might be remarried, so we'll continue to look for her."

"Not dead." Then it wasn't logical that Angelo would have a child living with him. She paused, realizing it could be his present wife's child. "Finding her will answer a lot of questions," Joanne said, discouraged.

"We checked Angelo's home. No one's there. It looks empty. No fresh tracks. We sent an officer to the trucking company, and according to them, Angelo's on vacation with his family."

Her skin prickled. "Do you believe them?"

"We're checking with the Department of Motor Vehicles. We'll get his car registration and then keep an eye out for his license plate. If he's in the area, we'll bring him in for questioning."

"What about the dead woman in Dearborn?" Joanne asked. "Any news on her identity?"

"None, that I've heard. No one's filed a missing person's report. They're still out there combing the area. Something will come up."

"Thanks for filling me in." She couldn't keep the disappointment from her voice.

"By Monday we should have some news on the e-mails."

"Benjamin said you've found a suspect? Who is it?"

"We haven't questioned her yet. We will and I'll let you know."

"That's it, then?"

"That's it," he said.

She hung up and told Benjamin what she'd learned. "I forgot to ask if they think the person e-mailing is the caller."

"You'll know more on Monday."

But Joanne wanted more. She was tired of unanswered questions. "Do you realize they still have nothing concrete to go on?"

He didn't respond. She didn't need him to. They both knew the truth. They returned to the living room, where the coffee and muffins were cold.

Benjamin finished his muffin but pushed the mug aside. "What's on your agenda?"

She didn't know.

"Would you like me to leave?"

"That's the last thing I want." She leaned her head against the chair. "What I want is my life back."

"Be patient. I think it's close now." He stood and carried their mugs into the kitchen while she sat there feeling miserable.

When he returned he'd refilled the mugs.

"Let's decorate the tree," he said, handing her the hot coffee. "We need to do something cheerful."

She hooked her finger into the mug, then took a careful sip. "It's on my list of things to get done."

"Great," he said, setting his drink on the coffee table and rubbing his hands together. "Ready?"

She wasn't, but Benjamin was and she figured she had little choice when he'd set his mind to something. She rose and crossed to the pile of boxes beside the tree.

He spread the cartons in front of them and lifted a lid. "Aha! Christmas balls—all sizes, all colors." He dangled one from each finger.

His silly expression made her chuckle.

"See. You've cheered up already," hc said.

She forced her despondency aside. "Where's the music? Something jolly and loud."

He set the balls back into the carton and crossed to the CD player. She watched him crouch beside the stack of choices, shuffling through her myriad of Christmas disks. Why she had so many she didn't know. Considering how short the holiday season was, she'd spent a fortune, but she loved the festive tunes and the lovely carols.

Soon the spirited music rang out in the gloomy atmosphere and before she knew it, Joanne surprised herself by joining in the chorus. "*Fa la la la la, la la la la.*"

Benjamin burst in on the last few *la*'s, his rich voice booming.

Joanne pulled balls and whimsical trimmings from the carton, and while he hung ornaments on the higher limbs, she filled the lower branches. When she unwrapped a white baby cradle with a pink design that said, "Baby's First Christmas," she faltered.

Benjamin noticed and stepped to her side. Running his finger over the delicate ornament, he said, "I'm sorry, Joanne. I feel as if I forced you to do this. I thought it would help, but maybe it's too soon."

"No," she said, caressing the tiny cradle. "It's me. It's everything going on—but don't blame yourself. I'm glad you goaded me into decorating for the holidays. I need to get my life back to normal, Benjamin, and I wasn't doing a good job alone."

"I hope you mean what you're saying."

Joanne rested her hand on his arm. "I wouldn't lie to you. I mean it from the bottom of my heart." She brushed a tear from her eye and released a soft chuckle. "You might have to put up with my whimpering a bit. Just be patient."

"I'd think less of you if you had no feelings."

His comment surprised her. Most men she knew hated women who cried and clung to the past. Benjamin came from a different mold.

They worked side by side, periodically bursting into choruses of "Joy to the World" or "Go Tell It on the Mountain." As they added color and beauty to the tree's limbs, Joanne's thoughts drifted back to their earlier conversation when she'd asked him why he hadn't married. He'd been evasive, and it still made her curious.

He'd stuck by her side since his return, never questioning her emotions or her wild deductions. When she had first heard the voice, most people probably thought she'd flipped. She was sure the detective had thought so, but Benjamin had listened as though she made sense.

"What about icicles?" Benjamin asked as they pulled the last few balls from a carton.

She shook her head. "I never liked them. Sometimes I've added bows and ribbon garland, but I like to see the ornaments—and icicles block them."

She leaned over to pick up one of the last

ornaments, and her gaze drifted to the floppy eared dog, still sitting in one of the boxes. She felt a pang in her heart thinking about Mandy. She felt certain her daughter was alive. Now she feared Mandy had been put in danger, and she had no control over the situation.

She picked up the worn plush toy and held it in her arms. "She seems so close, Benjamin."

He faced her, an ornament suspended in his hand. "She's in your heart, and if God wills it, she may be back in your life. But it's not a certainty, Joanne. I wish I could make it all come true for you, but it's in the Lord's hands."

"I know, and you've done so much. I couldn't ask for nothing more." She gazed at him, drawing in his strength and being soothed by the tenderness in his eyes.

"I'm doing what my feelings tell me to do." He turned toward the tree and attached the last ornament to the limb, then backed away.

The balls and trimmings caught the lights' glow, and Joanne felt comforted by the familiar Christmas scene.

Benjamin crossed to her side. "What do you think?" He gestured toward the colorful branches. "Pretty nice, I'd say."

"You and the tree," she said, wrapping an arm around his shoulders. "You're helping me find Christmas again." It felt so natural and tonight, filled with so much emotion, she needed to touch someone. She'd lived too long with only memories.

Joanne pivoted toward him. With his arm still across her back, she put her arms around his waist and bound her fingers together.

He stood so close she could feel him breathe, and she sensed the ripple of his muscles as he reacted to her caress.

Benjamin drew her into an embrace. They stood in silence for a moment, face to face, eyes searching eyes, until Joanne did what her heart led her to do. She reached up on tiptoe and her lips sought his.

She felt him tense, yet in a heartbeat, his mouth softened and moved beneath hers. The kiss stirred her longing. An exquisite depth of feeling flooded her.

Benjamin moved his hand upward and caressed her cheek, then ran his fingers through her hair. The unbelievable feeling caused her pulse to dance. When he eased his hold, his lips lingered on hers, then brushed feathery kisses on her nose and her eyelids.

A shudder coursed through her. Amazement, wonder and delight filled her.

Neither spoke. Joanne rested her head on

his chest and felt his heart beat beneath her cheek. With his hand he grazed her arm so tenderly that she wanted to cry.

When she shifted away and looked at him, he gazed at her with dark hooded eyes that flickered with deep emotion. "You're an amazing woman."

"And you're an amazing man."

He seemed embarrassed and shy as he stepped back. Instead of speaking, he crossed the room and stacked the individual ornament containers into a larger box. "Where do you want this?" When he turned and looked at her, she could see his mind was not on the decorating.

"Let's put it in the guest room. I'm not expecting any holiday company." She gestured, but knew she didn't need to show him. The room was right next to Mandy's bedroom, still pink and white with rosy balloon wallpaper and shell-colored curtains, white furniture, and toys on the shelves. She hadn't had the heart to change it.

Benjamin loaded the boxes into his arms and carried them through the archway.

Joanne slipped into a chair, amazed at what she'd done. Her lips still tingled from Benjamin's mouth on hers. She couldn't believe he felt as she did. He'd joined in the kiss with the same eagerness she had felt, as if they'd waited forever to seal their friendship—their relationship... She didn't know what it was, but her heart knew it was special.

As the warm, lovely feeling enveloped over her, guilt pulled at her like an undertow. Benjamin had been Greg's friend, and hers. How could these feelings have grown and blossomed into something so different from friendship?

The reality was that Greg had been gone for three years. He would want her to love again, to find someone special to share her life with, to laugh and enjoy the sunrise.

When she heard Benjamin's footsteps, she forced the thoughts away.

"Done," he said, brushing his hands together as he stepped into the room. "What now?"

She shrugged. "How about some food?" But it occurred to her that the same question could be asked about them.

What now?

Chapter Seventeen

Joanne sat in the recliner, her feet raised and her Bible on her lap. She'd been uplifted by the morning's worship service, and the pastor's words continued to ring in her ears.

After church, she'd carried her Bible to the chair and opened it to Mark 11:22 without taking off her Sunday clothes. The Scripture she'd needed had been the focus of the service. She was often amazed at how God worked His wonders.

"That's why He's God," she said aloud as she flipped through the pages of her Bible. Her eyes sought the Scripture again; she knew she needed to hear it and live it. She read through the passage, pausing over the last sentence. "Therefore I tell you, whatever you ask for in prayer, believe that you have received it, and it will be yours."

Whatever you ask for in prayer will be yours. The words caressed her heart. This was God's promise, and Joanne had prayed for Mandy's safe return. The certainty filled her with hope.

Each time she looked at the Christmas tree, her hope grew. Benjamin had motivated her this year to bring Christmas back into her home.

Her gaze drifted to Floppy beneath the tree. She'd set him there last night after her emotional moment. The stuffed mutt and Christmas went together, especially this year as she prayed for Mandy's return.

There was a noise outside the house, and Joanne craned her neck to sec out the window. She hadn't expect Benjamin until later, but he often surprised her.

When the bell rang, she felt her smile fade. Benjamin never rang the bell anymore. He had his special rhythmic knock. Who'd be calling on her today?

When she pulled open the door, she was shocked.

"Mom! What are you doing here?"

"I decided to come," said Evelyn Ryan,

holding the door frame and hoisting her suitcase into the room.

Joanne felt her jaw sag. Her mother? She
grabbed hold of the luggage and moved it
away from the door, then gave her mother a
hug. "This is certainly a surprise."

"I didn't tell you because I knew you'd say
no. You already said not to come, but I'm
not staying away when you need family with
you."

Joanne helped her with her coat and hung
it in the closet. "I just got home from church,"
Joanne said, still too perplexed to think of
anything else to say.

"I figured."

Joanne's mother didn't attend worship.
Most of her family didn't. Joanne's introduc-
tion to her faith had come from Greg, a life-
long Christian who had a close walk with the
Lord. Joanne had fallen in step as easily with
God as she had with Greg.

"Please, sit," Joanne said, trying to relax
the frown from her face. "I'll take this into
the guest room."

Her mother wandered into the living room
and headed for the tree while Joanne maneuvered the luggage down the hallway. She
grinned when she came through the bedroom

door. Benjamin had piled the boxes in the middle of the room because she'd said she wasn't having company. Little had she known...

Joanne set her mother's suitcase on the bed, then shifted the boxes to the doorway. In the hallway, she opened Mandy's bedroom door. She felt a twinge when she glanced inside at the girlish wallpaper and white furniture. As she shifted the boxes from the guest room to Mandy's, loneliness swept over. She returned to the hallway and closed the door. This wasn't the time for melancholy.

"The house looks nice decorated for Christmas," her mother said, standing beside the tree as she entered the living room. "It's real, too. I can smell it."

"Thanks. It is real." Joanne faltered before continuing. "This is the first year I've decorated since..."

Her mother turned to her with a frown. "This is the first year?"

"Well, I was with you last Christmas."

"But you weren't yourself. I felt like a stranger came for the holidays."

Her mother's words struck her an unexpected blow. Joanne had felt as if she'd been *treated* like a stranger. "I'm sorry. It's a good thing I didn't agree to come this year."

Her mother looked away with a sigh. "I don't want to argue about it, Joanne. I just felt as if you were withdrawn. What's that word?" She pinched her lip as she thought. "*Aloof.* Is that it?"

Joanne thought back to last Christmas. She'd felt unattached to her family, perhaps withdrawn. "Yes. That's the word, I suppose."

Her mother didn't say any more, and Joanne decided to steer clear of the subject. "Please sit, Mom. I'll make some fresh coffee—or would you prefer tea?"

"Either's fine."

"Have you eaten?"

"I had a big breakfast before I left Cleveland. It isn't that far. Under three hours."

Joanne nodded and gestured toward a chair before heading for the kitchen. As she stood inside the room putting water on for tea, she wondered why her mother had come. They'd never been close—not that she hadn't longed to be, but her mother seemed focused on her sister and her own doings, and not on much else.

The teakettle began to whistle on the burner and Joanne set two cups on the counter plus the pot, then pulled out four teabags. She preferred real tea steeped in a tea ball, but this would be faster.

Joanne poured the water into her flowery teapot and set everything on a tray with the fixings, not remembering how her mother liked tea.

She lifted the tray and carried it into the hallway. As she stepped through the arch to the living room, she paused, seeing her mother standing beside the tree with Floppy in her hand.

Her mother must have heard her because she turned. "This was Mandy's."

"I found it in the tree-trimming boxes."

"She used to toddle all over the house, dragging this poor beat-up thing."

"I'm surprised you remember." Joanne's sigh rattled through her as she continued across the room.

"I don't suppose you remember who gave her this."

"I thought we did."

Her mother shook her head. "No, your dad and I did for her first birthday. I remember finding it at the department store. Mandy loved this old thing."

Joanne set the tray on the coffee table. Now that her mother mentioned it, she did recall the plush dog had been in the gifts her mother had sent from Cleveland. "She slept with it every night." She turned away so her mother wouldn't notice her sadness.

Evelyn returned the dog to its place beneath the tree and crossed the room to the sofa. She proceeded to pour the tea into the two cups, then lifted one and took a sip.

After Joanne took her cup, she settled across from her mother and waited, though she was filled with so many questions.

Her mother looked uneasy and didn't speak for a while. Then she said, "Maybe I made a mistake coming here. I should probably just head back home."

"I'm sorry you don't feel welcome. I'm just astounded that you came." Especially since she'd told her not to—but then her mother always did things her way. "I'm having a bad time with all this trauma. I'd begun to heal from the tragedy, and this has dragged everything out again. It's like living it all over, but this time with a precious hope dangling in front of me—the thought that Mandy might be alive."

"I don't understand how that could be, Joanne. Are you sure this isn't some kind of hoax?"

"Is that why you came? Because you thought I'd fallen for a hoax?"

Her mother looked startled, and Joanne regretted being so blunt.

"I came because you're my daughter and I thought you might like to have some family around for support."

Her mother's look had darkened, and Joanne couldn't really blame her. Her greeting hadn't been very welcoming.

"I have friends," Joanne said. "I can count on them." The dig slipped from her mouth before she could stop it, yet she knew she'd been honest. "But you're here now, so stay a couple of days if you'd like."

The word *friends* rang in her ears. She didn't have that many—Benjamin, Nita, a couple of people at church who were more acquaintances than anything.

"I'm glad you have friends, Joanne. I know we haven't been much help to you, living so far away."

She wanted to remind her mother that she'd mentioned the ride hadn't taken that long— under three hours. Where had her family been when Joanne needed support during those lonely months after the accident?

She opened her mouth to ask, but something stopped her. She recalled a lesson from God's Word—reckless words pierce like a sword, but wise words bring healing. She couldn't handle mending their relationship today, but she wouldn't close the door on it.

No matter how frustrated and hurt she was by her family's rejection, her mother had come on her own, with no prodding from Joanne.

She lifted her gaze to her mother's questioning eyes. "It was thoughtful to come, Mom. I don't think there's anything you can do to help. I know you're concerned about a hoax, but I don't think this is one. My heart tells me differently, and I have a photograph—"

"A photograph?" A frown settled on her face.

Joanne told her mother the story of finding the snapshot in her Christmas packages and having the conversation with the woman. "But she hasn't contacted me further, and I'm afraid she was the woman found dead in the Dearborn park."

Her mother paled as she listened. "I can't believe all of—"

A familiar knock on the front door halted her mother midsentence, and Joanne felt a flush rise to her cheeks.

"Company?" her mother asked.

Uneasy, she glanced at the door and then her mother. "It's Benjamin."

She watched her mother's eyes widen. "Benjamin?"

"Maybe you'll remember him once you see him again," Joanne said as she hurried to the door and pulled it open.

"You have a visitor?" Benjamin asked, gesturing toward the car in the driveway.

"My mom."

He felt his eyebrows arch, but he said nothing as he stepped in. "Hello," he said, crossing the living room toward her mother with his hand extended. "We met years ago. You probably don't remember me."

Her mother rose and took his hand. "I do now that I see you."

Benjamin slipped off his jacket and tossed it on a small chair by the archway. "You've come for the holidays?"

"No, I'll have to get back—but Joanne told me about her ordeal and I had to come."

"I understand," he said, giving Joanne a sweeping glance.

"I told her no," Joanne said, "But Mom surprised me and came anyway."

Her mother nodded. "I couldn't leave her going through all this without family."

Benjamin looked from Joanne to her

mother, trying to read what had happened between them. "That was thoughtful," he said finally.

In Joanne's face he saw the usual tension when she spoke of her mother. Yet hope wore through his thoughts. He believed things had a purpose, and perhaps this visit, even though unwelcome by Joanne, was a means of resolving some of the issues between them. If the trials Joanne had been going through accomplished one thing, resolution and forgiveness would be a good reward.

The conversation shifted to Joanne's sister and family affairs. Joanne's edginess seemed obvious, but her mother plugged along, and Joanne joined in even though she seemed stressed. Benjamin felt out of place, and yet they included him in the discussion. To his surprise, as the time ticked by, they chuckled occasionally, and the more he watched the more he felt hopeful about the possibility of healing between them.

When the telephone rang, Joanne gave him an urgent look, then rose and left the room. He tried to carry on casual conversation with Evelyn, but his attention was drawn to Joanne's voice coming from the kitchen. She didn't sound upset, so he hoped it was a friend calling.

"It was Cortezi," she said when she returned. "He asked me to come down to the station today."

He noticed nervous tremors in her hands when she gestured, her focus shifting from him to her mother.

"I'm afraid I'll have to leave you here for an hour or so. We'll talk about dinner later, but make yourself a sandwich or something if you're hungry."

"No problem. I'll unpack and rest while you're gone." Her mother gestured toward him. "Benjamin can go with you, I hope." She looked at him pointedly.

"I sure will," he said, relieved she'd accepted his friendship with Joanne. "And don't worry about dinner, I'll take you both out to eat when we get back."

Joanne crossed the room to the foyer closet, and he followed.

"What did Hank say?" he whispered as she pulled out her coat.

"He wants to talk to me about the person who sent the e-mails."

His stomach jarred with the news. The answer they'd been waiting for could be only minutes away.

Chapter Eighteen

"Thanks for coming here on a Sunday," Cortezi said as he steered them into a private conference room.

Joanne eyed the tired-looking man and wondered why he never seemed to have a day off to rest. Benjamin held the chair for her and she sat. "What did you find out?" she asked immediately, her gaze darting to his desk for some sign.

"Do you know Melissa Shafer?" he asked.

Joanne's heart sank. "Yes, we work at Solutions, Incorporated." She thought of her promotion and Melissa's envy, but she had never believed Melissa could be involved. If it were Melissa and if the calls and e-mails were connected, Mandy being alive was a hoax.

"She's the person e-mailing you—from

her home. She'd already deleted the e-mail address and the files on her computer, but the server was able to trace it to her anyway. When we confronted her, she admitted what she'd done."

Joanne had to gather her thoughts. "I'd just gotten a promotion. Melissa was very envious, but I didn't think..."

She felt Benjamin's hand on her arm, giving it a squeeze. He'd warned her, and she hadn't listened. Even Nita had mentioned Melissa. It seemed obvious now, but she'd been so determined not to believe it could be anyone at Solutions. "And the calls? She did that, too?"

Cortezi's head snapped up. "No. She's not your caller. It's a coincidence that both of these things happened at the same time."

"A coincidence?" The news confounded her. "So what happens now?"

"That's up to you."

"What?"

"You can press charges against her. The messages had undertones of threat. We can prosecute and she'll probably get a year in jail or maybe probation."

Joanne felt sick. "Press charges?"

"I don't think she meant to carry it this far,"

Cortezi said. "We've talked to her. She had no idea you were going through this other situation."

"I know," Joanne said. "I only told one friend at work. She wouldn't have said anything."

"We can prosecute without you," Cortezi said. "What she's done is against the law. But I think I'd like to leave it up to you. You can speak with her if you want."

His suggestion surprised her. "Melissa? You mean at work?"

"No. She's here. We have her in another room."

Joanne squirmed, wondering if she wanted to speak to the woman. She turned her gaze to Benjamin, who sat in pensive silence, his hands folded in his lap, his jaw tensed.

When she caught his eye, he shook his head as if to say the choice was hers. It was, but she didn't know what to do. Then out of nowhere, she remembered that the Lord taught compassion and forgiveness. "Are you positive she has nothing to do with the calls?"

"Positive. We know the time the calls came in, and she had a solid alibi for two of them—a dentist appointment, an engagement with someone from Solutions. I think you should speak with her."

Joanne hesitated before answering, but she knew what she should do. "I'll see her," she said finally.

"Good."

Cortezi eyed Benjamin. "Will you—"

"I'll wait outside," Benjamin said. "This is between Joanne and this woman."

She heard protectiveness in his voice, but she understood.

"I'll be fine," she said, rising. "Where do you want me to go?"

"Wait here." Cortezi held up his hand. "I'll bring her to you."

Benjamin gave her a reassuring look as Cortezi headed for the door. Benjamin followed and gave her a final nod before he left the room.

Joanne sat alone with thoughts running through her head. All her tension had piled up like gray sludge along the roadways. Now she'd experienced a partial warming: one question had been answered, clearing away a little of her icy concern. Yet she still couldn't believe Melissa hated her so much.

Moments later she heard the knob turn, and her gaze lifted to the opening door. Cortezi's face was the first she saw, followed by Melissa's tear-streaked one. Her co-worker looked pale and haggard, not the vivacious sashaying young woman she knew at the office.

"I'll let you two talk," Cortezi said, staying near the door. "I'll be right outside if you need me." He slipped out and Joanne faced her nemesis—or one of them.

Melissa sank into the chair across from her and opened her mouth to speak, but instead, a sob broke from her and she covered her face with her hands.

Joanne stared at her, not knowing what to say or what to do. She wanted to be angry, but she'd been through too much to feel anything but bewilderment. She waited until she heard the woman's sobs fade and then subside.

"All I want to know is why?" Joanne asked finally. The question was an obvious one. Melissa was envious, but how had that led her to be so vicious?

Melissa didn't speak for a moment. She remained bent over, her face hidden behind her trembling fingers. Finally she raised her head. Her eyes were bloodshot and fear was emblazoned on her face. "I don't know, Joanne. I wanted that job so badly, and I..."

Joanne watched various emotions cross her

co-worker's face. Her own feelings knotted and twisted inside her, but she held on, staying strong. She'd fought so long to keep her sanity, and today, she would stay in control. She needed the Lord's guidance and she could only hear Him if she remained calm.

"This is no excuse," Melissa said, her voice breaking the silence. "I'm spoiled. I always have been. I've used my body to get what I want, but it didn't work this time. I thought I had your job. I thought the interview was only a procedure to cover tracks. When you were promoted, I realized I'd been used. You'd accomplished success with hard work and ability while I'd failed. I'd lost my morals and respect for myself in the process."

"I'm sorry for you," Joanne said, truly angered that this woman had been used by someone in the company. She couldn't even imagine it. She'd only been treated with respect—but then, she respected herself. She thanked God for that.

"I had no idea what you'd been going through," Melissa said. "I had no idea you'd been harassed by a telephone caller. That wasn't me, Joanne. I only sent the three e-mails, and I realized they were wrong after we had lunch together. I deleted everything and hoped I'd be forgiven."

Joanne let the word *forgiveness* wash over her. "You are forgiven, Melissa, when you repent and ask God to pardon your sins. The Bible has taught me to forgive so that I can be forgiven. It's not easy. I'm very angry at you, and I know I could press charges and your life would change beyond belief, but I can't."

"You can't?" Her eyes widened.

"My life changed one November evening when I lost my husband and daughter. I don't want anyone to live with that kind of grief and sorrow. What you've done is very wrong, but I think you'll suffer enough just knowing what you did and how much it affected my life."

"I am sorry, Joanne." She shook her head as if trying to awaken herself. "I can't believe you're not going to press charges after what I've done."

"I can't, either, but I'm not." Joanne felt the air empty from her lungs and she gasped for breath. Still, her heart felt uplifted by her decision. "This is between us. I only hope that you've learned that the only thing that makes life worthwhile is your hanging on to your values and faith. Please give that some thought."

Melissa sat as if stunned.

Joanne rose and walked to the door. As soon as she stepped into the hallway, Benjamin came to her side and Cortezi asked what she wanted to do.

"Let her go. I think she's suffered enough. I know I have."

Cortezi touched her arm. "You're sure?"

"Positive. I just want to go home."

"You can go," he said, giving her shoulder a squeeze.

"Keep us posted," Benjamin said, making no comment about her decision.

"It can't be long. He can't stay hidden forever, especially not with a child."

With a child. Joanne's pulse sped up as fear flooded her. Was Mandy still alive? Her silent prayer rose to heaven.

They said goodbye, and by the time they had left the police station, snow was falling.

"I'm glad you came with me," Joanne said. "I felt more secure knowing you were there."

"You're welcome."

He didn't say any more, and Joanne noticed that his jaw seemed tight. She wished he'd be more open tonight. She didn't want to play guessing games. "Are you upset I didn't press charges?"

"No. That was your decision. I don't think the woman had any idea how serious her actions were."

"She's used to getting her own way, and it didn't work this time." She didn't mention how the woman had used her feminine wiles to get what she wanted. It sounded too catty. "I'm doubly worried now about the calls...or lack of them."

He nodded but remained silent.

"What's bugging you, Benjamin? Please tell me."

He shook his head. "It's none of my business, Joanne."

"Yes, it is. If it has to do with me and it's upsetting you, then it is our business to get it settled."

"It's about your mother."

"My mother?" Her mind reeled. "What do you mean?"

"She came to support you, but you're not treating her as if you're happy she's here."

"You think I'm supposed to jump up and down with joy that my mother finally showed up to support me? Where was she all the years I was alone?"

"I can't answer that. But the Bible tells us to turn the other cheek, to use encouraging words rather than harsh ones. You just showed compassion to a co-worker, Joanne. The woman visiting you is your mother It's not only your words with her. It's your attitude. It's not like you to be so hard."

Hard. That's how she felt—hard-hearted and unforgiving.

"You're soft and beautiful, Joanne. That's how I think of you. You're kind and thoughtful, but seeing you with your mother shows me a side I don't like."

She flinched. "I'm sorry I've disappointed you by expressing my feelings."

"What I think doesn't matter," he said. "You're not accountable to me."

Then who was she accountable to? Herself? God. That's what he meant. Questions rolled through her mind. Joanne knew she had an attitude. It had become her defense against being hurt, but why hadn't she been big enough to let it go?

They rode in silence while she pondered what Benjamin had said. She'd clung to her anger for too long, and she knew she should be forgiving. Each time she asked God to be merciful, she paid little attention to the biblical truth that showing mercy begat mercy.

"I care about you so much," Benjamin said, breaking the silence. "You're too good a person to harbor bad feelings. Try to accept your mother's visit as a good thing. Think of forgiveness as the purpose for her visit."

Joanne hadn't been able to shake Benjamin's words as they sat in the restaurant. Her dinner hadn't sat well, but she'd tried to be pleasant, as Benjamin had suggested.

When they arrived home, Benjamin jumped from the car and helped Joanne's mother from the back seat. To avoid slipping when she got out, Joanne kept her focus on the deep snow that had already piled up along the edges of the driveway. When she came around the car, Benjamin grasped her arm, too, and guided her and her mother up the stairs. Joanne unlocked the door and stepped inside, greeted by the house's warmth.

Her mother slipped off her coat and thanked Benjamin again for the dinner, then meandered into the living room, but Benjamin didn't move past the doorway.

"Aren't you coming in?" Joanne asked, curious as to what was wrong now.

"No," he said. "You and your mom have lots to talk about. I think I'll get home. I have a court date tomorrow and I need to check over my brief before bed."

She really wished he'd stay, but she understood. He'd given her so much of his time, she couldn't ask for more. "I'll see you tomorrow, then?"

He nodded and leaned into the living room. "Good night, Mrs. Ryan."

"Good night, Benjamin," her mom called, then chuckled. "How about Evelyn? That sounds better."

"Sure thing," he said, giving her an amiable smile. "See you tomorrow."

To her delight, he leaned down and brushed her cheek with a kiss. He opened the door and the cold washed in as he stepped outside. Joanne wanted to call out, *I love you.*

"Drive carefully," she said instead.

When his car lights faded into the night, she closed the door and turned back to her mother.

"I'm exhausted," Evelyn said as she stepped into the room from the foyer. "Would you mind if I call it a night?"

"Not if you're tired." She felt relieved, and this would give her more time to think.

"Good night, Joanne," her mom said, giving Joanne a hug.

The hug was a surprise. "Good night, Mom." Miracles happened, and Joanne wondered if this could be one of them.

She heard her mother's footsteps heading back to the guest room, and she sank into the chair, her mind churning over what had happened that day.

Melissa's involvement had made Joanne question everything. She longed for reassurance that her daughter was alive and safe, and she'd begun to question if Carl Angelo had any connection. She had nothing positive to go on, and she was certain the police were only pursuing him because he was mixed up in some kind of stolen car racket.

She walked to the window and looked out at the flakes flitting past the windowpane in a spirited dance, twirling on the wind, but she didn't feel so sprightly. The desire to look for Mandy hammered in her thoughts. She remembered Angelo's address.

Should she do some investigating of her own?

She walked down the hallway and listened at her mother's bedroom door. No light came from beneath, and she assumed her mother had already fallen asleep and would sleep soundly until morning.

The decision came to her. She wanted to look at Angelo's house. Benjamin had driven past and had said there was no sign of a child, but she wanted to see for herself.

Joanne took only a second to don her coat, grab her gloves and handbag, then slip out the back door.

In the car she didn't turn on her headlights until she'd pulled out onto the street—so as not to disturb her mother. The snow sailed past the windshield in a sheet of white. She tested her brakes to make sure she didn't slide. So far so good.

When she reached I-94, she stayed on the freeway and followed it to Telegraph, then Cherryhill. She began watching the street names, then made her turn. Her hands gripped the wheel so tightly they began to cramp, and she released the steering wheel, one hand at a time, spreading her fingers to ease the ache.

What am I doing? she asked herself as she headed down the snow-covered side street. Her eyes pierced the darkness looking for the address. When she spotted the house, her heart raced, and she drove past a few houses before pulling over to the curb.

She sat for a moment peering back at the darkened house. Could he be inside? Her hands trembled as she pulled the key from the ignition and opened the car door. She hit the lock, then walked casually toward the house.

The night was quiet at this late hour, and as she passed a house two doors away from the Angelo's, she could see light from the television flicker against a wall. When she neared the Angelo residence, her pulse pounded in her ears. She avoided the driveway and walked along the high shrubbery toward the back of the building.

As she approached, no sound came from inside, but she stood for a moment, listening to make sure. The only sound she heard was the distant roar of traffic on the main road. She moved closer and glanced into the darkened windows. No lights were on, and she could see nothing.

When she reached the backyard, she stopped and scrutinized the house. No light. No sound. She felt confident no one was home, but she didn't want to arouse neighbors. A dog barked inside the house next door, and she ducked back into the shadows, waiting for the animal to quiet.

Nothing happened. No porch lights came

on. She moved with cautious steps closer to the back door. Beside the porch, Joanne spotted two large trash cans. Something inside might give her a clue to the residents.

She cringed, thinking of delving into someone's trash, but she would do anything to find her daughter. She brushed the snow off the lid and lifted it.

Inside she peered at a jumble of trash bags. She untied one and looked inside, then shifted the contents. A brown banana peel slipped lower in the plastic sack. She shifted the bag and eyed an empty box of pancake mix, then another carton. She shook the container and looked again. Then she saw it. She slipped her hand into the plastic bag and pulled up a cereal box—sugarcoated, chocolate puffs. She couldn't imagine an adult eating that type, but a child would. Her deduction was foolish, she knew, but she felt triumphant.

She dropped the box to the ground, then slipped the trash can lid back on. She hoped no one would notice that she'd moved it. Fresh snow would help.

Joanne picked up the cereal box and tiptoed toward the side of the house. But as she turned the corner, a hand gripped her arm.

Chapter Nineteen

"What in the world are you doing here?" Benjamin whispered in her ear. "Get inside."

He pulled Joanne to his side and steered her through the shadows toward his car. He'd lost patience with her—something he'd tried not to do.

"I'm sorry," he said, once they were inside, "but I can't believe you took a chance like this. For what?"

She handed him the snow-dampened cereal box. He stared at the cartoon pirate on the front and shook his head. "It's cereal, Joanne."

"I know, but kids eat this, not adults."

"You took a chance on getting yourself hurt for an empty cereal box?"

"For a clue that a child lives there. *My* child."

His heart broke for her. "This isn't going to convince anyone that Angelo has your daughter. You know that."

She turned away from him and stared out the passenger window without responding.

He knew she was angry. "Look, I didn't mean to frighten you, but you scared me. I couldn't believe it when I saw your car parked on the street."

"What are *you* doing here?" Her voice challenged him.

"Checking the house, but at least I do it from my car and not traipsing around the property, trespassing—it's careless and against the law. I only got out of my car when I knew you were there."

"I'm sorry." She folded her arms across her chest. "I want my daughter back."

"I know you do, but—"

"And you hurt my arm," she said, rubbing her coat sleeve.

"I didn't mean to. I grabbed you to get you out of there."

In the streetlight he saw her flash him an angry look. He shook his head, not knowing whether to laugh or cry. He'd never known a woman so determined. "Please, don't be angry. Don't you understand how much I care?"

He'd caught her attention finally, her frown softening as she looked at him. "I didn't mean to do anything wrong. It appeared no one was home, and I—"

"Appeared? What happens if he's inside? If the man's a killer, you could be next. I don't think you realize who you're dealing with."

"That's the horrible part of it all. We don't know if he has Mandy, or his own child, or if this is a hoax. We don't know if the dead woman is his wife or someone else. The poor man might be on vacation with this family for all we know."

"He might. But he might not be," he said, keeping his emotions under control. "It's late, and you drove here in a snowstorm. I'm going to follow you home, and I want you to promise me—"

"I'm not promising anything, but I'll heed your warning."

He felt grateful for that. "Okay," he said, not willing to argue tonight. "I have to get home and read through my briefs, but I'll follow you back first."

"I'll be fine," she said, unlatching the passenger door.

"I know you will."

She stepped outside, and he watched her climb into her car and drive away from the curb. He moved in behind her. She could rant in that car all she wanted, but he was determined to follow her home. He loved the woman, whether she knew it or not. He'd spent years hiding his feelings, struggling with guilt and remorse. No more. He'd release the reins of his emotion. He'd loved her too long to hide it again.

Joanne had waited all day hoping to hear from the detective, but she'd received no telephone call. Melissa had taken the day off so she didn't have to face Joanne, but the day dragged with her wondering about Carl Angelo and Mandy.

Benjamin had sent an apology e-mail that gave her a smile and then later he'd telephoned just to make sure she wasn't angry for grabbing her so roughly. Tonight she had to find out how long her mother planned to stay. She felt that she should do something special to entertain her, but her mother had stated up front that she wanted nothing special—she was there for Joanne's support.

Her mother's visit still amazed her, but also

gave her food for thought. Since Benjamin's comments the night before, Joanne couldn't help but review her unhappy relationship with her family, and she'd begun to ask herself questions.

When the clock hands moved to five p.m., Joanne breathed a relieved sigh and gathered her belongings to leave. An idea struck her, and since it was daylight and she wasn't *exactly* going to the Angelo house, she didn't think Benjamin could get upset with her. An idea had niggled all day.

She gave her mother a quick call to say she'd be home a little late and then she hurried to her car. Pulling out of the parking area, she headed onto I-94 again toward Dearborn. This time she hoped she would find some information. The traffic backed up along the freeway and then inched along on Ford Road. Telegraph moved better, and finally, she turned on to Cherryhill.

Her nerves heightened as she approached the Angelo home. It looked less formidable in the early dusk than in the dark, but tension still throbbed, remembering the night before. She pulled to the side of the road a few houses before Angelo's, and slid from her car.

As she approached the house next door, she heard the same barking dog that she'd heard the previous evening. Before she could knock, a woman peeked at her through the small window, then opened the door a crack. The dog's barking grew more ferocious.

"May I help you?"

"Hi, I'm looking for Donna."

The woman frowned, then inched the door open wider. "You have the wrong house. She lives next door."

"I know, but I haven't been able to get hold of her for a few days. No one seems to be home." She hated making up the story, but she didn't know how else to get the information. "Have you seen her?"

The woman opened the storm door. Warm air traveled from the house and curled around Joanne.

"No, I haven't." The woman looked into the air as if thinking. "I haven't seen her since last week sometime. I usually notice her when she picks Connie up from school."

Connie. Her breath caught in her throat. Did they call Mandy "Connie," or had she been totally wrong?

The woman grinned. "Connie loves Ralph."

"Ralph?"

"Our golden retriever."

Joanne looked down by the woman's hand

and saw a wet nose poking out. The sharp barking had stopped, and when the woman moved aside the dog's tail wagged in the warmest welcome Joanne had seen in a long time.

"How about Connie?"

The woman frowned. "She loves the dog."

"No, I meant, have you seen her?" She held her breath.

"Not since I saw her mother."

Joanne's stomach churned, and panic charged through her. Though her legs turned to mush, she forced her body to remain steady.

"I have seen Carl."

Joanne tried to keep her voice calm. "Recently? I could ask him about Donna."

"He's been gone since Friday. Maybe Saturday. I haven't seen hide nor hair of any of them, now that you mention it."

Filled with fear, Joanne took a step backward. "Well, thanks for the information. I'll try calling her again tomorrow. I'm sure she'll show up." *In the morgue,* Joanne thought.

She gave the woman a friendly wave and hurried from the porch. She'd learned something important, but the something scared her. The woman had seen Carl but not Donna or Mandy.

Joanne couldn't bear to think of what that could mean.

* * *

"The detective wants you to call," Evelyn said as Joanne walked into the house.

"Sorry I'm late. I had to take care of something."

"I understand."

She smiled at her mother, who was standing in the kitchen making cookies. That's one memory she had from her youth: her mother seemed to live in the kitchen. Perhaps it was there that Evelyn Ryan found her identity. Her mother had always been a good cook.

Joanne slipped off her coat and dropped it over a chair, then went to the telephone. She checked the number posted on the cork board nearby and dialed.

She waited while the call went through, wondering what Cortezi wanted. Within minutes she knew.

After hanging up, she said to her mother, "He wants me to come to the police station tonight. I'm really sorry about this. How about if I pick up some dinner on the way home?"

"I'll cook," Evelyn said. "I noticed you have a nice slab of beef. I can make Swiss steak. Do you have potatoes?"

She had to think before answering. "You'll find some in that cabinet."

Her mother's behavior seemed to contradict what had gone on between them for the past few years, and Joanne felt as if she were walking in a fun-house barrel. The floor seemed to roll out from under her as she tried to balance and make sense out of their relationship and all that had been happening between them since her mother had arrived.

"I think I'll let Benjamin know where I'm going," she said, but instead of using the kitchen phone, she went to her bedroom.

Not knowing if he were home or at the office, she rang his cell phone. It took a few rings before she heard his hello.

"Benjamin, Cortezi wants me to go down to the station now. I'm heading that way. Mom's making Swiss steak if you want to come for dinner later."

"I'm just leaving. How about if I meet you at the station."

"I'd like that."

"And tell your mom I'd love a home-cooked dinner."

She called to her mother on the way out the door, then drove the mile to meet with Cortezi.

When she arrived, the clerk opened the door and pointed to Cortezi's office. Anxiety coursed through her and she wished Benjamin would arrive before Cortezi told her his news—whether it was something she didn't want to hear or something wonderful that she wanted to share with Benjamin.

She glanced behind her before heading past the desks to the detective's office.

"Mrs. Fuller," he said as she stood outside his door. "Come in." He rose and shifted a chair for her.

"This must be important," she said, searching his face to see if she could read his expression.

"I have two things," he said without preamble. "One is we've finally located Rose Stella Angelo, now Bannicki. She's remarried and lives in Indiana with her daughter."

"Her daughter's in Indiana?" Joanne's heart thundered and she pressed her hand against her chest to hold back the ache. "I can't believe it. He has a child—" She stopped herself, knowing he would ask why she was so certain.

"We haven't verified that yet, since he's missing."

"You told me earlier that someone at the trucking company said he'd gone on vacation with his family."

"Family. Wife. We don't know for sure."

But Joanne knew. She'd found the cereal

box and later she'd talked to the neighbor. She was opening her mouth to tell him when she heard a knock on the door and then it opened. Benjamin. She reveled in seeing him come in. He'd become her hero.

"Do you mind?" he asked Cortezi.

"Not at all."

"Angelo's ex-wife lives in Indiana with their daughter," Joanne said in a rush.

Benjamin's eyebrows lifted. "Really." He looked at Cortezi.

The detective nodded. "Remarried. We finally located her."

"So what's happening now?" Benjamin asked.

"We're still looking for Angelo. He's managed to vanish for the time being."

Benjamin eyed Joanne. "Are you all right?"

"Sort of," she said.

Benjamin looked at Cortezi. "Is that all?"

Joanne turned toward the detective and saw him grimace.

"No. I hate to ask this, Mrs. Fuller, but we'd like you to look at the body. I know you don't know her name, but you said you saw the woman who put the photo in your package. Your ID might help verify if she is the dead woman."

Joanne caught her breath. "I'd have to go to the morgue?"

"No. We don't do it that way. I have a couple of photos. Can you handle it?"

Her stomach twisted with the thought. She sent a pleading look at Benjamin, but then realized she had no choice. "Yes, I'll look."

Benjamin stood behind her, his hands resting on her shoulders. "Are you sure you want to do this?"

She turned her head to see him. "It'll answer the question I've had haunting me for so long."

Cortezi pulled a file folder from his desk and flipped open the cover, then turned a photograph around to face her.

At first Joanne couldn't bring herself to look. If this *was* the woman, then her fear would grow for Mandy. No matter what anyone said to calm her, she would know her daughter had lived with that family.

Her breath rattled through her lungs and she felt her body tremble as she lowered her eyes to the photograph. In death, the woman looked different. Joanne stared at the head shot and her stomach tightened. She turned away, fighting nausea and thinking back to the two times she had seen the woman—once near her packages and once across the mall with her haggard look, the sagging jaw, the hair that straggled beside her ears.

"Try this one," Cortezi said.

The second photograph was from the side, and Joanne recognized her. "It's her."

"Positive?"

She nodded, unable to speak again without gagging.

"We need to do a dental check to be sure, and find a relative if this is Donna Angelo."

Joanne took a chance. "What about a neighbor? You know where Angelo lives. Couldn't you ask a neighbor to view the body?"

"If necessary. We'll have an answer for you soon," he said.

"Can we go?" Benjamin asked.

Cortezi nodded. "Thanks for coming in. And, Mrs. Fuller, I hope we have something for you in the next day or two."

With Benjamin holding her arm, Joanne rose, sickened by the pictures, but certain that the woman in the photo had known the whereabouts of Mandy.

Joanne had to leave her hopes in God's hands.

Chapter Twenty

"Nita, I'm leaving," Joanne said.

"Leaving? Are you sick?"

"No, I have a few errands to run. I decided to take off a half day."

Nita gave her a wry smile. "Christmas shopping? Buy me something nice."

Joanne smiled back and moved away from the door before her friend got too inquisitive.

The past two days had weighed on Joanne like a boulder. Her mother's visit, the news from Cortezi and the reprimand from Benjamin had taken their toll. Today she would do one more thing that would send Benjamin into a tirade when he learned what she'd done.

She left the office building and climbed into her car, then aimed its nose toward Dearborn. The photograph of Mandy was in her handbag, and she had a good idea what school Mandy must be attending. She'd checked out the Dearborn school district on the Internet.

The traffic was light in the afternoon, and she made her way to Stevenson Elementary in less than an hour. She sat for a moment to collect herself before going inside. The deep premonition that had led her on this journey hadn't subsided. Donna Angelo had not phoned again about their financial agreement. In the past three days, the urgency had grown. She couldn't stop now.

She got out of her car and made her way up the walk, thinking she'd learned so much in the past few days. Angelo had a child he claimed was his daughter—though she knew it couldn't be his birth child. She'd discovered that the dead woman who'd been found in the park was the woman who'd given her the child's photograph. And she now knew that Donna and Mandy had not been seen around the Angelo home for the past couple of days. Too many things pointed to the fact that her daughter was in danger.

Facing the school building door, Joanne drew in a deep breath and stepped inside. A sign pointed to the nearby office, and she stopped there first.

"May I help you?" said a young woman walking toward her from a file cabinet.

"Yes. I'm looking for a first grader named Connie Angelo."

The woman's face puckered at her question. "And you are…?"

Joanne scrambled for a response. "I'm an old friend of the family."

"I'm sorry. We can't provide information about our students without proof that you represent the family and you have a legitimate reason for asking."

"I *do* have a reason," Joanne said, irritated by the woman's scrutinizing look. Then she had second thoughts. The woman was following the rules—and wise ones, too.

"I'm sorry," the secretary said. "If a parent calls to tell us a friend is dropping by or we have some other form of proof it's fine, but otherwise my hands are tied."

"I understand," Joanne said, backing toward the door. "Thanks anyway."

She gave the woman an accepting smile, then made her way to the corridor, but instead of going back outside, she looked up and down the corridors. Seeing no one guarding the halls, she walked as if with purpose down the hallway, glancing at doors and reading the signs outside each room: teacher's name and grade.

Perfect.

After passing the kindergarten room, she spotted another sign across the hallway: "Mrs. Price, First grade." Her pulse quickened. She tapped the door, praying the teacher, too, wouldn't chase her away.

When a woman opened the door, children's voices hummed in the background as she gave Joanne a puzzled look. "Yes?"

"I'm looking for Mandy Angelo. She should be in your room. She's in the first grade." Her heart missed a beat. She'd called the child Mandy Angelo. She'd made her first mistake.

The woman's puzzlement deepened. "There's no Mandy in this room, and I know Mrs. Desantis doesn't have a Mandy, either, but she does have a *Connie* Angelo. Her room is the next one across the hall." She pointed in that direction.

Joanne swallowed hard. "Thanks so much, and I'm sorry to have disturbed you."

The woman sent her a curious look and stepped back into her classroom. Children's voices quieted as the door closed.

Joanne stopped outside the opposite door to regain control. Slipping her hand inside her pocket, she felt the small photograph, then sent up a silent prayer. *Lord, I need Your help and strength.*

Her hand trembled as she rapped on the door.

Voices rose inside the classroom, and she heard the teacher shushing them before she answered.

"Hello," the teacher said, her expression shifting from pleasant to questioning.

"I'm looking for Connie Angelo. I believe this is her classroom."

She glanced down the hallway as if to see if Security had followed her there. "Connie's absent today."

Joanne's chest tightened. "Absent?"

"Yes, she's been out of school since last Friday, I believe. Who are you?"

"I'm an old friend," she said, continuing her masquerade. She put her hand into her pocket and pulled out the photo. "Would you mind looking at this photo so I know for sure we're talking about the same child?"

The teacher took a step backward, obviously startled by the request. Though it probably didn't make sense to the woman, this was vital information for Joanne. The woman's gaze lowered to the photograph, then lifted to Joanne's face.

"That's her—but I don't understand."

Joanne's knees weakened and she had to struggle to remain standing. "It's a long story," she said, though her voice sounded breathless. "Thank you." She slipped the picture back into her pocket and turned.

She sensed the woman watching her as she made her way along the corridor. Escaping was Joanne's focus. She wanted to get out of the building before someone called the police or school security. She'd have too much to explain.

By the time she was inside her car, Joanne felt panicky. Her heart throbbed. Carl Angelo had raised her daughter as Connie. He'd abducted Mandy, then caused Greg's death. Joanne didn't understand it, but she knew it had to be the truth.

But she still didn't know if Mandy was alive. She turned on the ignition as tears poured from her eyes. Her body quaked. She knew the Lord had promised not to give her more than she could handle, yet today she questioned that. Her thoughts turned to a prayer. *Father, I want to see her living. Please keep her safe. Protect her and give her strength.* Grasping for inner strength, she shifted into reverse and backed out of her parking spot.

As she drove, her thoughts became more rational. Though it had seemed forever, only four days had passed since she'd heard about the dead woman in Dearborn. Now she had to face Benjamin with her secrets, and her mother with an open heart. She didn't know which would be harder.

Since Mandy's body hadn't been found at River Rouge Park, she prayed that meant the Lord had moved Carl Angelo's heart to spare her daughter's life. Surely the worst villain would have compassion for a child he'd raised as his own. Hope swelled inside her, and Joanne prayed for God's mercy. Mandy had to be alive. She had to.

Benjamin's mind would not focus on the merger papers spread across his desk. He'd read the last page twice and nothing had registered except thoughts of Joanne and Mandy.

He hated being away from Joanne, partly because he had no idea what crazy thing she might do next. She'd gone to the Angelo house without thinking. She'd agreed to give the woman caller money. She'd kept important information from him. He suspected she still had more to tell him than she let on.

He hadn't taken long to be convinced that Joanne's feelings about Mandy were legitimate. He'd seen evidence. The photograph seemed proof positive, unless that child was Mandy's double. The girl in the photo had Joanne's coloring, shape of face and eyes. The only difference between mother and daughter was that Mandy had her father's mouth, smile and faint dimples.

Benjamin had to stop himself twice from calling Cortezi. He had assumed they would have learned something by now—either the dead woman's positive identity or Carl Angelo's location. It wasn't Benjamin's place to call. Although he'd done it before, he now decided to back off and let Joanne handle it.

Joanne. Her face hung in his thoughts. His feelings had deepened far more than he would have believed. He'd always been drawn to her, and he had chastised himself for that attraction. Finally he had done the right thing and had gone away. He'd found no other method to keep his feelings under control. He'd prayed and talked to himself. He'd tried to close his mind and heart to her, but it hadn't worked. Away had been easier.

Joanne didn't seem to suspect. Benjamin sensed she cared for him, but how much was still a mystery. He knew he'd become her companion—but what about love?

Benjamin had hedged with himself about how to handle this evening. Though he wanted to see Joanne every day, he knew he needed to give her and her mother more time alone. He'd decided to work late and catch up on some long-neglected files.

He pushed his chair away from the desk and stood to face the window. The winter sun lit the blue sky. Positive weather. Positive thoughts. That's what he needed.

After circling his chair, he sat again to face his work. *Concentrate,* he told himself.

Joanne couldn't sleep. She watched the clock hands inch their way past midnight, then twelve-thirty, then one. She shifted her legs to the edge of the bed and slid her feet to the floor. Her mind had been filled with worries. Cortezi had called to tell her that the dead woman had been identified by a neighbor as Donna Angelo.

Joanne's chest ached at the news. Donna had been her connection to Mandy, and now

Donna had been murdered. Joanne knew her daughter was in the hands of a madman.

She'd been disappointed at Benjamin's absence that evening. He'd called before she'd heard from Cortezi to tell her he had a corporate meeting early the next morning and had too much to prepare. He'd also mentioned that he thought she and her mother had plenty to talk about. She figured that was his real motivation for staying away.

She recalled his criticism last night and asked him about it, but he denied his avoidance had any connection. He insisted he wasn't angry. She wondered if that were true.

Tonight she'd tried to open her heart to her mother. It had been difficult, but she'd done her best to be thoughtful and amiable. Yet Joanne realized she'd held back. She didn't want her mother's pity. She wanted her love— the kind of unyielding love she had felt for Mandy all these years.

A thought had niggled all evening. The police were looking for Carl Angelo's car, but what if he'd hidden his car somewhere and borrowed one from a friend? Far-fetched, perhaps, but she sensed he'd done something. She now knew for certain that Angelo's wife was dead, and she speculated he was hiding Mandy somewhere. Joanne needed to do something—to act, to find her.

She dressed in silence, then made her way down the staircase. Her mother seemed to be a sound sleeper, and Joanne would be back before she was missed. She backed the car out of the driveway and followed the road to the freeway. She'd driven there twice before, and tonight, though the spotty traffic seemed a blessing, patches of ice and frozen snow were hidden in the blackness and she strained her eyes for danger.

As she drove through the darkness, her thoughts shifted back to Benjamin and his affect on her life. Since she had spoken to him on the telephone earlier, an unreasonable fear had grown in her thoughts.

Benjamin would be furious, but that couldn't stop her. She'd been wrapped in self-pity and grief for too long, and now she longed to be the old Joanne again—strong, determined, intelligent. She had a goal: find Angelo. Then she would find Mandy.

Benjamin's homecoming had changed her life, yet since her mother's arrival, he'd acted differently. Although she had calculated he might still be miffed at her, her greater fear was that he didn't care about her as much as she hoped. Was his only purpose to be a friend to the friendless?

Joanne had come to realize that she'd given her heart to Benjamin without his asking, and tonight she suspected a deeper relationship with him might be unattainable.

Yet her mind couldn't dwell on that concern. Finding her daughter was taking all her energy.

Joanne turned onto Cherryhill and looked for the side street. She started at every shadow, and Benjamin's warning returned to her. She could be in danger, but she didn't care anymore. She wanted to find Mandy.

She bristled as the house came into sight, seeming as dark as it had been the night before. But as she inched the car past, she spotted a faint light flickering at the back of the house. Her stomach rose to her throat as she pulled the car to a stop.

When she pushed open the car door, the night wind fluttered through her hair and icy air surged around her. As she approached the house her knees weakened. She followed the shrubbery to the side, farthest from the front door.

As she inched her way in the darkness, she

listened, hoping to hear something from inside, but only her pulse thundered in her ears.

When she reached the back of the building, Joanne crept closer to a window and saw the flickering light inside—from a bedroom, perhaps. A television…?

Her heart cried out. Was her child inside? Gooseflesh tingled along her limbs. Something wavered behind the drawn shade, and Joanne feared she might be discovered.

She needed to get away from there and notify the police that someone—presumably Carl Angelo—was home. Her rarely used cell phone was in her glove compartment. When she got to her car, she would call Cortezi.

She darted from the window and in her hurry, bumped the trash can, sending the lid tumbling off with a *clang*. Her heart rose to her throat, and she stood paralyzed.

Finally she found momentum, but as she moved, the porch light flared, illuminating the yard. As the back door opened, she darted around the side of the house. A deep bellowing voice assailed her as she raced across the snow-covered lawn. She stumbled on ice, her foot slipping out from under her. As her ankle turned, pain rolled along her leg and a cry shot from her, but she forced herself forward.

As she neared her car, Joanne hit the remote, but she could hear the man pounding behind her, his angry voice demanding that she stop. She heard him skid behind her, then his profanity split the night air.

Her ankle throbbing, she fought for breath, and silently her prayers rose to heaven. As she clasped the handle and yanked the door open, her pursuer's shadow lengthened beside her. She hit the lock and pulled on the door just as his body darted forward toward her.

The telephone's ring jarred Benjamin from his sleep. Panic charged through him as his gaze sought the clock. Two in the morning. *Joanne.* He gripped the receiver and pulled it to his ear.

"Hello," he said, knowing he sounded raspy from sleep.

"Benjamin?"

The voice sounded unfamiliar, and he tried to gather his senses. "Yes?"

"This is Evelyn Ryan."

Words tore from his throat. "What's wrong, Evelyn?"

"Is Joanne with you?"

"With me? No. I didn't see her today. She's not home?"

"I've looked everywhere. I went to bed early, and then I had an unpleasant dream. Something must have disturbed me, and when I woke I had an eerie feeling. I went to check on her and her bed was empty. I've looked all through the house. And her car is gone."

Dear Lord, he pleaded, *protect her.* He could only image what she had done. "Don't panic, Evelyn." His words to calm her did nothing to allay his own terror. "I'll find her. I'm sure it's nothing." But his heart said it was. "I'll call when I find her, and you do the same if she shows up."

"I will, Benjamin. I'm sorry to disturb you but I didn't know who else to ask."

His hand shook as he clutched the phone. "I'm thankful you called."

"I'll wait here by the phone," she said. "She's my daughter and I don't want anything to happen to her. She's been through too much for a young woman. I can't bear it."

He only wished Joanne could hear her mother's concern. "Do you pray, Evelyn?"

"I've never been one for religion," she said, "but I found myself asking God's help tonight."

"That's what you can do for her. God says

if we believe, we'll receive what we ask for. He'll answer our prayers."

"That's in the Bible."

"It sure is. In the Book of Matthew."

"I'll be praying, Benjamin."

He sent a thank-you to the Lord. "I'll get back to you as soon as I know something."

He disconnected and then sat on the edge of the bed trying to gather his thoughts. Where would she go? *Out for fast food?* He knew better. She had barely eaten enough to keep her alive lately. *To see Cortezi?* Not in the middle of the night. *To look for Mandy?* That made sense. *Where?* He knew the answer, and he felt sick.

She'd done it once before—gone snooping around Angelo's house. Would she go there again? He'd told her never to go back, but he'd already learned that Joanne was a stubborn woman. When she had her mind set on something, he could insist, plead or demand, and it would be fruitless.

If he left the house to find her, he wouldn't be home if she called him. He could call the police—but was she really in danger? He sat staring at the telephone, torn by what to do.

Chapter Twenty-One

Terrified, Joanne slammed her door, flinching as the man's body hit the side of the car. It had to be Angelo. Her hand quaked as she slid her key into the ignition. While he yanked on the door handle, she shifted into gear and tore away.

In her rearview mirror, she saw him reel from her acceleration, then rant, shaking his fist above his head. Then, in a heartbeat, the mirror showed another image. He'd regained control and now darted toward his driveway. Before she had even reached the end of his street, she saw his headlights glaring in the distance and gaining on her.

Fear gripped her as Angelo's SUV closed the distance between them. Gunning the motor she spun onto the highway, her car wheel slamming into a snowy rut. She struggled to hold the steering wheel steady and pull her vehicle back onto the highway.

Her mind raced. She needed to lose him or get help. She'd stored her cell phone in the glove compartment, but she had no time to find it and punch in the numbers. She'd have to slow down, and she couldn't take the chance. If she didn't decelerate, she would roll the car on the black ice.

Her prayer rose that God be her pilot. Terror pounded through her veins and her head swam with horrible imaginings. As if her heavenly petition had been answered, Joanne spotted a police car heading toward her from the opposite direction. She flashed her headlights, hoping he'd realize something was wrong.

Her hand trembled as she turned the knob. *Blink. Blink. Blink.* The police car drew closer and her hopes rose, then he veered to the right and up the ramp. Had he seen her and would he come back, or hadn't he noticed her at all?

The light-colored SUV stayed on her tail. The traffic was the only thing saving her from his getting into a dangerous position beside her. She feared he would run her off the road and into the freeway barricade.

As Joanne approached a ramp, an idea struck her: she needed to find a police station. Finally she recalled that if she took the next exit she could make her way to Vernor Avenue and the Detroit Third precinct. There she would find help.

Traffic thinned, and Angelo's vehicle moved into the left lane. She saw him gaining speed, and her only hope was to take the next ramp, or he'd force her off the road. She waited until the last minute, hoping to dodge him, and then turned her wheel and took the ramp. A car followed her, but it was dark colored, and she knew Angelo had missed the exit or had fallen behind.

She got her bearings and made a right turn. For once she hoped the police would pull her over for speeding, but none stopped her. She tried to play the lights. Halting for a red would be her undoing.

Behind her, she spotted a vehicle picking up speed. Tension assailed her as she struggled to keep her wits. She spotted Vernor Avenue and made a quick right. Ahead of her sat the Third precinct building. She wheeled into the parking lot, and the light colored SUV slowed, then shot past.

An officer was coming out of the door and

heading to a squad car. She put her hand on the door handle, ready to call to him, then changed her mind. It would only delay her. Her body felt like gelatin as she leaned over and hit the glove compartment button. She pulled out her cell phone and punched the numbers.

Benjamin. He'd know what to do.

When the telephone rang, Benjamin answered, and relief flooded him when he heard Joanne's voice.

"You did what?" he said, astounded that she would take such a chance.

"I couldn't sleep, and I—"

"You'll be sleeping permanently, Joanne, if you keep doing things like this." He knew how much she wanted to find Mandy, but her way just wasn't wise. "Let the police do their work. Now tell me about the car, and I'll notify the Grosse Pointe police."

"I couldn't see the license plate, but it was pale-colored—an SUV—and I know it was him. When I pulled into the police station, he slowed, then zoomed past. So, he's somewhere in this area."

"I wish you'd seen his license plate."

"He was behind me. All I could see was the glare of his headlights."

Benjamin understood, but having the numbers would have made the job easier. "Which police station?"

"Third on Vernor."

"Listen to me. Don't move from where you are. If you want, go inside the station, but otherwise stay there. You're safe and I'll come to get you."

For once she didn't argue, and when he hung up, he put in an immediate call to the Grosse Pointe police. Cortezi wasn't there, but he knew the department had a bulletin out to look for Angelo's vehicle. "She said it was a pale-colored SUV," he reported, "but she didn't catch the license plate."

"Pale-colored?" the detective asked. "There's the problem. Angelo owns a black sedan. He must be driving a borrowed car or a rental. We'll get on it."

Relief surged through him as he hung up and called Evelyn. Her voice quivered when she answered the telephone, but he heard relief when he told her Joanne had called.

"Will she be safe?" she asked.

"I'm going there now. I'll bring her home, but if anyone calls or comes to your door, don't answer—and call the police immediately. Do you hear me?"

"I hear you," she said, strained amusement in her voice. "I'm not as stubborn as my daughter."

"I'm glad to hear that," he said, grinning to himself.

He disconnected, then hurried to his car. He'd dressed over an hour ago and had waited by the phone, hoping Joanne would call him or her mother, saying she was safe.

Some people talked disparagingly about the "weaker sex," but Joanne was a gender of her own. She had the stubbornness of a bull and the gentleness of a lamb. The woman surprised him at each turn. He'd read about parents giving their lives for their child, and Benjamin could see this in Joanne. She held no fear.

He backed out of his driveway and headed down Lakeshore Drive toward Detroit. Each time he drove along the lake he'd remember Joanne's frantic call three years earlier. He wanted to rid himself of the memory.

Tonight Christmas wreaths and garlands decorated the streetlights and he had to remind himself that everywhere people were excited about the coming celebration of the birth of the Savior. All he'd had time to think about was saving Joanne. He had growing hopes that tonight God in His mercy would bring an end to this horrible situation.

To distract himself, Benjamin snapped on the radio. He pushed station buttons until he heard Christmas music ringing through the speakers. *"God rest ye merry gentlemen,"* he sang along. *Let nothing you dismay.* The words hit home.

He'd been dismayed. He'd found it easy to forget Jesus' birth with so much going on. The truth saddened him. How many people around the world were faced with difficult times so the impact of God's love had been watered down to nothing. Christmas should be a time of jubilation and thanksgiving.

When all Joanne's trials ended, he prayed they would have time to rejoice. Benjamin knew he had much to be thankful for. Every day, he praised God for bringing him home to Detroit, for bringing Joanne back into his life, for giving him so much more than he ever could have dreamed.

He turned onto Michigan Avenue, and then left onto Vernor Avenue. A few minutes later, he spotted the Third precinct and Joanne's car.

Joanne sent him a grateful look when she saw him. He parked his car nearby and slipped into the passenger seat of hers. She fell into his arms. Her tears soaked into his jacket as he held her close to soothe her. His heart swelled.

"Thank you," she whispered once she'd calmed. "This was horrible."

"I don't doubt it, but what I want to know is, what were you thinking of?"

"My daughter."

Her answer was short and honest. She'd given no thought to herself. He wanted to ask her to promise never to do something this foolish again, but he would cause her to lie. Joanne would do what she needed to, to locate her daughter.

"I called the police about the vehicle following you. Cortezi wasn't there, but I know they're looking for him."

"I should have listened," she said, resting her head against his chest. "He is a madman. I have no doubt he could kill again." She shifted her head upward. "I heard from Cortezi earlier tonight. The dead woman was Donna."

"Why didn't you let me know?"

"You didn't want to be bothered. You said you had work to do."

He knew she'd been disappointed. "My mind has been filled with you and your problems, Joanne. I've neglected my own work, even though I've tried to concentrate. You're taking up every bit of my attention."

"I'm sorry, Benjamin. I've asked too much of you."

"Not by your asking. It's me. You're in my every thought."

She gave him a curious look, and he realized this wasn't the time or place to discuss the future. "We need to get you home."

"I hope my mother's still sleeping. She'd be—"

"She's been going crazy, worried about you. She called me in the middle of the night. That's why I was up and dressed when you called."

"She called you?"

"She woke and noticed you were gone. I phoned her after I heard from you. She was very thankful."

"Thanks. I'm sorry I scared both of you."

He gave her a final hug before opening the car door. "I'll follow you home so I know you're safe."

"Stay behind me."

"I will," he said, stepping out into the cold night air. He closed the door and patted the window reassuringly.

Her look melted his heart.

Seeing her house had never felt so good. As she pulled into the driveway, Joanne realized her mother had stayed up. Lights glowed in the living room and kitchen. Benjamin's car rolled in behind hers.

After parking she slid from the car and locked the door, then turned to find him at her side. Her mother opened the door before they hit the porch.

"I've been so worried," she said as she pushed back the storm door, then embraced Joanne.

Touched by her mother's concern, Joanne hugged her back. "I'm sorry, Mom. I didn't mean to scare anyone."

"You were right," Evelyn said, her eyes on Benjamin. "I felt better talking to God. I knew Someone was on our side."

"I told you," he said, and gave her quick hug.

A grin spread across her face. "I made a pot of coffee for you—decaf—if you want some. I'm exhausted, but I want to know what happened."

Joanne gave her a brief explanation and watched her mother's eyes weigh with sleep.

Evelyn patted Joanne's arm. "I'm grateful, but now that you're home safe, I'm going back to bed."

"Get a good rest," Benjamin said. "I'm going to sleep on the sofa. You two ladies aren't going to be here alone tonight."

Her mother looked relieved and headed down the hallway, while Joanne protested.

"I won't have you sleeping on the sofa, Benjamin," Joanne said. "You can go home. We'll be fine."

"I'm sure you will, but I'm not taking any chances."

She knew he could be persistent, so she saw no sense in fighting him. "You can sleep in Mandy's bed." Hearing her words surprised Joanne. No one had touched the room since the night of the accident. She'd gone in occasionally to dust her daughter's belongings but that was all.

"Let's have some of that coffee," Benjamin said, seemingly ignoring her offer.

Too wound up to sleep, Joanne led the way into the kitchen. She poured the coffee her mother had made, then checked the cookie jar and found some homemade chocolate-chip ones and set a few on a plate. Then she and Benjamin carried the snack into the living room.

Benjamin sat first and patted the sofa cushion beside him. A look of tenderness glistened in his eyes.

She walked to the tree and turned on the Christmas lights, then dimmed the lamp and joined him, happy to feel close to someone. Earlier she'd felt so alone, even though she had known God had her in His keeping.

She lifted the mug and took a warming sip. Her hands embraced the ceramic, the heat helping to alleviate the chill she'd felt since earlier that evening when she'd struggled to fall asleep.

"What can I say?" She gave Benjamin a ponderous look, wondering how angry he was.

"You can say you'll be more careful. You have no idea if he can trace your license plate here. The man's a criminal and apparently a murderer. He's killed twice now."

"And a kidnapper." Her heart skipped a beat at the thought that her daughter had been raised in Carl Angelo's home.

"I'm sure his picture is splashed all over the television," Benjamin said. "You know what that means."

She did, and it frightened her. "He'll be desperate. You know that. He won't want to drag a child all over the country trying to hide out from the police." Her pulse raced. "If someone doesn't find her soon, it'll be too late."

"God is with her. That's all we can count on, Joanne."

"I've prayed." She paused. "Every waking moment." She curled her legs beneath her and felt Benjamin's arm slide behind her back. He drew her closer, and she rested her head against his shoulder. "Why do you think Donna Angelo contacted me now? The kidnapping happened three years ago."

"He married her after he'd taken Mandy, and maybe she'd just begun to put two and two together."

"You think something might have happened to make her question whether Mandy was his daughter?"

"Something like that," he said. "Perhaps his first wife got in touch and said something about their child. She'd know then that Connie wasn't his."

Questions marched back into her thoughts—all the whys and hows that had plagued her. "Why do you think Carl Angelo kidnapped Mandy? Because Greg represented his wife?"

Benjamin rested his head against hers. "Greg handled not only the divorce but the restraining order. Then the permanent order became part of the divorce settlement. His abuse must have been terrible for her to give up child support and alimony to get away from him."

"Donna was doing the same thing. She was trying to get away."

Benjamin's face fell. "I've been wondering if Donna really planned to tell you where to find Mandy. She might have taken the money *and* her."

"I don't know. I had to trust her. But she did refuse to make a trade. She wanted the money and said she'd give me information." The possibility struck her. "This has been so difficult, so awful, yet it would be wonderful if—" Tripped by her emotions, she couldn't finish.

"It's been a horrendous journey, Joanne, and yet one that's changed my life." He tilted his head to look into her eyes. "And yours, I hope."

Seeing his face, her pulse kicked into high gear. "I'm awed at how important you've become to me. I lived in a box before you arrived, Benjamin. I didn't realize it. I worked and went to church, but I'd cut myself off from so many people. Inside, I felt very lonely and incomplete."

"And now?"

She avoided his question. "How about you?"

"Men aren't good with words."

"I know." She'd wanted to hear him tell her how he felt about her so often, but once again, she feared she longed for more than he had to offer.

"You're an exceptional woman. I've always admired you."

Admiration. That's not what she wanted. "Thanks," she said, hoping her disappointment wasn't apparent. "I've always admired you, too." She rested her head on his chest again.

"But my feelings have changed."

"Changed good or changed bad?"

"Neither. My feelings have grown. You've

become my focus—what's important in my day and my night."

She lifted her head, her heart pounding. "You're my everything, Benjamin. We've always been dear friends, but I've been amazed at your sacrifice for me. You've stood by me, even though I'm sure you thought I'd gone a little loopy, and all the while you've become my joy. Our friendship has changed and blossomed into a flower."

He brushed her cheek with his free hand, then ran his fingers along her hair, his eyes searching hers. "You're the flower. You're roses and orchids and violets gathered into one beautiful bouquet." His fingers slid to her chin and tilted it upward as he lowered his mouth to hers.

The kiss warmed her mouth, and she breathed in his scent. His lips moved beneath hers, deepening and caressing until her heart felt as if it would burst.

He eased away, and her mouth tingled, longing for more. She took what she yearned for, closing the distance between them and capturing his mouth again. The rhythm of her heart beat against his, and when he drew her even closer, she responded eagerly.

Benjamin released a sigh, startled and yet

amazed by what had happened. Like opening a well, sweet water gushed from an untapped spring washing him in a sparkling delight he hadn't expected, yet had dreamed of.

She looked at him, her eyes saying more than words could utter.

"I've wanted to do this forever, Joanne."

His stomach tightened with longing. He'd lost control of his emotions, and now, in the midst of all she'd been through, this wasn't the time to confess he'd loved her for so many years.

Instead he rocked her in his arms, feeling love swell in his heart. He hadn't spoken the words, but he would when the time was right. She wrapped her arms around him and closed her eyes. Nothing more needed to be said.

Chapter Twenty-Two

Joanne sat at her desk the next day and gazed at the surprise floral bouquet. They'd appeared shortly after she'd arrived at Solutions.

She'd felt ill at ease when she woke, remembering how Benjamin had awakened her and sent her to bed. She'd fallen asleep in his arms and had wandered off to her room without offering him a pillow and blanket. He must have found some on his own—so much for being a hostess.

She believed they had fallen in love. Benjamin hadn't said "I love you," but he'd shown enough in his words and actions to give her confidence that he felt as she did.

Her mother had made coffee and scrambled eggs for Benjamin, but Joanne had only had the coffee. She'd felt in a daze.

As Benjamin drove her to work Joanne recalled her mother talking to Benjamin about prayer. She'd never heard her mother speak of God or prayer, and she'd meant to ask him about it last night, but things had taken a different course. She was anxious to know what had transpired between them and when she asked, he surprised her with her mother's willingness to pray and curiosity about the Bible.

"Where'd you get the posies?" Nita asked now, coming through the doorway.

"Benjamin."

"Can I read the card?"

She didn't wait for an answer, but pulled the small note from the holder and eyed it. "Whoa! What's this mean?"

"What?"

She pointed to the scrawl: "'I meant everything I said last night.'"

Joanne couldn't control her grin. Instead of keeping everything hidden, she told Nita about the chase and then opened her heart about her feelings for Benjamin.

Nita smiled as she slipped the card back into the bouquet. She strode to Joanne's side and gave her a hug. "I'm thrilled about the romance, but—"

"I'm not positive it's a romance yet, but it seems to be heading in that direction."

Nita stood over her. "I'm happy about that, but I'm not happy to hear that the man followed you. You need to be careful. Did you drive yourself to work this morning?"

"Benjamin dropped me off. He said he'd pick me up tonight, or I thought if he can't make it I could hitch a ride with you."

Nita pressed her hand against her chest. "Sure, I'll drive you home. I wouldn't think of your driving yourself. Not now."

"I'm praying it will be over soon. The police had his mug shot all over the TV last night, when I watched television, but we didn't hear well." She looked at Nita's face and realized what she'd said. "We were talking."

"Right," Nita said, giving her a wink.

Joanne's stomach growled, and she covered her empty tummy with her palm. "I only had coffee this morning and forgot my lunch." She glanced at her watch. "It's almost noon. I think I'll run next door to the sandwich shop. Do you want anything?"

"No, thanks. I'm good."

Nita turned to go, but Joanne stopped her.

"Wait a minute. I'll walk with you to the elevator."

She grabbed her handbag and jacket, then closed her office door, but she got only a few steps before she heard her name coming from Melissa's office. She paused outside her coworker's door.

"Could I talk with you a minute?" Melissa called.

Her eyes pleaded, and Joanne gave her a nod. "Nita, go on ahead. I'll be a few minutes."

Nita waved and walked on as Joanne stepped into Melissa's office.

"Is something wrong?" Joanne asked, noticing how uneasy the other woman seemed.

Melissa rose from her desk and approached her. "I wanted to thank you again for what you did, and I want to say goodbye."

"Goodbye?"

"I've resigned."

Joanne felt her eyes widen. "Not on my account."

"No, on mine. I've created a reputation for myself here, and I realize I'll get nowhere. I made a big mistake and I've learned something important. From you, actually."

"From me?"

"From your kindness and your integrity. You worked hard to get where you are. My way didn't work. I realize that you could have sent me to jail or had me put on probation if you'd wanted to, but you didn't."

"I thought you'd suffered enough, Melissa."

"Joanne, had I been in your shoes I probably would have pressed charges. But you did the right thing—the moral thing. I'm not a slow learner. The writing is on the wall. I've decided to make a clean start somewhere else."

"Do you have a job already?" She should feel relieved, but she didn't. She felt responsible for Melissa's predicament.

"No, but I'll find one. I have some vacation time. I'll enjoy the holidays, get a grip on myself and then start looking. You could say a prayer for me if you would."

Joanne's chest tightened. "I'd be happy to."

"Thanks," she said, extending her hand.

Joanne took it in hers and gave it a squeeze. "I wish you the best, Melissa. Things happen for a reason. I like to think God teaches us His will in very dramatic ways sometimes."

Melissa nodded and stepped back.

Joanne didn't say any more. She stood

there for a moment, then turned and headed for the elevator.

Her mind was filled with thoughts of Melissa as she descended to the first floor. Perhaps a Blessing had happened with that horrible experience. If Melissa had learned that hard work and morals were the key to success, Joanne could write off the bad experience as having had a purpose.

In the lobby, she zipped her jacket and threw her handbag over her shoulder, then darted into the chilly air. The street seemed filled with Christmas. Carols drifted from nearby shops. A Santa stood on the corner beside his kettle, ringing a bell.

As she walked three stores over from her office building, the crisp breeze stung her face and she felt like Jack Frost was truly nipping at her nose. A snowflake fluttered down, followed by another. She'd always loved a white Christmas. Still it never seemed right without it.

This year she had greater hopes for the holiday. She hadn't said the words, but she'd felt in her heart that Mandy would be with her. She realized it wouldn't be easy—she loved Mandy with all her heart, but the child wouldn't remember her. Still, time would heal the wounds.

The cold wind burned in her eyes. She darted inside the warm deli, fragrant with the scent of hot soup and corned beef. After studying the menu board, she decided anything too rich wouldn't sit well. She selected a tuna sandwich with grated cheese and lettuce.

The clerk wrapped the sandwich, dropped in a big dill pickle and tucked it into a sack. Joanne paid the cashier and stepped outside. A chill rolled up her back as she strolled along the sidewalk. As she passed an alley, a man rammed into her. Joanne looked up, expecting his apology, and her heart cartwheeled with fear.

The man's grip on her arm was like a vise, his fingers bruising her flesh. "If you make a noise, I'll kill the kid."

The kid. Her knees weakened and the deli bag slipped from her hand as he forced her into the alleyway. The cream-colored SUV was there, and she could see a little girl peeking through the back window. *Mandy!* Her heart cried out and her fear flooded with pure joy.

Angelo hit the remote, then tugged open the back door and shoved her inside. As the door slammed, he jumped into the front seat and started the engine.

With her eyes forward, she slipped her hand to the door handle and eased it down. Child-proof locks. Disbelief washed over her as she looked at her daughter with blurred eyes.

Mandy huddled in the corner, her smoky blue eyes wide with terror.

Joanne fought the instinct to wrap her arms around Mandy, to kiss her cheeks, to tell her how much she loved her. Fear and wisdom kept her quiet. All she could do was try to catch Mandy's gaze and let her know she was on the child's side.

Mandy shivered against the opposite door, too far away for Joanne to touch her arm or whisper words of comfort. Her heart felt wrenched.

"Any funny business," Angelo said, "and it's the kid."

She wanted to beg him to let Mandy go, to kill her instead, but Joanne knew he wouldn't listen. Her stomach cramped with fear, but she gathered her wits. She knew who would listen to her plea.

"Lord, help us."

Benjamin felt his cell phone vibrate. He slipped it out of his pocket and glanced at the number. Joanne. She usually didn't call on his cell if it wasn't important, and today he was in a meeting. He waited for a break in the conversation. "Will you excuse me a minute?"

Five heads turned his way as he pushed his chair and rose. He darted from the conference room and hit Joanne's number.

The phone rang only once, but his breath caught in his throat when he heard a stranger's voice.

"You don't know me," the woman said, "but I'm Nita Wolfe. I work with Joanne."

"Is something wrong?" Benjamin asked, feeling his pulse escalate.

"She left here to pick up a sandwich at the deli nearby about a half hour ago and she's not back yet. It isn't like her. She can make the trip in fifteen minutes easy."

"Maybe it's crowded. Could there be a lineup at the deli?"

"I just called and they said it's not too busy. No line." A ragged sigh came through the wire. "I know she's been having serious problems and… I have a bad feeling."

"Thanks, Nita. I'll take it from here, but please call if she shows up."

"I will, and sorry to bother you."

"I'm glad you did." His body trembled as the truth hit. Joanne could be in trouble.

He punched the number of the Grosse

Pointe police and waited. Cortezi didn't answer, but finally someone picked up the line.

"Detective Ron Wieczorek here."

He rattled off the details. "It may sound far-fetched but—"

"Nothing's far-fetched in this business," Wieczorek said. "We have a stakeout at her home and the Angelo home. Let me check in with them. Hang on."

Benjamin clutched the phone against his ear, his heart pounding in terror. If Angelo had abducted Joanne, it could be too late.

Minutes ticked past. His hand began to sweat so he shifted the cell and wiped his damp palm.

"Sorry," Wieczorek said. "There's been no activity there. Are you sure she didn't decide to stay and eat lunch at the deli?"

Benjamin hadn't considered that. "Her co-worker just called there, but let me check and I'll get back to you." Benjamin called Nita and asked her to phone the deli, then he headed back to his meeting.

"I have an emergency," he said, as he bolted through the door. "You'll have to excuse me." He didn't wait for their response. He grabbed his papers and case, then pushed through the heavy door. He didn't care if he lost his job. He'd find work somewhere else.

He said a prayer as he darted to his car. His cell vibrated again. "She's not there," Nita said, her voice quaking. "The guy told me she'd ordered a sandwich, and on the way back, I found a bag kicked off the sidewalk next to the alley. It was a sandwich."

Benjamin's breath caught. "Thanks so much, Nita." As he slid into his car, he clicked off, then called the police. His mind spun. Where would Angelo take her?

The answer came to him in his heart the same way Joanne had heard Mandy. Angelo would take them to River Rouge Park.

"Wieczorek," the officer answered.

"She's not at the deli. Try River Rouge Park," he yelled into the cell as he raced from the parking structure.

"We're on it," Wieczorek said. "I've talked with Cortezi and he suggested the same. Angelo's driving a rental and we have the license plate. Officers are on the way."

"I am, too," Benjamin bellowed as he disconnected.

Joanne's mind spun like tires on ice. Fear had paralyzed her, but as they drove, she struggled to regain her wits. She would die and so would Mandy if she didn't.

Her concern was for her child. Joanne had inched her way toward the middle of the seat, making sure she didn't alarm Angelo. She could hear him ranting to himself, mumbling about "dumb Donna" and how he should have killed her a year ago.

He snarled at Joanne in the rearview mirror and evil darkened his eyes. Her skin crawled at his look, but when his gaze drifted, Joanne slid her hand closer to Mandy and patted her arm.

The child's tear-filled gaze caught hers, then darted to her hand. She brushed the child's jacket, hoping to soothe her, to let her know she would protect her.

Mandy shifted in her seat, and Angelo glanced over his shoulder and let out a filthy oath. "Sit still," he bellowed.

"Where are we going?" Mandy asked, her tearful voice fighting to sound confident.

"On vacation." Angelo let out a maniacal laugh.

Mandy seemed to gain courage. "Where's Mom? Me and her were going on vacation alone."

"She went without you."

"No, she didn't. She wouldn't go without me."

"That's all *you* know, kid. Now shut up."

His words stabbed Joanne's heart. Hearing Mandy's side made Joanne realize that

Donna had not planned to leave Mandy behind. Though angry, she couldn't help but ache for the woman who had apparently loved her daughter so much that she had planned to take her away from danger.

"Where were you going?" Joanne whispered.

"To Florida. We were going to Disney—"

"Shut your mouth," Angelo roared, jerking around to face them.

The vehicle veered with such speed that Joanne slid closer to Mandy. She took advantage by sliding her arm around her daughter. Mandy looked up at her with questioning eyes, and then overcame her fear and nestled in Joanne's arms.

Though petrified about the danger they faced, Joanne praised God for having her daughter in her arms once again. She studied the child's upturned face and saw her own eyes gazing back at her—Mandy had the same coloring and facial shape, but Greg's dimpled smile.

Grief overtook Joanne. She'd lost three years of life with her baby—her daughter—but now, with her age six, they would begin again, God willing.

As Mandy quaked in her arms, Joanne wanted to ask her so many questions. Had she been happy? Did she have friends? What were her hobbies? Did she know about Jesus?

With Mandy's warmth permeating her own quivering body, Joanne looked out at the scene flashing past the window. They had been traveling down I-94 toward Dearborn. She recognized the landmarks from her previous trips. Would Angelo take her to his house? She hoped the police would be there waiting.

But minutes later, she realized he'd left the freeway at Michigan Avenue. Angelo's driving was erratic, and Joanne hoped the police would pull him over. Did he have a weapon? The question strangled her, and she gasped.

Her daughter gave her a questioning look, and she tried to send Mandy the message everything would be all right.

Soon she read a street sign and knew they'd turned onto Hines Drive. Joanne didn't know that part of town well, but when they crossed the Rouge River, her heart seemed to stop. River Rouge Park. He was headed to the place he'd left Donna's body.

Dearest Lord, be with us.

Chapter Twenty-Three

Benjamin flew down the freeway, his eyes on the speedometer. If he got pulled over, he would lose time. He had to get to the park. His memory failed him. He'd only been to the park once, many years ago, and all he remembered was that it was divided by Outer Drive. The river rambled through the area with too many possible hiding places.

His frantic mind struggled to hang on to positive thoughts. The police were on it. He knew they would contact the Dearborn police. Would they get there before Angelo? He had a half hour on them. Benjamin tried to calculate how long it would take to drive from Joanne's office building to the park.

Then another thought struck him. What if they'd guessed wrong? Perhaps Angelo hadn't gone to the park. Benjamin's eyes misted with emotion. Why hadn't he told Joanne last night how much he loved her? He'd loved her forever it seemed, from the time he got to know her. His love had grown as naturally as the sun rose. He'd fought it. He'd prayed about it. He'd lost the battle.

But now he saw the purpose behind his love. He'd been here to support Joanne and to guide the police to her. If it was God's will, she and Mandy would be saved. If the Lord didn't mean for their love to come to fruition, Benjamin would have to live with that—but the thought pained him.

Evelyn came to mind, and he stopped himself from calling her. Why cause her panic when she could do nothing? Better to let her learn the outcome, which Benjamin could only pray would be cause for thanksgiving.

He veered up the ramp and onto Michigan Avenue, then made his way to Hines Drive. He wasn't far now.

Dearest Lord, keep them safe. That's all I ask.

Icy perspiration beaded on Joanne's skin. She drew in the scent of Mandy, so close yet so unattainable. She longed to whisper the truth to the child, but she couldn't speak without Angelo hearing her, and she knew Mandy would be confused and frightened by her admission that she was the girl's mother.

They'd reached the park, and the roads vanished as Angelo turned down a snowy rutted trail. Joanne longed to look behind her to see if she could spot anyone following, but Angelo would see her in his mirror, and she didn't want to push him over the edge. God would be with them. He had to be.

Angelo left the path and the SUV tilted and bumped through a snow-filled field. The tires sank and spun, but Angelo persisted, and finally the vehicle shot forward. He skidded to a stop behind a stand of leafless shrubs, the density of which partially hid the vehicle from anyone who might venture down the path.

Joanne could see the frozen river nearby, and she recognized a setting similar to that on the television news bulletin she'd seen the day she had lunch with Melissa. She recalled the police breaking through the mounds of snow and the emergency vehicles parked in the vicinity as they carried Donna's draped body to an EMS van.

Would she be the next news bulletin? She

and Mandy? Never. She'd give her life, but she'd do anything to keep her daughter alive.

Angelo climbed out and jerked open her door. He grabbed her arm and yanked her from the SUV. He slammed the door, leaving Mandy inside.

Joanne's only hope was to get Mandy outside, to distract him, then tell her to run. "Why are you leaving her inside?"

"What do you care?"

"She's my daughter," she said, twisting her face in the most vicious look she could. "You abducted her years ago and then killed my husband."

"Pretty good, wasn't I?"

"You're evil. You killed your wife." She knew if she riled him, he'd kill her. She had to shut her mouth until she could free Mandy.

"Poor dumb Donna. She should have let well enough alone. A few smacks now and again didn't hurt her, but she pushed her luck."

Joanne opened her mouth, then closed it and prayed for wisdom.

He dragged her closer to the river, then pulled duct tape from his pocket. "I lost my daughter because of your husband, and I thought I'd get even by taking his. Now you get to watch when you lose yours *again*." A vicious laugh erupted from his throat.

Joanne struggled against his hold, but his grip was ironclad and she didn't have the strength. He leaned over and shoved his face into hers as he bound her hands around the tree. Joanne flinched at his stinking breath while she fought to keep her hands loose in the tape.

But he wound the tape around twice, three times, and she worried she'd never get free. She hoped he wouldn't cover her mouth. She needed to warn Mandy.

A distant sound distracted him, and he reached beneath his jacket and jerked out a handgun.

The sight sent chills through her. She'd been sure he didn't have a weapon. He'd strangled Donna and run Greg off the road into the lake. She'd expected the same treatment. Joanne craned her neck to look through the barricade of limbs to see if rescue had come, but the sound they'd heard faded, as did her hopes.

Her heart thundered against her chest, and she feared she would faint before she could help Mandy get away. She watched Angelo tug open the door and pull her daughter from the back seat. Joanne's panic rose when she saw the terror in Mandy's face.

While Angelo's back was turned, Joanne worked her hands to try to release the tape, but it only seemed to get tighter the more she struggled.

Angelo pushed Mandy forward, and she slipped into a rut and fell. He yanked her up by her coat neck and pushed her ahead of him, his pistol wagging toward the ground as he stalked forward.

Mandy's fear-filled eyes searched Joanne's, and Joanne sent her daughter a fervent look, shifting her gaze toward the road and hoping Mandy would understand to run when she could. Joanne sought a diversion, anything to distract Angelo long enough for Mandy to get away.

As he shoved Mandy nearer, Joanne continued to try to wrestle her hands free of their binding to the slender tree trunk. She sent up a prayer and then, in desperation, cried out, "I hear them." She didn't know why she'd said that, but she hoped he'd look around. "I knew they'd come."

"I don't hear nuthin'," he said, his hand still clutching Mandy's arm, but Joanne noticed a flicker of confusion on his face.

"You're not listening. I heard them over there." She used her head to indicate the brush to his left. "I had a cell phone. You didn't see me call."

He faltered, his brutal look aimed at her. His gun waved in the air as he marched away from Mandy and stuck his face into Joanne's, his breath assaulting her nostrils, his voice harsh. "You can watch your daughter die now." He grabbed the collar of Joanne's coat.

"Leave her alone," Mandy screamed. "You always hurt people."

"Oh yeah," he said, turning back toward her, his pistol aimed at Mandy.

Tears rolled down Joanne's face from the sting of his hand and from despair. "Shoot me," Joanne screamed. "Kill me and get it over with."

He pivoted toward her and aimed the pistol.

"Run!" Joanne screamed to Mandy. "Run!"

He swung back toward Mandy and a shot rang out.

And then Joanne knew only blackness.

Benjamin heard a shot reverberate across the bare landscape. His vehicle skidded to the side of the rutted road and he leaped from it. Noise sounded from the right, and his pulse raced as he darted through the ice-covered snow, slipping as he ran.

"Joanne," he screamed. He knew Angelo could be aiming the pistol toward his voice but he didn't care any longer. What was life without the woman he loved? If Angelo killed her— He stopped his thought. He didn't dare give way to hopelessness.

"Joanne!"

Through the branches he could see movement. A dark jacket flashed between the bare limbs of a tree. He crouched, running as low to the ground as he could. His suit pants dampened at the ankles and icy slush seeped into his shoes as his feet broke through the crusted snow.

"Joanne!"

As he broke through the brush, he skidded to a halt.

Joanne lay on the ground, her lifeless body twisted. Medics hovered over her while another body lay sprawled on the ground.

Then he saw the child. Tears streamed down the child's cheeks as an officer held her in his arms.

Benjamin darted past them and pushed his way through the officers, then kneeled at Joanne's side. Tears burned his eyes as he bent closer. His prayers soared, asking God why. *Why?* Then he saw her eyelids flutter, and his heart skipped a beat.

He scrutinized her body, searching for a wound or signs of blood. "Was she shot?" he asked the officer.

"I think she fainted," he replied as a medic bent closer.

"Stand back," the other said, pushing Benjamin away. He moved as the emergency technician kneeled to check Joanne's pulse, but before he finished, her eyes opened.

She focused on Benjamin with dazed eyes. "Mandy?"

"She's okay. They've put her in a squad car."

"I heard a shot." She lifted her head and gazed at the lifeless body of Carl Angelo being lifted onto a litter. "What happened?"

"We shot him before he hurt the child," the officer said. "He's dead." He turned and waved toward the EMS ambulance. "Another gurney here."

"I can walk. I'm fine." She struggled to shift herself upward, pulling away excess duct tape from her hands.

"Don't fight them, Joanne," Benjamin said,

his mind so rattled he could barely think. "I'll follow you to the hospital."

He stepped away as they lifted her onto the gurney. His mind reeled at the thought of what could have been, and he knew the Lord had granted his request.

He'd kept Joanne and Mandy safe.

Joanne stood outside the hospital door watching Mandy through the opening. The child had fallen asleep, and Joanne felt grateful. She'd said a prayer of thanksgiving. God had heard her prayer, and the horror had finally ended.

She'd been delayed arriving. She'd asked Benjamin to call Nita while she gave her statement to the police and dealt with her physical examination, and finally they'd released her.

"How long will she be here?" she asked the physician as he jotted notes onto the clipboard.

"She's been through a horrifying ordeal. After she has a full examination, we'll still want to keep her a couple of days. We'll have a social worker talk with her and a therapist."

"Can I talk with her? Can I tell her who I am?" Joanne asked.

Benjamin pressed her arm as if to urge her to be quiet, but she couldn't.

The physician shook his head. "We need the DNA first, just to make sure."

"I am sure. I know my daughter."

"But the courts will need proof. You can visit her later, but don't confuse her. She needs to rest, and we need to help her deal with this."

Joanne wanted to be the one to help her. She'd waited three years to have her daughter back in her arms and now she had to wait again. Her nerves jarred with frustration.

Benjamin leaned close to her ear. "Be patient, Joanne. She'll be with you soon. Give it time. Not for them, but for Mandy. She needs to be ready to hear what you have to say."

She knew he was right. "Can I at least take her home when she's released?"

The doctor looked frustrated with her question. "I just told you we need DNA. She'll go into a foster home."

"A foster home? No. She's been in a foster home for three years."

"Joanne, please," Benjamin said.

She heard the urgency in his voice and quieted. "For how long?"

"We should learn the results from the DNA test in three or four days. It won't be long."

"You've waited three years," Benjamin said. "Another couple of days won't matter. You can get her room ready, and go Christmas shopping."

"I don't care about that. I want my daughter." She realized what she was saying and closed her mouth. "I'm sorry. Benjamin is right. I can get things ready for her and make it a real homecoming."

"I know you're anxious," the ER doctor said, his tone softening. "I'm sorry, but we have to follow procedures, and I know you want to make sure she's healthy."

Joanne nodded. "Can I visit with her? We talked in Angelo's car. She knew I was worried about her. She might want to see me."

He glanced at Mandy through the doorway. "Let's say tomorrow. You can see her before we send her to foster care." His expression softened. "I promise, if the DNA proves right, you'll have her before Christmas."

Before Christmas. The words washed over Joanne. She took a final look at Mandy before she let Benjamin move her away from the door.

Chapter Twenty-Four

At home, exhaustion overcame Joanne as she sank into the sofa with her cup of tea. Her mother sat across from her, her eyes swollen from crying, her face pale from hearing the lengthy story of what had happened.

"I thank God you're both okay," her mom said. "I suppose I should head for home now that I know you're safe."

Her gaze searched Joanne's, and Joanne understood what her mother wanted to hear.

"Wouldn't you want to see your granddaughter?"

"With all my heart, but I didn't know if—"

"You can see her tomorrow. We can't tell her anything yet, but you can talk with her. I'll tell her you're my mother and that's all."

"If I won't be in the way, I'd give anything to see her."

"You've given enough, Mom. You came here when I was in trouble, even when I told you not to come, and you stood by my side." The conversation astounded Joanne. She and her mother had not talked so openly in years.

"I would have been praying if someone had told me."

Joanne looked at her with amazement. She'd only heard her mother talk of prayer the night Benjamin had made reference to it. This wasn't the mother that Joanne had grown to resent.

"I didn't know you believe in God," Joanne said, being blunt and hoping not to start an argument.

"I was not raised in the church, but I knew about God. I just never took much stock in leaning on anyone but myself."

"So what happened? What changed you?"

"Benjamin told me a few things in the Bible, and it felt right. We talked about prayer. While I was here alone during the day, I started reading the Bible. I have a long way to go, but it makes sense to me."

"I'm happy to hear you say that."

"Only the New Testament. I started the Old

Testament, but it got too confusing. I love the part about Jesus in the newer Scripture."

"Scripture is beautiful. It's a guide for living."

Her mother ran her hand over her cheek. "I can see Benjamin's a man of faith. He's strong and confident. He's a good man, Joanne."

"I know he is. His faith is stronger than mine."

Her mother shook her head. "I doubt that. You've been involved in church since you met Greg."

Joanne's heart lurched at the reference. "I was, but that has nothing to do with believing. Church-going is an outward symbol. Believing happens right here." She pressed her hand against her heart. "We all sin, Mom. Even Christians. We make big mistakes. We get angry at God. I certainly was, after Greg and Mandy were gone."

"I can only imagine." Evelyn looked thoughtful. "I've made a few big mistakes myself," she said as an expression of remorse darkened her face. "Sometimes I wish I could erase how I've lived and do it over."

"We can't back up, Mom. We just have to make the future different." Though she said the words for her mother, they had a strong meaning for Joanne.

Her mother didn't respond, but Joanne noticed her brush her fingers across her eyes. She'd never seen her mother cry. That thought triggered another. Perhaps her mother had cried about things alone. Joanne had judged her without knowing her.

"I'm so sorry you've been going through all of this pain alone, Joanne."

Joanne opened her mouth to remind her mother that she had Benjamin, but she stopped herself. Right now, she and her mother were talking as two caring people. She wanted to cling to the rare moment. She recalled how miserable she'd often been when she visited with her family. She'd become an outsider.

"I've been neglectful," Evelyn said suddenly.

Joanne didn't respond. What could she say? She'd believed exactly that of her mother.

"To tell you the truth, Joanne, I didn't know what to do or say to you after the accident. I should have said more, but words just didn't capture the sorrow I felt for you." She turned her head toward the window and rose, walking across the carpet to look outside. "Mandy was my granddaughter. My flesh and blood. I gathered my personal grief and clung to it like a selfish man to his money. I guarded it like some kind of treasure."

Her words spun through Joanne's head. Was this the same thing she had done?

"You probably felt the same," her mother said, her face burdened with sadness, "and instead of joining together in our sorrow, we both hugged it to our breasts and made it our own."

Her mother's explanation smacked Joanne with the truth. She had hugged her misery to herself. She'd guarded it, unwilling to share. She'd resented anyone saying they understood, because no one understood. No one felt her pain. No one had had his life pulled out from under him like she had.

"You're right, Mom. I felt just like that. I didn't even want you to feel the grief that I felt. Now that I think about it, I put myself on a pedestal of sorrow. I became untouchable."

"So did I."

"But, Mom, right in here, I wanted to be touched." She rested her hand above her heart. "I wanted to be sheltered and cared for. I wanted my husband and child to reappear."

Her mother turned from the window and

opened her arms. Joanne joined her, and they stood, wrapped together in a tight embrace, tears dripping from their eyes while Joanne unleashed the hurt from her heart.

"I'm sorry I didn't understand," Joanne whispered into her mother's hair.

They stood together in silence as forgiveness enveloped them. Joanne knew total healing would take time, but today her mother had taken a step forward and so had she. The step felt wonderful.

When they eased away and finally settled into their seats, Joanne gathered strength to take one more step. "I felt so lonely for so long. It wasn't just you who seemed to turn your back on me. Friends did the same thing. Couples. I became a threat, or maybe they didn't like the fifth-wheel idea, but I drew into myself even more. My only escape was my work at Solutions, and I drown myself in it."

"I wish we'd talked this out a long time ago," Evelyn said.

"I do, too. It wasn't only you and friends who turned their backs. I realize now it was me. I'd turned first and made it harder, but I wish someone had persisted. I needed people so badly."

"I'm sorry I didn't, Joanne. You know I've always been a private woman. Expressing my feelings hasn't come easy. I probably seem self-centered."

Joanne smiled, recalling her conversation with Benjamin. "You don't have to say any more, Mom. Like I said, humans make mistakes, and that's why we need God's love and forgiveness."

She saw her mother's gaze shift. "I'm not trying to evangelize, Mom. It's what I feel in my heart. My faith has kept me sane. I felt anger at God. I felt betrayed by Him, but He stood by my side anyway. We should learn from God's abiding love. He never turns His back."

Her mother's eyebrows rose a little. "That's a good lesson. Something all of us should keep in mind."

Joanne agreed. She'd experienced it fully. God had not turned His back on her. He'd answered her fervent prayer and He'd kept her daughter safe.

"Why didn't Benjamin stay?" Evelyn asked, changing the subject.

"He had things to do. He'd walked out on a meeting, and he needed to go back and settle some work projects."

"He'll be back later?"

"I'm sure he will. He and I have some things to talk about."

"I'll stay out of your hair, then."

Joanne grinned. "I know you will. And now we have work to do."

"Okay." Her mother rose. "What can I do?"

"We need to get Mandy's room ready for her."

"Wonderful. I'll get the cleaning supplies," Evelyn said, and darted to the kitchen.

Joanne stood, but staggered by the reality of what had happened, her joy exploded into tears. God's gift to her was unbelievable, amazing. An early Christmas present. The Father gave His only begotten Son to a world of sinners one Christmas night long ago. Today God had given her another gift, her daughter, offered out of His love.

She sank back into the chair and wept with gratitude and thanks.

"Sorry I'm late," Benjamin said, coming through the door. "I had to undo some problems I created by vanishing. When they heard what had happened, I've been forgiven."

"We can all use a little of that," she said,

anxious to tell him about the talk with her mother.

He slipped off his jacket and hung it on the closet doorknob. She loved it there. That spot had become a symbol of Benjamin's presence in her life and heart.

He wandered into the living room and stood for a minute in front of the Christmas tree. She'd turned on the tree lights and had even started a blaze in the fireplace. She walked beside him and nestled her hand in the crook of his arm.

"We cleaned Mandy's bedroom today," she said after they'd stood in silence for a few moments.

"I'm sure it felt wonderful to get it ready for her."

She squeezed his arm. "Like a miracle. I packed up her little clothes and baby toys. Now I can fill it with all kinds of new—" Unbidden, the tears rolled from her eyes. She had cried much of the time she'd packed the old things away. "I'm sorry. I'm being a baby."

"You're being a mother. God has given you the most precious gift a woman could ask for. You have every right to cry." He gave her a sly grin. "I've done a little of it myself."

"You have?"

He nodded, and she noticed the mist rising in his dark brown eyes. She turned toward him and opened her arms. He gathered her against his chest, and she felt as if she'd finally found her way home.

Joanne rejoiced in the moment as they stood together in a silent embrace beside the glistening Christmas tree. Each ornament held a memory—baby's first Christmas, the nativity, the whimsical ones she and Greg had given to each other. Perhaps this year, she and Benjamin would do something to begin a new set of memories.

She felt Benjamin ease back, his gaze capturing hers. "I think we should sit a while and talk."

Talk. The word shuddered through her. Would this be his goodbye? Mission accomplished? In thirty seconds, their relationship could self-destruct.

"Sure," she said, trying to sound casual and confident, but she prepared herself for the worst.

Once they'd settled on the sofa, she sensed his tension. He fidgeted without speaking and she felt her world being torn apart again. *Lord, You've given back a daughter and now must I lose a—?* She paused her thought. A what? Friend? No. A man she loved. She loved him with all her heart. The relationship had blossomed like a wildflower in the forest— unseen and in the shadows, but there and beautiful, until one day a wanderer stumbled upon the rare bloom.

"What is it?" she asked, unable to wait any longer.

Benjamin faced her and the truth. He needed to tell her. He'd kept it to himself far too long. "I guess I need to get something off my chest."

Her face reflected her concern.

"I have to be honest with you before I can say any more," he said. "When I was racing to the park, praying you were there and alive, I wished I had told you all of this yesterday. I was so frightened that if something happened, you'd never know."

"Know what?" She gazed at him.

He leaned forward and rested his hands on his knees, his fingers twined together. He couldn't look at her for fear she would react negatively. He feared he would disappoint her.

He heard her sigh. She rubbed her arms as if she'd felt a chill, but he suspected it was more than that.

"Remember a few weeks ago," he said, "when you asked me why I'd never married?"

"Yes. You said you'd been in love but it was a love that couldn't be."

"That's right." He tilted his head and gazed at her. "Did that make any sense to you, Joanne?"

"Not really. I guessed she might have been engaged or maybe married, but that didn't seem like you, Benjamin."

"It's not like me, but that was the problem."

She tried to cover her shock, but he could too easily read her face.

"Do you want to talk about it?" she asked.

"The woman was married, and I was ashamed of my feelings. I couldn't control them no matter what I did, and I finally put it in God's hands. He solved my problem."

"Was that while you were in Seattle? Or was it during college?"

"Neither. It was only a few years ago, when I should have known better. I know God has forgiven me, but I hope you can."

"What is it? Do I know her?"

"Yes. It was you, Joanne. I'd fallen in love with you."

"Me?" Her voice was a whisper. "You fell in love with me."

"I loved you and Greg both. I treasured our

friendship, and I had no idea that my admiration and feelings for you would grow into something I could hardly control."

She searched his face as if waiting for a punch line, but he had none. "I did as I said. I asked God to get me out of the problem. The offer came for me to move to Seattle and take over the project there. When Greg died, I felt almost as if God were punishing me for my improper feelings. I knew better, but I could hardly face you. That's why I was gone so long. I felt ashamed and guilt-ridden."

She reached out and touched his face. "I had no idea."

"I tried to hide it, but I feared it was emblazoned on my face." He held her fingers beneath his palm. "Just as it's emblazoned on my heart."

"You've loved me all this time."

Her dazed look would have made him smile if he hadn't felt such agony.

He nodded.

"How could I not forgive you? You did everything you could to make it right."

"I dated in Seattle, but I could never find a woman who compared to you. You were the epitome of what I wanted in a wife."

"And now?"

"My feelings haven't changed, Joanne." He felt ready to open his heart. "I love you now even more fully than I did before. You make me feel complete. You and Mandy would bring me such joy if you'd consider being my wife."

"Your wife?"

"I don't mean tomorrow..."

A smile eased across her face. "Why not? I love you, too. It sneaked up on me like sunshine bursting through a rain cloud. You brought purpose and joy back into my life. I cherish you as a friend and I'll cherish you as a husband."

He rose and drew her into his arms. His mouth touched hers in a tender blend of joy and awareness. One day she would be his wife, a dream he'd owned for so long. Today he could embrace the love he felt, and he prayed that if Greg could look down from heaven, he would be pleased to know that Joanne and Mandy would be loved and cherished as long as he lived.

What more could he ask? God had been his guide. He'd led Benjamin on a long journey, a frightening journey, but he'd arrived home. Nothing could be more precious than to have Joanne and Mandy by his side forever.

Chapter Twenty-Five

Joanne sat in the waiting room of Foster Care Services with her hand in Benjamin's. God had given her far more than she had ever expected. The days had flown past, unbelievable and wonderful. Even before she learned that the DNA matched, she'd filled Mandy's bedroom with new clothes, toys and games and a pile of gifts. It was as though she felt she could make up for the three years her daughter had been missing from her life.

"Did you get a chance to look through the envelope Cortezi gave me?" Joanne asked.

"The one from Donna Angelo's luggage?"

She nodded, remembering her shock.

"I glanced at it—divorce papers, restraining order, newspaper article and the old photos. She must have put two and two together."

"That's what I figured. Now I understand how this happened so long after the accident."

"Attorney's mind here, but I wonder why she was taking it. I suspect either to black-mail Angelo for more money or to protect her from him if he found her."

"Probably the last reason. I don't think she was a bad woman, Benjamin. I think she was petrified—scared to death that he might harm Mandy."

"Domestic abuse cases do go awry. I've seen cases where the complaint goes no-where, and the woman's left facing her hus-band's wrath. We see it in the paper all the time when it's someone famous."

She understood, and her mind slipped back to the haggard face she had seen across the mall.

"You have a kind heart," Benjamin said, giving her hand a loving squeeze.

Joanne's spirit lifted as she looked at him. Benjamin had been at her side, with his staunch faith and his wisdom, helping her to keep her head on straight.

She could still picture her mother's face when they went to the hospital to visit Mandy the day after the rescue. Joanne and her mother had struggled to keep their identities hidden from the child. The social worker had guaranteed that they would prepare the child ahead of time for the news. Joanne knew Mandy would continue therapy. She'd found a wonderful Christian counselor to give her daughter support as she adjusted to life in her real home.

Joanne's next greatest joy was Benjamin. He'd professed his love and she'd admitted hers. They'd sealed their confession with a kiss that had made her heart flutter like a schoolgirl's. Her love for Greg would never fade, but she had so much love to give—love for Mandy, Benjamin, and, God willing, another child to fill their home and heart.

The door opened and the social worker beckoned them inside. Joanne carried the plastic bag she'd brought from home as the woman led them down a corridor to another smaller lounge. When they entered, Mandy was there waiting for them. She gave Joanne a shy look and seemed more withdrawn than she had on the last visit, but that was to be understood. The adjustment would take time, and Joanne would let nothing detract from this moment.

"Hi," she said. "Are you about ready to go?"

Mandy nodded. "Mrs. Allen said my name is really Mandy."

"It is. What do you think about it?"

"I like it better than Connie, but it sounds weird."

"It will for a while." Joanne sat beside her on the love seat.

Mandy stared at the floor before speaking again. "I'm supposed to tell you when I'm mixed up or scared."

"I hope you do. I get scared, too. Very scared sometimes, but Jesus is always on my side."

"Jesus is with me, too."

Joanne's heart leaped when she heard her daughter's statement. "Did your other family teach you about Jesus?"

"No, but my friend did. She told me all the stories. She got to go to Sunday school. I never did."

Joanne brushed her fingers along her daughter's shining hair. "Would you like to go to Sunday school?"

"Uh-huh."

"We'll go next Sunday. It's Christmas Day."

Mandy gave her a shy smile and nodded. "Do you remember me?"

Joanne's heart stuttered. "I've never forgotten you. *Ever.* I remember everything about you. You loved to sit on my lap while I read you a book. You liked to play with blocks, and I even remember the little heart birthmark on her leg."

Mandy's eyes widened. "You remember that?"

"I loved it. I used to kiss it when I changed your diaper when you were a baby or when I gave you a bath."

Mandy giggled as her hand touched the heart-shaped mark on her leg. "I don't remember all of that."

"I know, but when we get home I'll show you photographs of you when you were little."

"Okay." Her gaze shifted to the sack Joanne held on her lap.

"This was something else you liked when you were young. It's pretty beaten up, but I thought you might like to have it. I've kept it for you."

Mandy gave her a curious look. "Was it my toy?"

"It was. When you were two and three. You slept with it." Joanne handed her the plastic bag.

Mandy unfolded the top and looked inside. She delved down into the sack and pulled out the bedraggled plush puppy. Mandy stared at the dog, then at Joanne. She brushed her hand slowly over the stained, worn coat, then extended his frayed ears.

Her eyes filled with amazement as she cradled the dog in her arms. She looked into Joanne's face and searched her eyes as she murmured the name. "Floppy."

"What?" Joanne said.

"It's Floppy."

Tears inched from behind Joanne's eyes, and she looked at Benjamin, astonished at what she'd heard. One day Mandy might remember more. If not, they would create a whole new set of memories.

Benjamin leaned closer as if he didn't want to miss a thing.

Mandy removed one hand from the toy dog and raised it to Joanne's cheek. "You're my mother."

"Yes. I'm your mother, Mandy." She did everything she could not to cry. She felt her cheek tick and her lips tremble with disbelief.

"Can I call you Mama?"

"Oh, my darling girl, you can call me anything you want."

She wrapped her arms around her daughter and let the tears flow in silence. At that moment, Joanne knew her life was whole and complete. She looked up and managed to give Benjamin a reassuring smile.

When she saw tears roll down his cheeks, her heart swelled with the love that she felt. Nothing seemed more precious at that moment than to gaze at the man she loved and hold her child in her arms.

Joanne sat on the floor beside the Christmas tree and grinned at Mandy, who was nearly hidden behind the pile of boxes she'd received from Joanne's family and the gifts she and Benjamin had bought her.

Mandy had spent the past few days with her, and though Joanne knew the relationship would take time, they had already bonded. Her daughter had shied from Benjamin for the first couple of days, but his love had been so full and open that Mandy's fears had melted away, and she'd opened her arms to him, too.

"I've never had such a nice Christmas," Mandy said, her eyes glowing in the tree light.

"I like my presents, too," Joanne said, admiring the thoughtful packages her family had sent, and Benjamin's lovely gift, a gold chain and cross pendant studded with Mandy's birthstone.

"I love my books," Mandy said, pulling out a pop-up book that Benjamin had given her. The pages lifted to depict the Christmas story. Mandy flipped through the leaves, then turned the nativity scene around to show them. "This was where Jesus was born. See the cow? It's a stable."

"Yet He's the king of heaven and earth. It doesn't matter where we're from or where we're born. What matters is what's in our hearts," Joanne said.

"My heart has good things in it now," Mandy said.

Benjamin chuckled and lifted her into his arms. "Come with me, young lady. You can help me with a surprise."

"A surprise?"

"It's for your mama."

"Goody," Mandy said, as Benjamin carried her down the hallway.

Joanne rose and added a CD to the player. Christmas music drifted across the room as she settled back onto the floor. After a moment they returned, whispering to each other.

"What's the secret?" Joanne asked.

"You have another present," Mandy said, her hands behind her back.

"Is it from you?"

She nodded. "Benjamin said it's from both of us."

"Can I have it?" Joanne gazed at Benjamin and saw his smile broadening.

Mandy hurried to her side and set a box in her lap. When Joanne opened it, her chest tightened. She knew what it was immediately by the size and shape of the velvet box.

"It's a ring," Mandy said, apparently too excited to hold back.

Joanne opened the lid and gazed down at the lovely diamond cluster. The tree lights caught in the facets and the ring shot fire. "It's gorgeous."

"Okay, it's your turn," Mandy said, pulling on Benjamin's sleeve.

He shifted forward and bent on one knee as Mandy hovered beside him. He took the ring from the box and held it up to her. "Joanne, I would be honored if you would be my wife."

"Don't forget the other part," Mandy said.

Benjamin chuckled. "And Mandy would be my daughter."

"You'd be my dad," she said.

"I would be. What do you think?"

"I think it's a good idea, because then we'd all get to know each other at the same time."

"I want nothing more than this," Joanne

said, opening her arms. Benjamin and Mandy joined her. They kneeled on the floor together, arms wrapped around one another, beside the Christmas tree. "Silent Night" drifted from the CD player, and Joanne knew that finally her night would be silent but her heart would be full. Today she'd found Christmas in the eyes of her child.

* * * * *

HOME on the RANCH

READERSERVICE.COM

Manage your account online!

- Review your order history
- Manage your payments
- Update your address

> ### *We've designed the Reader Service website just for you.*

Enjoy all the features!

- Discover new series available to you, and read excerpts from any series.
- Respond to mailings and special monthly offers.
- Browse the Bonus Bucks catalog and online-only exculsives.
- Share your feedback.

Visit us at:
ReaderService.com